Shivering in the Sun

Also by William Fadiman

Hollywood Now (nonfiction)
The Clay Oscar (fiction)

Shivering in the Sun

A Novel by
William Fadiman

Wilshire House
Los Angeles

© William Fadiman, 1988

Cover: Edward Hopper, *People in the Sun*
Reproduced by permission of the
National Museum of American Art,
Smithsonian Institution, Gift of S. C.
Johnson & Son, Inc.

Design: Katie Messborn

Library of Congress Cataloguing in Publication Data

ISBN: 1-55713-043-4

---

10   9   8   7   6   5   4   3   2   1

Published by Wilshire House
6148 Wilshire Boulevard
Los Angeles, California
(213) 857-1115

For Irving Wallace
With profound affection

I

It was a magnificent day, even for California, where eternal sunshine was taken for granted.

As Judd Haber stood in front of his mirror he could see reflected the sun-dappled edge of the neatly shorn dichondera lawn and the array of petunias, azaleas and yellow roses in the front garden. The roses were especially beautiful; Judd knew Milly loved them.

His Mercedes stood gleaming in the driveway; Albert, their combined houseman-butler-chauffeur, had seen to that as he always did, and Judd was sure there would be two new packs of Shermans in the glove compartment.

He knew that Milly was getting ready in her dressing-room and that Kerry and Suz were undoubtedly doing the same thing.

He crossed the room and picked up the dark blue Nieman-Marcus tie that complemented the blue-black suit from Brooks, both of which the inimitable and ever-reliable Josie had ordered for him only a few hours after the word came.

Good old Josie: She was really invaluable; he must remember to check with Jim Banton on the last time she had received a raise.

The tie was finally firmly knotted into place, and then Judd began to rummage in his top bureau drawer. He discarded several wallets, three or four pairs of cuff links, and his father's old-fashioned silver knot stick pin before he found what he was seeking. There it was: a small round emblem-pin of black enamel with gold letters in a circle around its edge: Global Talent Associates, Inc. it read, and there was a gold number 25 in the center. Judd had only worn it a few times after Rudy had given it to him. He'd always known Rudy was a little on the sentimental side—never in business, of course—but it was one of the few times in his life that Rudy had really surprised him with anything quite so unexpected.

Opening the mirror-door of his closet, he saw his full-length image revealed. His hands went to his belt and he loosened it a notch, grimacing ruefully. He smoothed his grey-flecked black hair, felt his face for any trace of stubble, and adjusted his black-framed glasses more firmly on his nose (he never wore glasses except for driving and always whipped them off as soon as he got out of the car).

He fumbled in the closet for his suitcoat, and as he did so, his silk dressing gown tumbled to the floor. It was a deep shimmering blue with a coiled red dragon emblazoned on the breast pocket, and a discreet J.H., also in red, embroidered below it.

Replacing it on its hanger, he recalled the day Milly had bought it for him in that elegant shop in Hong Kong on Nathan Street. It was a birthday present,

Milly had assured him playfully, even though his birthday was months away. It had been an especially lovely day, as he remembered it, and they had celebrated that evening by dining in the candle-lit splendor of Gaddis's at the Peninsula Hotel. He grinned and wondered what Milly would think if she knew that an exact duplicate of the robe hung in another closet across town.

He slipped into his jacket and carefully adjusted the emblem to his lapel, snapping the tiny bar-lock tightly. As he fingered the 25-year service pin, he was certain that Rudy would have wanted him to wear it, especially on this particular occasion, for this was a very special day: September 14, 1963, the day of Rudy's funeral. Watching the pin's reflection in the mirror, he remembered the time he'd received it.

It had been very late in the day, about 7:45, and the only ones left in the office were Jenny, the new switchboard operator, and Alex—Alex Deming, the brown-nosing eager beaver who had joined Global about seven years before. Judd had never felt comfortable with Alex—Rudy had hired him while Judd was away on a deal in London—but he had to admit that a hell of a lot of contracts, and good ones, too, originated with him. He was particularly effective with actresses; the fact that he wasn't married and that his free time was his own may have helped in that respect. He was a handsome bastard, wavy brown hair always scrupulously combed, tall and athletic-looking—he was one of the few employees who took advantage of the gym room Rudy had installed for the staff—and he presented a direct, forthright personality that Judd knew concealed a devious and cunning mind. In the office everyone called him the cocksman-agent, often to his face. The appellation didn't trouble him in the least.

The only other office light that had been on was Lettie Mallon's; but Judd knew that Lettie was leaving. Through his open door he could hear her bantering with Jenny, whom she seemed to like.

Why, Judd could never understand. To Judd Jenny seemed a typical breezy eighteen-year-old with over-red lips and too much makeup, but Lettie thought she was "cute and sassy," as she put it. Lettie had greeted him as she passed by his office on her way to the elevator with her usual disarming "Good night, mother-fucker." Judd was no longer jarred by that; Lettie's foul mouth was part of her stock-in-trade and apparently served to put clients at ease with her immediately. Rudy had hated her language; he had once threatened to fire her when he overheard her conversing in four-letter words with a vice-president of ABC; but she'd talked him out of it. Rudy knew that she had the makings of a hell of an agent even in those early days. She wore her hair very short, affected oversized sunglasses that concealed her luminous blue eyes, and was rarely seen in anything but slacks. She hadn't been with Global long enough then to earn full executive status, but she was learning fast—and profitably. Even at this restricted stage she had developed a fiscally rewarding ability to turn up with other agent's clients, and although Rudy always piously intoned, "Global never steals clients, as you know" at the Monday morning staff meetings, he rarely questioned the source of Lettie's list since she always swore they had come to her and to Global of their own free will.

It had long been a custom for Judd to come into Rudy's office for a few minutes just before the place closed for the night. Rudy was always there, no matter how late the hour. He liked to say, "It's my store, and I like to be the last one out. Never can tell," and he chuckled, "might be a last-minute sucker come in looking for an agent, and I wouldn't want to lose him."

This time Judd and Rudy chatted a little about the three-picture deal Judd had just closed with Paramount for Ron Winner.

"Good job, Judd, good job," Rudy had said, puffing at his cigar. "Winner can't act worth a damn; but he's got the kind of balls that jut out on the screen, and that's what Paramount will sell. And if not, that's their problem, not ours. Thank God—and you—that their front office boys never saw that last spaghetti western he did for Maggiori in Italy." He paused. "I forgot. What did we pay Maggiori not to showcase it for a releasing deal until you clinched the Paramount thing?"

"Five thousand and a promise to give them first look at our properties. But it was worth it. We'll get it all back and then some from Paramount on the overtime clause: Winner gets twenty thousand a week for overtime, and knowing Paramount, there's bound to be a hell of a lot of overtime when you spread it over three pictures. Once the Maggiori picture is released, we couldn't have sold Winner for an animated cartoon; all we'd have to represent would be an ex-actor. I saw the rough cut. Jesus!"

Rudy leaned back, puffing slowly on the cigar. "And what about that first-look business? Did you have to do that?"

Judd grinned. "Frankly, Rudy, it was that or more money and I knew you'd prefer that. You see, Maggiori's on the edge of bankruptcy; I checked with their bank in Naples." He smiled. "You'll see that on my expense account." Rudy smiled and Judd continued. "They won't have a quarter to bid on one of our properties, anyway, so why not let them have first look? That's all it'll be — a look, and even on that I was careful. It's only for twelve months."

Rudy smiled appreciatively. "As I said, Judd, good job. This one calls for a reward." He coughed, adding as soon as he recovered, "No, it's not a bonus. Something better."

"There's nothing better than a bonus, but maybe I'm wrong," Judd answered, and waited while Rudy drew out a small box from his pocket and handed it to him. Judd opened it under Rudy's benevolent gaze. It was the 25-year service pin.

"There's a small speech that goes with this, Judd." Rudy said. "First place, you're the only guy at Global who's been around here that long except for me, of course. Second, it means a lot to me for you to have this, a lot to me and Global." He went on before Judd could think of anything appropriate to say. "You know, Judd, I always used to call you my right-hand devil. You don't shit me. I don't always like what you say, and I don't always agree with you; but I know you don't shit me."

Rudy got up from his massive mahogany desk, walked ceremoniously to Judd, twirling the little pin in his hand, and shook hands with him in solemn silence. Judd didn't say anything until Rudy had eased himself back into the black leather chair.

Then Judd spoke. "I'm grateful, Rudy, grateful for the pin, grateful to Global, grateful to you. That's all I can say." Judd grinned mischievously. "And I'm not shitting you."

Both men laughed. The tension of the moment was broken.

Rudy leaned back and the ceiling light above his desk gave his white hair the effect of an aureole; the gold rims of his old-fashioned glasses twinkled. He almost looked benign, this man who had bulldozed his way to the top of the heap in a town where deceit and integrity were frequently interchangeable if one wanted to succeed, this man who headed the largest talent agency in the world, an agency with a half-dozen European branches and as many in key cities in the United States.

Judd remembered the scrubby office Rudy first had in New York. 1260 Sixth Avenue was the number, fourth floor rear, a shabby brown rug on the floor, a battered desk with three equally worn-down chairs, and a reception office, so-called, where Rudy's secretary performed on the rented typewriter. Judd shared the room with her as the file-clerk-cum-office-boy. He was barely twenty at the time, and what he really wanted to be was a writer, but he had early discovered that the necessity of eating took precedence.

Judd's first name was Jacob then; it was Rudy who named him Judd. "I never heard of an agent called Jake, leastwise one who ever really made it," he said when he first hired Judd. "Let's call you Judd, and forget the Jacob business."

Judd got the job because of Milly. Milly was Rudy's secretary, and they met at Cooper Union where Judd was taking a night course in creative writing. Milly was there to brush up on her typing and shorthand. Their first dates were at a cheap restaurant deceitfully named Freddie's Fine Food. That's where he first heard about Global Talent Associates, Inc. and Rudy Ruttenberg. Milly was highly enthusiastic about the whole agency business, and it wasn't long before she'd introduced him to Rudy.

The intercom buzzed and Judd picked up the phone. It was Milly, asking when he wanted to leave for the services. He glanced at his wrist, then awkwardly put down the receiver so that he could use his other hand to press the stem on his digital watch. The time and the date, 1:30 on September 14, both lit up.

"We have plenty of time, Milly; we don't have to go for at least another thirty minutes. There's no problem about parking; everybody from Global has a place reserved." He put down the receiver.

That was just like Milly, he thought to himself, always concerned about being on time. That reminded him of the watch—a twentieth anniversary present from her—and how he detested it, but of course he had never said a word to her about it. What an idiotic idea! A watch that required the use of both hands to tell the time. Milly had once overheard him comment idly on it as he was thumbing the pages of the *New Yorker*, and she'd wrongly assumed it was a gadget that would interest him. She never neglected an opportunity to please him in those days; he thought of the blue dressing gown again. He still had occasional, but infrequent, twinges of conscience when he realized how little she meant in his life now, except for being Mrs. Judd Haber.

He wondered what she would think if she ever saw him with Mira. As a matter of fact, this was one of his afternoons with Mira, and she probably missed him. He knew he missed her. They had good times in bed together, very good; she made him think he was twenty-five again, and not a man of fifty who took testosterone injections. She hadn't complained when he called up and explained about Rudy's death and the funeral, but he thought he sensed genuine disappointment in her voice. "Are you sure you can't come over afterwards?" she had asked. "No," he told her, "chances are some of the staff will want to meet when it's finished and hash over the whole thing. We'll make up for it, for sure. I'll phone you." "I'll be here," she said. "Love . . . you . . . very . . . much," and she hung up. That was the way she ended every phone conversation; every time he left, she told him "love . . . you . . . very . . . much," each word spaced out and meticulously separated. Judd liked that "love . . . you . . . very . . . much." There were times when he wondered whether she really meant it, but once he was with her and her soft, full lips closed over his prick while one slender hand moved gently and inexorably up and down and the other pressed gently on his balls, he didn't give much of a damn whether she meant it or not.

Another buzz of the intercom. Milly again. This time she wanted to know whether he'd remembered to send flowers. Judd controlled his irritation. "Don't worry, Milly. Everything's been attended to. A wreath from you and me. Flowers from Kerry and Suz, sent separately. Josie did it all. I'll be down in about fifteen minutes," and he hung up the receiver, being careful not to bang it, as he would have liked. Milly and her flowers.

In a way, it was her love of flowers that triggered the first time Judd had slept with Milly, and it took almost a year of persistent wooing on his part to persuade her that fucking was all right, even though they weren't married.

Naturally, they saw a lot of each other at Global once Judd got the job, and they spent a lot of evenings together. Milly had auburn hair—Judd always liked to call it red—and when she shook it loose the first time they slept together, Judd got the best hard-on he had ever had in his whole life up to that moment.

It happened the day Rudy called Judd into his office and told him he was being fired. Rudy was unsmiling when he made the announcement.

Judd found himself suddenly sweating profusely. "I don't understand, Mr. Ruttenberg. What have I done? I don't understand."

Now Rudy smiled; then he began to laugh. "I guess I have a rotten sense of humor, and somebody else ought to write my comedy lines when I think I'm being funny. Anyway, Judd, stop worrying. What I'm trying to tell you is that you're too damn bright to be an office boy, and I'm going to promote you to another spot."

"What's that, Mr. Ruttenberg?" Judd asked, relief flooding his whole being.

"You won't believe it," Rudy said, "but we're going to have an accountancy department and you're going to be it."

Judd was no longer frightened, but still bewildered. "But I don't know anything about accounting."

"You will, Judd, you will," said Rudy, "because starting next Monday night you're going to enroll in the accountancy courses at New York University, compliments of Global Talent Associates, and once you've got that under your belt, one of these days you're going to go out and be a real agent for this outfit. In the meantime, beginning next week you've got a twenty-dollar raise. Any objections?"

Judd grinned and put out his right hand. "None that you'll ever hear. And thank you—very much."

The two men shook hands. "And now, Judd, since you're going to be handling the figures, and you'll see the books anyway—that is, once you learn how to read them—you'll want to know what's going on at Global. You remember Ed Garrell, that guy I met at Vegas? You remember we sold him that Spanish picture, the dirty one, the one Manuel Ortega made and couldn't unload anywhere." Rudy chuckled. "You know how I hate the whole porn business; Global never would have handled it if I'd known how filthy it was, but Ortega kept calling it a period film and never showed me the finished picture until the contract was already signed. Anyway, Garrell liked it—I guess he likes dirty pictures—and we got our ten percent from Ortega, and Garrell tells me he made a tidy bundle on it in the X circuit."

Judd had met Garrell in the office, a tall thin-faced unsmiling man. He nodded.

"Well, Garrell's a strange guy and I wouldn't want to know where his money comes from, but he's fascinated by the picture business and specially by the agency end of it. He thinks I've got a lot on the ball and he liked the way we handled that deal for him. Anyway, he wants to put some money into Global Talent Associates. He feels the agency business, and especially Global, is going to be big one of these days, and he thinks he can make a wad of dough for himself as well as getting an in on anything we have to offer that comes along. And—this is the best part of it all as far as I'm concerned—I've got the right to buy out his interest in Global anytime on six months' notice with a thirty percent profit. Of course, he's got the right to say he'd rather stay in than take the money; but I'll gamble on anybody accepting a thirty percent profit on an investment, and besides he won't be in the way. All he wants is to make dough for himself. How does that strike you, Mr. Accountant-to-be?"

"How much is he putting in?" Judd asked.

"Fifty thousand now, fifty thousand at the end of the year, and fifty thousand next year."

"I think it's just great, just plain great, and with you at the top I know we'll go places and do things."

"We will, Judd; we will. We'll do just that, and now get the hell out of here and let me do some work!" Rudy grinned as Judd shut the door behind him.

Judd went out that afternoon and bought one dozen yellow roses—and they were beauties, too. When he showed up at Milly's apartment for their movie date, she was staggered. And when Judd told her about the raise, the accountancy course at NYU, and the chance of becoming a real agent, she was elated.

And that was the night they became lovers, the night he brought her yellow roses.

Judd had slept with a few whores and knew a little about what to do in bed, and since Milly knew absolutely nothing, his paltry experience seemed sophistication to her, and she became an adept pupil.

It was only about a year and a half after that that they were married at City Hall. It was Rudy who made it possible. Judd had never forgotten that particular day which led to his marrying Milly.

It was a hot afternoon early in July that Rudy called Judd into his office. He waved him to the chair opposite his desk, lit the inevitable cigar, and twirled the match in his fingers before dropping it into the ash-laden tray on his desk.

"You're through, Judd. I've just taken on a new man—fresh out of school and raring to go—to handle the accounts. He comes in next Monday. I figure you ought to be able to teach him the ropes in about two weeks. That okay with you?"

This time Judd did not sweat. He knew Rudy a lot better by then.

"Two weeks is plenty if that's what you told him." He waited.

"Good. That's what I thought you'd say. And now, about you. I've been watching you a lot and you're ready to move on. First, your own deal. I'm doubling your salary and you'll be getting a cut on anything you bring in and close yourself. We'll work out the percentage later. Okay?"

Judd smiled. "Are you kidding? It's better than okay. It's terrific. When do I start?"

Rudy put down his cigar, took a letter from the pile on his desk, and shoved it forward to Judd to see.

"Now. You begin right now, Judd. What does that say?" he asked.

Judd started to turn the letter around; but Rudy's hand closed tightly over his and stopped him.

"But I can't read it, Rudy. It's upside down."

Rudy chuckled. "That's right. It's upside down." His voice took on a note of total gravity. "Judd," he said, "I'm going to make an agent out of you, a real agent, and you're going to earn this raise and a lot more unless I'm wrong about you. Starting two weeks

from today you're going to contact publishers, pro-
ducers, film companies, anyone and everyone where
you can get information that will help Global make a
buck." He leaned forward and peered into Judd's eyes.
"And one of the first things you're going to learn to do
is to read letters upside down. Get it? Upside down!"
And then he laughed, relaxed in his chair, and picked
up the telephone. "That's all. It's your first lesson in
agentry." He dismissed him with a cheerful wave of
his disengaged hand.

The wedding wasn't much of a ceremony. Judd's
mother was dead; his father was there, wracked with
arthritis, obviously ill at ease. Milly's mother and father came in from Idaho for the event, and Judd was
glad to see how eager they were to get back to their
farm. Judd knew he would never have gotten along
with them, though he never mentioned this to Milly
who talked a lot about her parents' "endurance and
survival instincts." Some cousins came, and Milly's
twelve-year-old sister came with her parents. Judd's
only brother Benny was working with an oil company
in Bangladesh, but he sent a cable of congratulations;
since Judd hadn't seen him for many years, it didn't
matter very much one way or the other. And of course
there was Rudy, Rudy and Mag, his wife, already in
the terminal stages of leukemia. She seemed even
frailer than she was standing next to the robust figure
of Rudy, who dominated the entire ceremony.

Three years after that Global Talent Associates
moved its main office to Hollywood, and it was on its

way. Judd was on his way with it, and so, in a sense, was Milly. Milly never really liked Hollywood; she understood the nuances of her new role as the wife of an ambitious executive, but she never seemed to enjoy that role. At least that's how it seemed to Judd. She functioned superbly as a hostess, but only Judd knew how glassy her smile was as she chatted with the various clients and "quasi friends," as she always privately termed the carefully screened guest list.

She was a good wife in that she never protested Judd's long hours at the office, and his business meetings at home at strange hours of the day and night. She accepted the various material testimonials to Judd's increasing success: the big house in Bel Air, the charge accounts, the two Mercedes (Judd had bought her one for herself), the costly clothes Judd insisted she wear, the jewels; but the key word was "accepted"—she never demonstrated any real enjoyment of them or what they represented.

Judd could never pinpoint the day or the occasion when he knew that his love for her had slipped easily and gracefully into companionship and tolerance. Nor did he really know whether Milly still loved him. In fact, he knew less and less about Milly as the years went by, and this was true even before Mira came into his life. It must have happened after Suz was born, he thought, but he wasn't sure. Suz was nineteen now, a junior at Occidental, and was as beautiful as Milly had been, those long years ago when she shook loose her auburn hair and slipped into bed next to him for the first time. Or maybe it happened because of Kerry.

Kerry—his real name was Kerment—was twenty-four, handsome, easy-going, and possessed of considerable charm. He was an adopted child. For some years after their marriage Milly was unable to become pregnant, and finally they had adopted Kerry from an orphanage in Illinois. Suz had been born to them some two years later as an unexpected but welcome bonus.

Milly's only sign of disinterest in, or perhaps disapproval of, the life they led as husband and wife was her return to college once they knew she couldn't have a child. That was early in their marriage. She'd enrolled at UCLA and she now had her B.A. and an M.A., too, in English literature. Even after she had her degrees she continued to go to UCLA, taking extension courses that interested her.

Judd was convinced by now that that was the beginning of their spiritual divorce. At first Milly had brought home books for him to read; she wanted to discuss them with him "in depth," as she liked to put it, and Judd never seemed to satisfy her on that score. He had early learned not to ask her whether she thought the book in question had a movie in it. Not that he felt there was anything reprehensible about that question—after all, that's what they made a living from, wasn't it?—but her irritation was so manifest, her contempt so stinging that he quickly realized the maladroitness of that conversational opening. It wasn't long after that Milly ceased recommending books to him. He recalled the incident that made her stop. She had recommended a novel by Alain

Robbe-Grillet and Judd had started it twice, only to admit to himself that it both baffled and bored him. But to preserve peace and to be able to discuss it "in depth" with Milly, he had borrowed a studio synopsis to give him enough familiarity with the story to hold up his end of the discussion. Milly was elated, until she found the synopsis on his desk the next morning. She didn't talk about it at all; she merely handed him the synopsis just before he left for the office, and it was never mentioned again.

It wasn't long after that that she moved into one of their guest rooms, telling the half-listening Kerry and Suz that her migraines kept her awake and it was unfair to Judd.

Rudy had always liked Milly and used to make heavy-handed jokes about not being smart enough to have tried to lay her himself when she had been his secretary back in those early days of Global in New York. Actually Rudy was grateful to her mainly because she'd been so good to Mag during the last few years of her ebbing life. It was Milly who used to come to see Mag, three times a week; she used to read to her in the half-dark of the bedroom while the older woman would listen and smile and occasionally reach out a gaunt hand to tap Milly's wrist affectionately. Milly had even been friendly with Janie, Rudy's second wife, until he divorced her after finding her in bed with Duke Morrow, a fourth-rate actor and one-time wrestler. But Milly never seemed to get along very well with Jackie.

Jackie was Rudy's third and current wife, a former

Vegas line-dancer, almost thirty years younger than
Rudy, strangely beautiful. Her green-gray eyes, dead-
white complexion, and her body that moved with fe-
line and calculated grace gave her a predatory
loveliness.

Judd had never been able to understand Milly's an-
tipathy to Jackie. After all, she was the boss's wife,
and if he wanted a young wife, it was not Milly's business to pass any judgments on his choice. But Milly
was adamant. Not that she wasn't polite and well-
bred when they met at industry parties, but she made
it clear to Judd that she had no intention of establish-
ing any rapport with Jackie Ruttenberg under any
conditions. The closest she ever came to explaining
her dislike was her straightforward answer when
Judd had pressed her for an explanation. "I like
Rudy; I don't like whores. Jackie's a whore even
though I can't prove it. But someday she'll slip and I
don't want to be around when Rudy finds out."

Secretly Judd agreed with Milly's statement though
his loyalty to Rudy would never permit him to say so.

There was something whorish about Jackie, the
same quality that Mira had: an extraordinary ability
to please men, a fantastic sexual talent.

Judd had first met Mira one drunken evening in
New York at the Plaza Hotel. He was there for the
buttoning-up of a deal for Wendy Macrin at Warner's.
It had been a difficult negotiation, mainly because
Wendy didn't know how to keep her mouth shut.
When the session was over and he had gratefully de-

posited her in her suite on the seventh floor, he knew
he needed something to remind him he was alive. He
also knew it wasn't Wendy, even though she had assured him in unmistakable terms that she felt grateful. Judd didn't. He was bone-tired, but even after a
few drinks from the bottle he always kept in his room
he found himself restless.

He called Grace's number and asked for Danielle, a
cute French girl he'd had on several previous trips,
but Grace explained that Danielle was no longer with
her; she had committed the inexplicable (to Grace)
folly of getting married to one of the house's clients.
And that's how Mira Dalloway became an important
part of his life.

Grace explained to him that Mira wasn't one of her
regulars; she was a dress model who turned a few
tricks now and then for the extra money. Grace went
on to tell Judd that she had asked Mira to join her establishment many times, but Mira preferred only
part-time engagements. She had class, real class, said
Grace.

Judd understood what Grace meant when he first
saw Mira. Her entrance was really spectacular. When
Judd opened the door in response to her anticipated
knock, she looked up at him and questioned, "Mr. Haber?" and when he nodded and put out his hand for
her coat, she slipped out of it herself and she was completely naked.

After she'd gone down on him for the second time
he knew that everything he'd ever experienced before
was second-rate. She was a sexual genius; every move

she made was for his pleasure.

Mira was a blonde with hair that glistened like liquid gold. Her legs were long and slender, her breasts full and round, and her pubic hair was thick and pale and curly. Her ruby-red toenails matched her long fingernails and her thick lips were wet and inviting.

He stayed in New York as long as he possibly could, spending every spare minute with Mira, who'd wangled a few days off from her modeling work when he told her what he was prepared to pay (and it was worth it). When Rudy's phone calls from the coast became more and more insistent, Judd realized he couldn't do without Mira.

It wasn't easy to persuade her to leave New York and her job and the life she liked. She kept raising the ante and insisted that she wouldn't go under any conditions unless she could continue modeling. She'd be damned if she would just sit around in some apartment in Hollywood no matter how elegant it was, waiting for him to visit her when he could. This was no problem, he assured her; one of Global's clients was Florence Jenkins, who headed the wardrobe department at Columbia, and Florence knew all the designers in town. He went on to explain that Florence owed him a favor. What he didn't tell Mira was that Florence's fabulous jewel collection had been bought with kickbacks from many of these designers, and that Judd had personally okayed the cashing of a number of checks drawn on Florence's account. No question about it, Florence would get her a job if that's what she wanted.

The minute Judd got on the plane he knew that he'd been right. He couldn't live without her. Every time he thought about her he got an erection, and he could taste her breast in his mouth. His whole body ached for her.

Once back in Hollywood, he talked to Florence; she listened, and she heard so well that within three days after his return he was able to phone Mira and tell her that she had a job as a model with Mirabelle Meredith, one of California's top designers. And then he told her about the furnished apartment he'd rented for her.

Four days later Mira Dalloway stepped off a plane at the Los Angeles International Airport and took a taxi to 747 Spalding Drive, Beverly Hills.

II

The drive to Temple Israel took about a half hour. It was a hot, humid day, and Judd was grateful for the air-conditioning in the car. Milly was quiet and subdued, and when Judd glanced over at her now and again and their eyes met, he could sense that her mind was far away. He was grateful for her silence; he too was immersed in his own reflections. Only once—usually it was much more often—did she admonish him about driving too close to the curb as he made a right turn. Her warning irritated him as it always did. He had explained to her before that he was a careful driver; that he had not been in an accident or even been warned by a policeman in the last fourteen years; but even as he spoke he knew that she would do the same thing the next time they went out in the car. It was inevitable. She was convinced he was a rotten driver.

Kerry was talking to Suz in low tones, sobered or at least impressed by the solemnity of the occasion; under ordinary conditions Kerry was aggressively expansive both in movements and in speech. Blond with gray eyes, tall, and always superbly dressed, he toyed absently with his gold lighter as he spoke. Judd could see Suz's face in his rear mirror, the soft waves of her auburn hair framing her expressive brown eyes. She didn't appear to be listening with any attention to whatever Kerry was saying. Like Milly, she seemed to be thinking of other things.

Judd was sure that Milly was remembering moments with Rudy; after all, she'd been the old man's secretary way back and it was natural. But he was equally certain that neither Kerry nor Suz gave much of a damn. They weren't thinking about the funeral at all, he was sure, except as an interruption of their usual activities. Certainly none of them were thinking about what was occupying Judd's mind: when he would take over the presidency of Global Talent Associates once a decent period of mourning had elapsed, and when he could get away to see Mira.

Judd was wrong about Suz and Kerry; they were indeed thinking about Rudy and Global Talent Associates and the subsequent role of Judd Haber in its international affairs, but he would have been surprised at the tenor of their thoughts. He was right, however, about Milly.

Milly

So it's all over for Rudy, she thought. No more parties for two hundred and fifty "friends" who would drink his liquor, eat his food, dance to his band (always clients of Global Talent, of course), smoke his cigars smuggled in from the London office, laugh at his jokes, flirt with his sex-driven wife when his back was turned, swim in his blue-lit pool, toast him at least three times during the evening as the "Mr. Hollywood" of the film industry, and calumniate him viciously in groups as a bastard, a tyrant, a thief, a confidence man, an opportunist, a parvenu (no, Milly corrected herself, they wouldn't know that word), a bloodsucker of other people's talents and America's all-around shit. None of them really knew or understood Rudy, and that went for Judd, too, she was convinced. After all, she reflected, I was the only one who knew him when he was only a frighteningly ambitious young man in that shabby Sixth Avenue office.

It wasn't the time that counted; it was the kind of man he was then and the kind of man he'd become since. Rudy loved power, he loved it with a genuine passion; it was his reasons for wanting power that intrigued Milly at that period. "You've got to understand what I mean, Milly, when I say I want to be the biggest agent in the whole goddamn business. Of course I want money; who doesn't? But I want something else and maybe nobody will understand that but you. I love this damn business; I love every son-of-a-bitch in it who thinks he can crack it. I love them because they have talent. That's what I worship, that's what I want to see rewarded, that's what counts. I'm smart, but Jesus Christ, is that a talent? A talent is something God-given, something that happens when one of these bastards we're trying to place gets a chance to stand in front of a camera and later on an audience looks at him and something happens to them—something strange and wonderful and moving—something—Jesus, Milly—something unbelievable. And I'm the guy sitting in that same audience who made it all happen. I suppose you think I'm talking like I want to be a god. That is how I want to feel, like a god. If you ever tell anybody I said that, I'll fire you five minutes after I find out. I sound like a sentimental slob, but that's the whole of it, Milly, and I'm never going to change, no matter how big I get. I am going to be big, really big, the biggest there is in the business, and I'm going to do it without shitting all over everybody to get there. There's no need for that, believe me. You just wait and see."

Maybe Mag, his first wife, feeble, ill, adoring, maybe she had understood what first drove Rudy and what mattered to him. But Milly wasn't sure about her, either, for Rudy was a different man outside the office. Besides, Mag needed all her waning energies just to stay alive, and she was content to continue to love the Rudy she'd married, the young Rudy, Rudy the believer. And he'd done just what he said he'd do— become the biggest in a town where every morning there were twenty people scheming and plotting and planning to be what he'd become and ready to tear him apart. It had been a hard thing to accomplish. He'd done things that Milly hated to think of; he'd ruined competitors; he'd stolen clients; he'd double-crossed his friends; he'd swindled and cheated and connived; he'd used every honest and dishonest trick that the industry offered, and while doing it he'd forgotten all about the reasons that drove him that afternoon in the office with his feet on the desk, his vest open, and his cigar burning unheeded in the ashtray. He'd forgotten about talent and its miracle and what joy it brings to an audience. He'd forgotten everything except the one thing his success gave him—power. All the people who hated Rudy were right. He had became hateful: he was cruel, vindictive, resentful; he had become everything he once knew was wrong and destructive, and all to hang on to the power he'd fought so hard to get. He'd become the kind of man who'd marry a whore like Jackie and be proud of her.

Maybe he never knew she was a whore; but Milly was convinced that even if he did, he didn't give a damn as long as nobody said it. And he knew nobody would. He was Rudy Ruttenberg, President of Global Talent Associates, and they all knew it.

And now they were on the way to Temple Israel, all of them, including Jackie. And there would be speeches, eulogies about Rudy Ruttenberg, the Mr. Hollywood of the industry, encomia about his charities, his kindness to young actors and writers and directors, anecdotes about his generosity, his virtues, about his love and passionate devotion to the industry, about Rudy as a wielder of miracles—all patently lies, lies about the man who had just died.

The tires squeaked against the curb, throwing Milly to one side.

"For God's sake, Judd, you're driving like a fool. You know how I hate it when you're careless at the wheel," she said angrily, looking at him with open resentment.

"Sorry Milly, I guess I wasn't thinking. But you needn't be so dramatic about it. Jesus, Milly, all I did was scrape the tire."

"I know, but that means you're not watching the road, as usual," Milly retorted and drew back once again into her own thoughts.

Now it was all over, finished: the cheating, the venality, the deceit, the corruption, the slime that was Rudy's everyday domain. She glanced at Judd's still-trim figure, his hands' firm grasp of the steering wheel, the watch she had given him visible on his wrist. Would the same thing happen to Judd when he became president? Would he go the same way? It had been years since she and Judd had talked about anything except the dinner parties she had to give for clients or the places they would go to with clients. But she still thought she knew Judd pretty well, at least the Judd she had married years ago. She knew he was weak, but she also knew he was basically a honorable man. Did she think so because he was that way when they had first met? When Judd became president would he become another Rudy, give the same parties Rudy had hosted, the same banal, empty, noisy, vulgar parties? Would he triumph by destroying, as Rudy had done? Or would he be chastened when he realized that it all ended the same way, in a garishly decorated coffin at the Temple Israel? God knows they had enough money right now for Judd to do anything he wanted. But what did he want? Was it power just like Rudy?

Judd had once wanted to write; she remembered that first and only play of his, so filled with bombast and polysyllabic words; but it had a chaotic beauty, too, and a passionate floundering sense of tragic reality. It was inspired in part by one of Shakespeare's sonnets (Judd had just discovered Shakespeare then, encouraged by Milly). She recalled the title, "False Colors," and the dedication, "For Milly, who else?" She'd explained to him that most playwrights did not dedicate plays, that it was unusual to do so; but he'd said, "I'm not most playwrights," and that was that.

The play never got anywhere, of course; it was amateurishly written, and besides, it was very soon after he'd finished it that she got him the job with Rudy. And he'd never mentioned it again, not once. Nor had she, though she'd thought about it now and then when he'd return from the office drawn, almost white, the skin around his eyes tense. She'd tried to be a good wife to Judd, but she didn't wonder why they'd grown apart. She knew. It wasn't really that they'd grown apart; it was sadder than that. He'd stopped growing altogether.

He'd gone ahead in the business; he'd moved up the corporate ladder; he'd confirmed Rudy's belief that he would become a top agent; but Milly didn't consider that to be growth. That was just being smart in business and getting smarter through experience. But everything else had stopped dead. It was not only that Judd never wrote again; it was as if he had never wanted to write. Nor did he read anymore except for business and for conventional dinner-table chatter;

he never went to plays or movies unless they offered
business prospects. In his own way, sitting there driving his shining Mercedes to Rudy's funeral, he was as
dead as Rudy.

She glanced at his handsome profile, this man she
had married, who had once written a play and had
wanted to write others, this man who had once—it
seemed such a terribly long time ago—made passionate, tender love to her and she to him. They still had
sex now and again, perfunctorily, ritualistically, pas-
sionlessly, dishonestly. Did Judd have a mistress?
Milly wondered. No. She knew him too well for that. If
he did it was Global Talent Associates. Of that Milly
was absolutely sure. Would he have cared that she
was having an affair with Jerry Horton, the English
professor who had taught her at UCLA? Probably not,
she reflected. Nice, gentle, timid Jerry Horton, scared
of his termagant wife, scared of their clandestine relationship, scared of losing his job, scared of meeting
her once every week in that grimy motel room, always
scared, scared of life. No, Jerry wasn't the answer to
anything, but he helped to fill a void, a void left by a
fiery young man who had wanted to conquer the
world. "It's not that I think I've got more to say than
any other playwright—I just know it. I've got a million ideas racing inside of me, Milly, maybe more, and
I know they're good, and that I'm good. I'll be the best
goddamn playwright in America before I get through,
Milly, maybe the best in the world, and you'll be up
there next to me when they call out for the author.
And that'll be me!," and he grinned and buried his

head between her breasts. How long ago was that? How many years? Had Judd really said that? Had it ever really happened?

Kerry

"You're not even listening to me, Suz, I don't think you've heard anything I've been saying for the last five minutes. Don't tell me you're taking this funeral seriously. I can't believe it."

"It just so happens that I *am* taking it seriously, and if I were you I'd shut up before Dad hears you," she answered. "Rudy meant a lot to Dad, so you might at least pretend to care a little for his sake." She eased away from him to indicate her disapproval.

"Oh, shit!" was Kerry's answer, reaching into his pocket for a cigarette.

At that moment the wheels scraped against the curb and Kerry listened to Milly's sharp admonition to Judd about his careless driving. Kerry grinned; he knew how the old man hated to be corrected when he drove. Poor dumb bastard, the old man. All he could ever do in his whole life was make money. Not that he'd ever learned how to spend it. Hell, no. He was so busy making it that he'd never given any thought or time to having any fun with it. Jesus, he must be a dull guy to live with. Kerry closed his eyes, puffed on his cigarette, and tried to imagine his old man and Milly-Mom (that was the name Milly had asked him to call her when he was adopted) making it together. I

bet the old man calls his night switchboard just before
he puts it in to tell them he won't be available for fifteen minutes. And Milly-Mom. Wonder what kind of
tits she has and whether she has a tight cunt. Kerry
reached into his own immediate past to give color to
his images. Did they do it the way he did it with Colette, from the back? Did Milly-Mom ever go down on
him? I doubt it. The old boy was too conservative for
that. The images vanished. No use. They probably
hadn't fucked each other for years, anyway. Did they
love each other, whatever the hell that meant?

From somewhere deep inside his memory, Kerry
plucked out a hazy recollection of a very handsome
tall man with a very cheerful voice sweeping up a five-
year-old boy, holding him high in his arms, and then
swinging him down again to hand him to a beautiful
lady with gray eyes and a nice smell. "You're a handsome boy, and we're very proud to be your new mother
and father, aren't we, Judd?" The tall man had nodded and kissed the boy on his cheek. "And we're going
to call you Kerry, if it's okay with you. Kerment is a
very nice name, and we like it; but Kerry sounds more
like our son. Kerry Haber. How does it sound to you?
You'll like it a lot better than Kerment Callahan
when you get used to it." At that bewildering moment
in his life, Kerry had no idea how it sounded. All he
knew was that this tall man and this beautiful lady
were going to get him out of the Clement Hill Orphanage and that he'd never see it again. That was good
enough for him. Kerry was fine. Kerry Haber was fine.
Why not? What difference would it make anyway?

A cigarette-ash dropped on his carefully creased trousers, and he brushed it away irritably. He glanced at his watch. Almost two-thirty. Maybe he'd have time for some tennis and a massage at the Club, and a quick one later with that new manicurist, the one with the big boobs. Kerry could feel his erection. A hell of a thing to happen to a guy on the way to a funeral, he thought, and he giggled aloud. Suz shot him a look of disapproval and he stopped. Christ, why was everybody so grim? So Rudy was dead, his godfather Rudy, as Dad had asked him to call him for no goddamn good reason except he thought it would please his boss.

Kerry hadn't seen Rudy very much when he was growing up,except on birthdays and Christmas,when the old bastard would appear at cocktail time, bringing extravagantly useless presents, and pat him on the head absently while talking to Judd about business. In fact, Rudy was a cloudy figure to Kerry except for two memorable occasions, and Kerry clenched his fist in anger as he remembered them. The first was three years ago when Kerry had dropped out of Santa Monica College. Actually, he had been "encouraged to leave," as his advisor put it, when he had been caught cheating on an exam. He'd always thought the whole college bit was a crock of shit, anyway.

The thing Kerry most wanted to do was to get a job acting and become famous. It was bad enough to endure the hullabaloo Judd and Milly-Mom raised when he'd told them (but he knew how to handle Milly-Mom). Judd was not so easily persuaded, and he must have discussed it with Rudy at the office. That's when Kerry saw red, because the next thing that happened was a command-invitation to lunch at the Ambassador Hotel where the old bastard lectured him about the importance of education and how much he was hurting himself and Judd and Milly-Mom and on and on and on. Kerry had listened as politely as he could under the circumstances, but it spoiled his enjoyment of the highly priced French wine the old bastard had ordered. Several times during Rudy's exhortation Kerry had silently told him to go fuck himself even as he heard his own voice trying to explain and expand on his abiding love of films and the contributions he would make to the industry as an actor.

Not that Rudy gave him much of a chance to talk. "Kerry," he said in parting, "Your father doesn't even know I'm doing this, but I've known him for more than a quarter of a century and your mother even longer, and what you're doing to him and to your mother and to yourself is just plain rotten. You don't want to be an actor; you're just too damn lazy to go to school and you're lying when you say you aren't." Kerry didn't interrupt. If anybody was lying it was the old bastard when he said Judd hadn't asked him to do this. "One other thing, Kerry, my boy, if you think Global or anyone in it is going to help you in your ambition to be an actor—and I'm sure you figure on that—forget it. And that includes your father; I'll see to that personally. We won't. If you're sucker enough to quit school, you can make it on your own. And I want you to remember that. No one at Global is going to help you do the stupid thing you're doing. I may be your godfather but I'm not a damn fool." Kerry hated him after that. The old bastard had been right; Kerry had assumed that with Global behind him he could easily get into acting.

Kerry never mentioned the lunch at home, nor did Judd. But after a couple of more heated scenes with Judd and a lot of tears from Milly-Mom, they'd given in. Kerry had enrolled at an acting school. He didn't last very long there. Then he'd gone to another one. Same result. At the second school he went to, he'd laid the director's wife and she got him a few jobs in a little theater in Glendale. It wasn't much of a theater, and the few parts he got weren't much either, and when he showed up on stage drunk a couple of times, they dropped him. By that time, the director's wife had dropped him, too, and Kerry soon found more interesting occupations, playing tennis at the Beverly Hills Club and frequenting the Beverly Wilshire bar where he ran up charges that Judd refused to pay, but that Milly paid in secret.

Judd offered to aid him in getting a job, any kind of job; but Kerry was adamant and kept saying that the only job he wanted was acting. He kept sullenly silent when Judd reminded him that he'd been fired from all the acting jobs he'd ever had. Conditions at home were ugly most of the time, but Kerry was always able to con Milly-Mom into defending him when the going got too rough. He could always get what he wanted out of her; some things were harder than others, of course, but he always won her over in the end. As the weeks and months went by the tension increased. Judd had stormed and refused to talk to him; Milly-Mom had cried and given in; even Suz got into the act with a serious sister-brother talk that had bored him silly. Right about then Kerry got his first break. It happened through one of the friends he'd met at the Beverly Wilshire bar, who introduced him to a guy with the unbelievable name of Prompton Warwick, a fat, florid, fast-talking man in his early fifties who turned out to be the president of Warwick Artists Representatives, a small agency that specialized in providing talent for porn films. Prompton eventually told him that he used to make porn pictures and was headquartered in Vegas before he decided that there was more money in providing the ingredients. He'd only come to Hollywood six months ago, but as he boasted to Kerry, "the chips were already piling up."

They first met in the sauna. After the introduction had been made, the two men exchanged pleasantries. Prompton took a look at Kerry, emitted a "Wow!" and then remarked, "Son, you've got the best-looking prick in town. Why not show it? Maybe I can help you." They both laughed. Prompton presented him to another man in the steam room, a man named Ed Garrell, whom he said was also interested in porn films. Garrell was an investor in Warwick Artists Representatives, but Prompton didn't mention that. Garrell didn't talk much except to say that he knew Judd when he heard Kerry's last name. It wasn't long after that meeting that Prompton kept his word and Kerry got his first job acting in a porn picture. It was shot in Tijuana to avoid union complications. The money was good; there was a lot of first-rate fucking available from the other cast members and he was acting. Kerry was very pleased with himself and with Prompton, who saw rushes demonstrating Kerry's prowess in a sex circus sequence and enthusiastically assured Kerry that he'd have no trouble getting further assignments.

The scene between Judd and Kerry in the Haber living room when Judd found out about Kerry's new career, and that he was a client of Prompton Warwick's, was explosive and catastrophic. It seems that the very day Prompton got Kerry his first job he went directly to Judd's office and asked to see him. When he sent in his name he did not mention that Kerry was his client, and the flustered Josie returned to him in the waiting room with a curt message saying that Mr. Haber had no interest in seeing Mr. Warwick. What the embarrassed Josie did not tell the infuriated porn agent was that Judd had told her to "get that scum out of the office."

As Judd described the visit, he walked up and down the room recollecting the scene with rising anger. "And then the son of a bitch sent Josie back to me to say that you, my son, were a client of his, and that I'd better see him. When the hell did that happen and have you gone out of your mind? My son, acting in porn flicks and represented by that slime!"

Kerry flushed, stifled his anger, and said with controlled resentment, "He's an agent and he got me a job in pictures. That's a lot more than you were willing to do at Global."

Judd stopped his nervous pacing, and stood directly in front of Kerry's slumped figure. "You're damned right it's more than Global would do. We don't sell our clients to filthy pictures. That's been Rudy's policy since he started Global, and he's absolutely right. We're agents, not pimps; and we don't call the people who perform in those filthy films actors. They're whores, male and female, and that's what you are, Kerry, a whore!"

This time Kerry did not respond; there was nothing to be gained by answering.

"And you know what that asshole did when I finally saw him? He had the gall to suggest that we establish a department at Global with him in charge. He said that if Warwick Artists was good enough for my son, it was good enough for Global, and that there was a lot of money to be made in porn. Jesus Christ! I finally threw the oily-mouthed shit right out of my office and if I never see him again it'll be too soon. As for you, Kerry, if that's what you want to do with your life, do it somewhere else. I don't want you around here. I'm ashamed to admit you're my son."

Kerry straightened up in his chair, rose to his feet, and sauntered slowly to the door. "That's okay with me; I'll send for my clothes later," he said, and slammed the door.

As Kerry drove away he clenched his hands on the wheel, and thought to himself it was his father who was a shit, not Prompton. Hell, he was glad to be out of the house; he could move in with Colette, she was always glad to have him around, and what with the dough he was making now he could have a ball. For Christ's sake, he could name twenty films with Global clients playing scenes just like the ones he was doing in porn films. Where did the old man get off playing the pure and moral with him? Who did he think he was anyway—God?

As for Prompton, when Kerry queried him about the conference with Judd all he would say was, "He may be your father, Kerry; but nobody—and I mean nobody!—can treat Prompton Warwick that way and get away with it. Who the hell does he think he is—God?"

The whole situation gnawed at Kerry. What the hell was everybody so damn excited about? He was getting paid for acting, which was more than a lot of guys he knew who hung around bars waiting for a phone call for a bit part. What did they want him to do, nothing?

It was right about then that dear old godfather Rudy saw him once more, only this time it wasn't lunch at the Ambassador, it was ten minutes in his office, and Kerry hated him more than ever. "I'm seeing you because Judd told me what you're doing. It's just to tell you that you're a prick, Kerry Haber, a first-class prick, and if you were my son I'd kick you out on your ass instead of giving you a credit card and buying you shirts from Saks and suits from Dick Carroll's. And if you don't shape up and do something else besides jerking off in porn films, you'll end up in the gutter where you belong. And now get the hell out of here before I forget I'm supposed to be your godfather."

The situation at home was nasty. When Milly heard the news from Judd, her sorrow over what Kerry was doing was soon replaced with irrational anger at Judd for having thrown him out, and it wasn't long before Kerry moved his clothes back from Colette's. Judd wouldn't speak to him at all if he could avoid it, and Milly went around for days as if she had been crying: but as time went by they both accepted the inevitable. After all, he was acting, wasn't he, as he kept reminding them. And maybe he'd realize what a grimy world he was working in and get out of it.

Kerry kept pretty much to himself when he was at home and absented himself as much as he could, usually explaining that he had to work. By now he had a role in his third picture and he'd begun to enjoy the camaraderie on the set. As soon as the performers and technicians learned that he was the son of Judd Haber of Global they teased him good-naturedly about not being able to get a better job than porn. Kerry answered their jibes with jokes, but they rankled.

His resentment of his father and of "Rudy's policy" at Global grew inordinately. He knew how powerful Rudy's agency was and how it could open any doors in Hollywood. A word from Global would have started his career instantly; he'd seen it happen to lots of actors with a lot less talent and looks than he had; but that word never came. His hatred focused largely on Rudy; he was sure his father would have helped him (he could always count on Milly-Mom to swing the old man around to his side) were it not for Rudy. It was Rudy he abominated; his father didn't have enough guts to do anything contrary to Rudy's wishes—the fucking jellyfish. It was all his godfather's fault, that shithead.

And now he was dead. Good! He, Kerry Haber, was very much alive. When Judd sat in the president's chair, Kerry expected life to change for him, too. Hollywood would soon be hearing of a new star emerging on the horizon.

Suz

She was really irritated with Kerry. She knew perfectly well that he'd disliked Rudy, but was that any reason for giggling on the day of his funeral? She'd succeeded in divorcing herself from Kerry's latest adventure into porn beyond one brief discussion. She had told him she thought he was a jackass and he had told her to mind her own business. But this was an important day for all of them, and she moved away resentfully from Kerry, pushing herself up against the door. She closed her eyes.

Rudy had always been wonderful to her. It was on her tenth birthday, the day he gave her that marvelous green and gold bicycle, with her name burnt into the side of the leather seat, that he'd told her why. "You see, Suz," he said, "I've had a lot of wives; three of them, in fact, and that doesn't mean much to you, I guess; but anyway, I never had any children of my own, not from any of them, and I've decided that you're the little girl I wanted to have." He caressed her hair with his tobacco-stained fingers. "I like little girls with brown eyes and auburn hair and I especially like them when they happen to be named Suz— that's my favorite name. And since your daddy and mom made me your godfather I'm going to take full advantage of that relationship. That is, if it's okay with you."

It was very much okay with Suz. She liked everything about Rudy: his flamboyant shirts, the heavy seal-ring he wore, the big Rolls Royce that his man, Chester, drove, his thinning white hair (Suz never knew him when it was coal black), his old-fashioned pince-nez glasses that kept slipping when he nodded his head in excitement or agreement, even the deep wrinkles in his neck that she used to trace with her fingers when she was a very little girl. She asked him whether they went down all the way to his feet. He laughed and laughed and laughed before he swept her up in his arms and hugged her.

She loved going to his house the few times Daddy and Mom would take her along, the huge house perched on a high hill in Bel Air with its carefully tended English gardens, its sparkling blue-white pool, its gleaming tennis court. She had learned to play tennis on that court, courtesy of Rudy; that was a gift on her twelfth birthday. And on her graduation from high school there had been a gift certificate, not from one store in Beverly Hills, but from three, and she and Mom had a wonderful day buying what Mom called "Rudy-clothes."

Mom would miss Rudy; she and Suz used to talk about him sometimes and Mom would tell funny stories about the time when she had worked in Rudy's New York office, long before the house with the pool and the tennis court. It was hard to think that Rudy was dead, gone, disappeared. I guess it will change a lot of things for Daddy at the office, she mused. I suppose he'll be promoted to head the agency, but that would hardly make any difference, except he'd probably work harder and not be home as much. As it was, there were many evenings that he didn't come home until very late at night; Suz could hear him pass her door on the way to his suite as she sat propped up in bed studying.

It had been a very exciting year at Occidental for Suz, especially because of Jake Isaacs. Jake was a senior, on an athletic scholarship to help pay the tuition he could never have afforded. He was the captain of the basketball team and at the same time maintained a straight A average. They spent as much time as they could together, hampered on his side by his job waiting tables at a restaurant near the campus. They made uncomfortable love in her Porsche and gravely discussed their future together.

Suz had known Jake for almost 10 months—9 months, 5 days, and 3 hours, as she had told him the last time they were together—but for some reason she couldn't quite fathom, she'd never been able to get him to come to the house and meet her mother and fa-

ther and Kerry. Not that she hadn't tried. He had always refused with the phrase, "It just wouldn't be a
good idea, and let's leave it at that." Was it, she wondered, because he knew his world was totally different
from hers? Was he afraid that her family would disap-
prove of him because of that? She had tried to make
him tell her about his home life, what his parents did,
what his brothers were like (he had once told her that
he had two younger brothers), but he had invariably
cut her off. "It's different from Bel Air," was all he
would say.

Actually her family knew about Jake, that is to say,
they knew he existed and that Suz saw a great deal of
him. Kerry had once found an open letter from Jake
on her desk when he was rummaging for some
stamps—that was the time she and Jake had been
quarreling about her money and he had written to
apologize—and had read it. Kerry had teased her
about her man, Jake, and after that Suz was more
careful about her mail. Knowing that Kerry would
probably tell her parents about Jake, she told them
herself, explaining that she was interested in a senior
at Occidental and might bring him around to meet
them someday soon. Milly and Judd hardly listened
to her brief recital except to say politely that they'd
love to meet him anytime she wished. That was
months ago, and by now what she had described to
Milly and Judd as "interest" had become a deep, satisfying, consuming love.

The car lurched against the curb and Mom went
into her predictable act of when-will-you-learn-to-

drive-carefully while Daddy, as usual, listened white-lipped and Suz could not hear his response. Poor Daddy. Did he really love Mom? Had he ever loved her? Had he ever felt about her the way she felt about Jake or the way Jake felt about her? Suz loved both her parents but it was really Milly who was her favorite, her confidante, her intimate, that is except for Jake, of course. She glanced at her watch. She had a date with Jake this evening; they were going to an early dinner and a foreign flick at the Fox Venice. She'd left a message at his place about the funeral and she hoped he'd gotten it. Wonder how long funerals take? After all, there was only so much anyone could say about Rudy. I hope it won't take too long. I don't like to keep Jake waiting.

Judd

He was sorry about disappointing Mira; she must understand that he had to go to Rudy's funeral. He wondered what she'd do. She never scheduled anything when he was to see her, so she would have to fill in the afternoon with something else. She'd probably go shopping; about thirty days from now Josie would be coming into his office with two manila folders, one labeled Mr. Haber To Do, and the other without any designation. It was some time ago that she had started that custom, almost immediately after she had entered his office one afternoon with puzzled expression.

"Mr. H" (Josie always called him Mr. H and by now it seemed so appropriate and normal that he hardly noticed it), "Mr. H, there are some charge items here from Juel Park that just arrived in the mail. They're for someone named Mira Dalloway and they seem to come from her. Of course it's probably a mistake, but before sending them back I thought I'd better check to see if it's one of our clients I don't know who asked the office to pay her bills."

Judd didn't look at the manila folder. Instead he looked at Josie and said, "It's no mistake, Josie. They're okay. They're for a friend. It's okay to pay the bills."

Josie actually blushed and lowered her eyes. "I understand, Mr. H, thank you." She scooped the offending folder from his desk and left the room without a further word. It was never mentioned again, even though thereafter the two folders continued to appear on his desk on the first day of every month with appropriate checks attached to each one awaiting his signature. Knowing Josie's loyalty to him, Judd was sure that the unlabeled folder was there merely as a convenience to him, for verification, and not as a note of moral disapproval.

Judd was well aware that he had no secrets from Josie, either private or professional. She had been with him for years; he'd forgotten how long ago it was that she'd come to be interviewed, fresh from some Kansas backwater, having just completed a course in secretarial school. She'd worn her hair in a bun then, used no make-up, and wore what he had later learned were called "sensible clothes." Nor had her appearance changed much since then. After she got the job she'd moved almost imperceptibly from routine secretarial work to confidential advisor and consultant.

Judd turned his head to look briefly at Suz and Kerry in the back seat. Suz's lips were tightly drawn and Kerry had that sulky look on his face that Judd found especially displeasing. I suppose the kids have quarreled about something, he thought; it would be nice if they preserved some sense of decorum on a day like this and didn't indulge in their little-child bickerings and disagreements. After all, this was an important day in their lives too; with Rudy gone, somebody had to take over the big office, and they should be interested in that for his sake, if for no other reason.

In all their years together, and they'd gone through a lot, he and Rudy, Rudy had never brought up the question of a successor. Only once Rudy had talked about mortality and then it was derisively. It was the afternoon of the day he'd come back from his annual physical at Dr. Morganstern's.

"Jews are the best doctors in the world. You know why, Judd?"

"No. Why?"

"Because they know best how to enjoy life, how important it is to keep alive. Maybe it's because they've suffered so much, through so many thousands of years, and lived so long and so closely with death. But whatever it is, they're the best. Take Al, for instance. Al Morganstern keeps telling me what to do to stay alive as long as I can. Of course, I think he's full of crap sometimes and if he thinks I'm ever going to give up my cigars and slow down on the brandy, he's an idiot. But I know what he means. To keep alive, that's the important thing." He leaned back in his chair and chuckled. "Besides, I've got to keep alive to keep Global alive. Hell, there's nobody here who could run this shop the way I do, and you know that, don't you, Judd? Nobody." He lit a cigar and puffed reflectively. "And that's why I'm going to live one hell of a long time. I don't want anything to happen to Global."

The car swerved. He hardly listened to Milly's sarcastic remarks about his driving, being so used to them by now.

Well, now Rudy was dead, finished. What was going to happen to Global now that there was no Rudy to sit in that big leather chair in that big office? He braked the car sharply for a red light and he could feel Milly's disapproving glance.

Global never had any vice-presidents. That was one of Rudy's many business oddities. He always said that there should be only one man in a business, and that man was the boss, the man who controlled the company, lock, stock, and barrel, as he put it. And that one man was Rudy Ruttenberg, as far as Global was concerned. The others were all executives, or associates or whatever they wanted to call themselves, but no vice-president stuff. Even though Global had over a hundred employees in its four-story building on Rodeo Drive, to say nothing of the dozens of others in its U.S. and foreign branches, Rudy had determined that the Hollywood home office would be governed by himself and a small staff. As he had once explained to Judd when one of the younger agents had requested to be considered for executive-level status, "Give him a raise, Judd, if you think he deserves it; but tell him I've got all the top people I'll ever want and that's the way I'm going to keep it."

The car jerked slightly as it started again. There were really only four "top people": Lettie Mallon, Alex Deming, Jim Banton, and himself. Judd had been with the firm the longest and had been very close to Rudy since his early struggling days in New York, and obviously he'd be the one Jackie would choose to head the corporation.

III

It was an impressive funeral even for Hollywood, a town not noted for restraint in any of its social events, merry or melancholy.

At least four blocks before the Mercedes reached the sycamore-lined driveway leading to the Temple entrance, both sides of the streets were filled with parked cars, and a number of people were walking up the Temple driveway. These were hoi polloi, the spectators, the onlookers, the voyeurs who had come to see the famous-name people whose cars were being parked by a corps of Temple attendants. The onlookers had cameras, tape recorders, autograph books. To them Rudy Ruttenberg meant little or nothing, but they knew that the most celebrated personalities in the film world would be flocking to pay him obeisances, and it was this quarry they were stalking. Judd remembered *Day of the Locust* as his car inched nearer in the cortege. The crowd thickened into masses of people on the long grassy knoll in front of the monumental wooden doors. Hundreds of camp chairs were in evidence—it was like a film premiere— and those without seats were lying on the available grass; a number were pressing against the velvet ropes, their cameras and recorders and autograph books at the ready as the Cadillacs, Mercedeses, Jaguars, Jensens, and Rolls Royces discharged their soberly garbed passengers.

The contrast in colors was arresting. The group outside the Temple was dressed in garish plaids, bright-colored T-shirts, pink shorts, green skirts and red sunglasses, some carrying faded parasols. There was a sprinkling of battered quasi yachting caps on balding heads. There were children there, too, dozens of them in their teens hunting for celebrities, and others, too young to be left at home, who had been taken along for the day.

The car jerked forward a few feet and touched the rear bumper of a gray Rolls. Almost automatically Judd turned his head to meet Milly's accusing glance, but this time she didn't say anything, and for that he was grateful.

Eddie Swenson, Paramount's Western star, emerged from a white Rolls that was first in line. He was immaculately garbed in his usual cowboy outfit complete with Stetson, but all in sombre black. Behaving with unusual dignity—his agent must have cautioned him—he waved aside the clamorous requests for a picture or an interview and merely smiled his fatuous toothy smile. Exiting from the other side of the car was his equally famous acting partner, Bo Jordan, also in a jet-black cowboy outfit, but hatless and obviously trying hard to control the infantile grin that his fans adored. He imitated Eddie's waving gesture of rejection to the autograph seekers and walked slowly up the outdoor carpet.

Francoise Goulet was one of Global's less-talented clients from France, where she had been a mistress to the American director Jeb Marley, another Global client and the reason for her being with the agency. She couldn't resist the crowd's blandishments and signed two or three autographs before her companion, Lettie Mallon, dressed this time in a decorous black dress, skillfully maneuvered her back into the slowly moving line of mourners. Lettie was good at her job; she did the right thing at the right time. Not that she exercised that wisdom in her own life; but she was a top-flight agent.

Rabbi Samuel Rosenstiel was an imposing man and relished his self-importance inordinately. Portly, with thick greying hair meticulously combed, he had developed the habit of rocking back and forth whenever he addressed his congregation, raising himself on his toes now and then to lend greater vehemence and resonance to his oratory, consequently giving the calculated impression of being considerably taller than his actual five foot eight.

He was aware of the importance of this moment. Global Talent Associates, Inc. had given large donations to the Temple on more than one occasion, and Sam Rosenstiel was not a man to forget that most of Rudy's own generous gifts had been donated to the Rabbi's Discretionary Fund, a fund that permitted considerable leeway in how the money was to be disbursed. Even as he looked around the crowded room and walked with careful solemnity to the rostrum he wondered whether he could anticipate further largesse from the company now that Rudy was no longer at the helm. Could he count on Jackie? He doubted it; he was most aware that any loyalty she had, either to him or to the Temple, was only a reflection of Rudy's wishes. He felt disturbingly certain that Jackie didn't have the slightest interest in religion and that she was perfectly capable of entirely eliminating any donations permanently. Jackie offered no shred of comfort as a future benefactress. His eyes sought her out in the front row, her tightly clenched handkerchief a striking note of white against the impeccable blackness of her dress.

Garbed in black, Jackie's appearance was striking. Her deep-set eyes, large and luminous, accented the smooth marble whiteness of her skin. The darting rays of sunlight filtering through the stained-glass windows made her carefully coiffed black hair gleam. She wore no jewels except for a single large emerald ring which she twisted nervously now and again. Apart from occasional darting dabs at her eyes with the white handkerchief—Rabbi Rosenstiel doubted whether they were caused by tears—she sat perfectly still and made no effort to talk to Judd, who was on her right, or to Lettie Mallon on her left.

Lettie sat very straight, her hands folded over her black suede purse, only shifting her position now and then to relieve the pressure on her back from the hard bench. As the mourners—Lettie instinctively checked off those who were Global clients— walked slowly down the aisles to the seats assigned them by the watchful ushers, she watched them carefully. She was curious as to how the ceremony was to be conducted. Lettie had never been inside a synagogue in her life. She'd never been in any house of worship, at least that she could remember. It was a strange moment for her.

Although Lettie was now an accepted denizen of Hollywood, there was a time when such a possibility had never even entered her consciousness. Born into poverty in Brooklyn to a slatternly Irish mother and a hard-drinking stevedore father who hated each other, Lettie's recollections of her childhood were bitter ones. She grew up neglected and ignored, learning from the streets. It was here that she amassed the amazingly profane vocabulary that marked her personality in Hollywood.

By the time she was fourteen and the neighborhood boys had begun to notice her pearly complexion and limpid blue eyes, as beautiful as they were deceptive in their innocence, Lettie had an experience that changed her life. It happened in the daytime when her mother was out earning a few extra dollars scrubbing floors. Lettie never recalled her father drinking before nightfall, but this time he had changed his habits. The reason was clear when he told Lettie that he'd just been fired for "standing up for his rights," as he put it. He paced up and down as he talked. "Bastards," he kept saying, "bastards. Who do they think they are? Bastards." Now and again he would stop his incessant pacing long enough to swig from a bottle he had in his pocket. Then he began to cry and sobs wrenched his gaunt frame. Tears ran down his stubbled cheeks and he threw himself down on the torn couch, his shoulders shaking. Lettie didn't know what to do; she'd never seen her father this way. She went over and hugged him, stroking his shoulders and kissing him, hating the foul taste of his mouth. He began to return her kisses, he stopped crying, he held her so tightly in his arms that it hurt her. She squirmed and kicked at him, trying to wrest free; but he never relinquished his grasp and the sound of his breathing was hoarse and rasping. He threw one leg over her struggling body, pinning her down with one hand while he tore feverishly at her dress until he ripped away enough to reveal what he sought.... The actual rape didn't take long, or so Lettie remembered it. All she could recall was that she kept trying to scream as his lips closed hard over her mouth before she fainted.

By the time her mother came home and listened to Lettie's hysterical story, her father had disappeared. Neither of them ever saw him again; neither of them ever wanted to. Lettie always felt that it must have been that day that made her hate all men; but whether it was or not didn't matter. What mattered was that she knew she was never going to let a thing like that happen again. No man was going to savage her as her father had done.

When Lettie was sixteen she apprenticed herself to a massage parlor and became a masseuse. Madame De Lys Massage Salon, it was called. She soon become proficient at her new trade. By that time her mother had died the doctors called it cardiac arrest, but Lettie knew she had died of hard work and too little money. Lettie didn't go to the funeral. What good would it do, she thought to herself, and besides if she took time out for that she might miss one of the sophisticated customers who tipped lavishly and whose hotel or apartment worlds were havens of the luxury Letty coveted so fiercely.

It was one of those customers who made the second big change in Lettie's life. Morna Darling was her name, and she had come to New York from Hollywood to star in *Lovely Lady* on Broadway. Morna was devoted to massages. She took a fancy to Lettie when Madame De Lys sent her to the Pierre Hotel, where Morna had an elegant suite. Lettie enjoyed the massage sessions with the ebullient, gossipy Morna, who chattered about the celebrities of Broadway and Hollywood even as Lettie's supple fingers stroked and pounded her body. Petite and golden blonde—Lettie learned on her first visit that the blondeness was not real—she filled Lettie's dreams with glamour. To Lettie Morna could do no wrong. It was an imperceptible step from massaging Morna's body to being seduced by her. At first Lettie was horrified at what was happening, but she soon began to love it. Morna was artful, and under her dancing fingers, enclosed in her scent, Lettie became an abandoned devotee of women's love.

It took very little persuasion on Morna's part to convince Lettie to come to the west coast with her when the play closed. Her exact role in the household was never made clear to her, but she became combination masseuse, lover, companion, and maid. The salary was good; Morna was as charming as ever; California was a welcome release from the grime of New York; and Lettie was completely content.

Part of her services as companion involved playing hostess at the lavish parties Morna gave, and Lettie was soon on casual terms with many of the beautiful people of Hollywood. Life went on pleasantly enough until the day—Lettie remembered it vividly because it was an unusual day for California, one of teeming, uninterrupted rain—when Morna announced that she was going to make a picture in England and had decided to live there for at least a year for tax reasons. But as she explained to Lettie, she didn't want to leave her without a job; she had told her agent, Rudy Ruttenberg, about how clever Lettie was, how many people she already knew in films and what a treasure she would be in his office. And Rudy, who had met Lettie at Morna's galas, was willing to gamble on her.

And that's how it all happened, how it was that she was sitting on a hard-backed bench in Temple Israel paying tribute to the deceased master of Global Talent Associates, Inc. As for Morna, Lettie later found out that she had told her the truth when dismissing her, but she had omitted mentioning that a certain eighteen-year-old singer named Nanette Rolande had suddenly given up her nightclub job and was en route to England with Morna as a companion. By the time Lettie found this out, she had already fallen in love with her new work at Global and it no longer made any difference. The only amusingly intrusive thought that occurred to her was whether Nanette knew how to massage.

Sitting rigidly in his seat Alex Deming noted by a quick sidewise glance that he was the only man in the row who had flung one leg over the other. He surreptitiously placed both feet firmly on the floor. Alex was the latest addition to the executive staff of Global Talent Associates. He was also its most ambitious and determined member. Even though Alex's five-figure salary was a far cry from the modest sum he earned in Vegas when he first met Rudy Ruttenberg, he wanted a lot more and he was finally going to get it.

Rudy had been a frequent visitor at The Dunes in Vegas. Many of his clients worked in the stage shows there, and besides, Rudy was an inveterate gambler and loved the tables with a compulsive passion. It was at the gaming rooms that Alex, working as waiter, had first started to cultivate Rudy, feeling that somewhere, somehow, he might impress this titan of the industry in a way that would be profitable. Alex had no intention of remaining a waiter, and one way of making a change might be via the president of Global Talent Associates. In any case, it was always worth a try.

Alex was always there when Rudy was gambling, attentive, serving him drinks—he had quickly learned that Rudy drank only Courvoisier—and the Beluga caviare he liked. At four in the morning, when Rudy finally turned in his chips, it was Alex who was there to sympathize or congratulate on the outcome of the evening's play. Rudy began to ask for Alex if he had been assigned to another station; he called him his good-luck piece. By the time Alex began to discreetly suggest the names of various girls with specific sexual talents, Rudy had began to think of him as an indispensable adjunct to his Vegas jaunts. Rudy was not surprised, one Friday morning, after a particularly profitable session with the dice, when Alex took his long chance and asked outright for a job at Global Talent Associates.

Rudy had always prided himself on his judgement of people, and although he was amused at the temerity of Alex's request, he was aware that Alex's mastery of flattery, cajolery, and obsequiousness could be important assets in an industry where all three were potent business weapons. Besides, he really liked Alex. He understood, as only he could, what fierce ambitions were driving this man, ambitions that might prove beneficial to Global Talent. Normally, he would have talked it over with Judd, as he did every other personnel addition on an executive level; but Judd was in Europe on a deal, and besides, he could always fire Alex if his performance turned out to be less than his promise.

And that's how Alex Deming, ex-waiter, became an employee of Global Talent Associates. He swiftly justified Rudy's gamble, as well as his own self-confidence. The crafty audacity that had led Alex to cultivate Rudy proved to be of genuine value in the day-to-day operations of agentry, and by the time Judd returned, Rudy could already point to several deals Alex had closed. He specialized in women clients and, having no wife to encumber his movements, he offered his sexual gifts to clients and buyers alike, and all parties were satisfied with services rendered. Alex Deming could barely recall his waiter days in Vegas. When he did, it was only to squelch the memory as rapidly as possible.

Rabbi Rosenstiel had begun to speak. Alex tried to concentrate on what he was saying, but again and again the vision of Rudy's big mahogany desk clouded his thoughts. He'd keep the desk, but the rest of the office would have to be changed. He liked bright colors, modern prints, an antique Persian rug, and the first thing he'd throw out was that damn black tin wastebasket that Rudy brought from New York as a souvenir of early days.

"Man of many talents . . . pioneer of the industry . . . beloved community figure . . . devoted husband . . . friend of the actor . . . " Alex caught some of the resonant phrases as Rabbi Rosenstiel warmed to his subject. Suddenly Jackie began to sob, wracking, high-pitched sobs, and Alex turned to look at her.

Bitch, he thought, bitch, she never gave a damn for Rudy, and he, Alex, was certainly the one man who knew it almost from the very beginning. He smiled a private smile. I wonder what would have happened if I'd walked into Rudy's office and casually mentioned the strawberry mark under Jackie's left tit. He almost chuckled aloud but caught himself in time. He knew Jackie would give him no trouble about changing the decor in Rudy's office. Hell, she'd probably help him. She was a bitch, but a very useful bitch, he reflected, and not bad in bed either.

"Pillar of the temple . . . dedicated his life to our industry . . . magnificent example of the American dream becoming a superb reality . . . ", the Rabbi droned on, and Jackie's sobs subsided to a gentle whimper and were finally silenced.

No; two or three Navajo rugs would be better than a single Persian carpet. And some pieces by that guy who did work in cement, the one Jackie liked. What was his name? Something like Breen. Yes, Breen. Ronald J. Breen. May as well please Jackie; after all, she *was* the boss's wife.

Perspiring despite the air-conditioning, Jim Banton stared straight ahead at Rabbi Rosenstiel's gesturing figure, looking neither to the right nor to the left. Heavy-set, balding, overweight by at least twenty pounds, he could feel the sweat gathering around his waistband, and he surreptitiously eased his belt buckle. His rubicund complexion was dotted with tiny glints of perspiration, but Jim felt it highly inappropriate to call attention to himself by wiping the moisture away.

The fact is, Jim Banton spent a good deal of his working life being as inconspicuous as possible. Jim had majored in business administration at a second-rate college in Florida, landed a job in the accountancy department of J.C. Penney and had been eventually transferred to one of their Los Angeles branches in a personnel shuffle. Jim was content at Penney's; he did routine work in a routine way and never questioned either his ultimate destiny or his

present way of life. It was sheer accident that he met
and married Margie Noland, one of his clerical subor-
dinates in the department. At least Jim thought it was
an accident; he never knew that Margie was pregnant
at the time and determined to snare a husband come
hell or high water. The child was stillborn, and afterwards Margie had persuaded him to have a vasec-
tomy, explaining that her doctor said it would be
dangerous for her to conceive again. Jim didn't care
much about having children either, so that he really
didn't mind. He accepted that as he did everything
else in life, passively and quietly.

It was really through Margie that he became a part
of Global Talent Associates. Margie knew Morty
Golden, the head bookkeeper at Global, and she also
knew he had a heart problem. This latter bit of information came to her attention during the course of a
brief affair she had with him, but that did not prevent
her from introducing Jim to him, and it didn't take
long before Jim sat at one of the four desks in the
bookkeeping department. Nor was it long after that
when Morty Golden died, and was buried and forgotten, Jim Banton was moved up to his big office and his
job. That was some years ago. Jim, ultimately promoted to office manager, was as content there as he
had been at Penney's. All he asked of life was to keep
earning a salary and to go through his days unno-
ticed.

Jim had always liked Rudy and he was sorry that
he was dead, but his only interest beyond that lay in
the hope that any management changes would let

him keep his job.

"Friends in every area of the community . . . integrity, probity, charity . . . highest ethical standards . . . unblemished reputation . . . citizen with pride in the world he lived in . . . "

Jim felt an insistent nudge on his right side; it was Margie holding a Kleenex in her left hand and motioning to his face with her other hand. Jim took the Kleenex and mopped his face, but he was irritated. Why did she have to call attention to him that way? He wished she would mind her own business. He smiled a false smile at her in acknowledgement of her attention and she smiled back. He put the Kleenex in his pocket, not knowing what else to do with it.

Rabbi Rosenstiel was still talking. "Creative imagination . . . man of many parts . . . dedicated . . . loyal . . . gentle and yet determined . . . " He was able to raise his eyes frequently from the typed pages in front of him because much of the text he was using came from an amalgam of at least a half-dozen other eulogies he had delivered about previous film figures in Hollywood. As he looked over the the crowded room, he could easily identify many of the mourners. There was Al Jackson, the slight tremor in his left eye quite apparent to the rabbi. He was head of National Agency Limited, a man who had hated Rudy all his life, now sitting with bowed head and twitching fingers, probably going over Rudy's list of clients one by one, checking off which ones he could lure over to National and which ones would be loyal. The front row included Eddy Rockham of Metro, Sid Schwartzman

from Paramount, Ronald Wright of Warners, Saul
Sidney of Columbia, company presidents all, and all
probably wondering whom they would be dealing
with at Global now that Rudy was gone. He could see
Eddie Swenson and Bo Jordan in their black cowboy
suits, Francoise Goulet's expressionless face, and
dozens of other film stars and personalities. He knew
all of them. They were either members of Temple Israel or they had come to other funeral services there
to pay homage to one of its members. Hollywood was
not a big place.

In one of the back rows sat Prompton Warwick ac-
tively enjoying himself. At his insistence—Kerry
couldn't understand why he'd wanted to come in the
first place—Kerry had arranged to get Prompton's
name on the list for the ceremonies. He'd wanted very
much to go; he wanted to be there and alive while
Rudy was there and dead. Even the probability that
Judd Haber, who had insulted him and whom he hated
even more than he did Rudy, would be the next boss of
Global did not dilute his pleasure at the death. His
eyes gleamed and he smiled openly as Rabbi Rosenstiel's laudatory phrases reverberated in the silent
room. He hoped Judd would know he was there—the
bastard!

Next to Prompton sat Ed Garrell, his face immobile, hands resting like limp rags on his lap. If he was
thinking about Rudy it was difficult to tell from his
quiet, relaxed demeanor.

"Devotion . . . forthrightness at all times . . . much
joy and happiness to the world . . . truly earned and

deserved the name of Mr. Hollywood . . . will not pass this way again."

Then sudden silence as Rabbi Rosenstiel concluded his peroration, his hands raised high above his head, his height magnified by his tiptoe stance at the lectern. The service was over. Rudy Ruttenberg had been properly eulogized. There was nothing more to be done.

At a gracious hand-signal from the rabbi, the hundreds of mourners rose slowly in straggling groups and edged their way solemnly to the exits. Nothing could be heard but the shuffling of many feet; there were silent greetings and quick perfunctory handshakes as the crowd moved forward, but no exchange of words until they actually left the confines of the hall and were released onto the sun-warmed sidewalk.

Rudy Ruttenberg was dead. The King was dead. Long live the King, whoever he may be.

On the short drive to the Ruttenberg house, where a carefully selected list of mourners had been invited to participate in a decorous reception for Rudy's friends and to express personal condolences to his widow, the passengers in the Haber car said very little to each other.

"It must be very hard for you, Dad; he was a good friend," said Kerry. I wonder whether Colette is free tonight; I could use a good fuck, he thought.

"He was almost like a big brother to me," said Judd. I hope Mira understood about my breaking our date; I'll call her as soon as I get back.

"He was a wonderful man, and I'm going to miss him," said Suz. I hope Jake got my message about the funeral; we've still got plenty of time to make the Fox Venice.

"Poor Rudy. I wonder what he would have thought about the services," said Milly. I guess this will hit Judd pretty hard, but he'll get over it as soon as he gets the top spot, she thought.

IV

As the Haber family were ushered into the main hallway of Rudy's house (now Jackie's house, thought Judd) by the butler, Joe Rando, who had been Rudy's houseman for over twenty years, they were met by an engulfing wave of sound that was strangely close to merriment. If this had not been the day of Rudy's interment, and if this event had not been devoted to a tribute to his memory, this would have sounded like any Hollywood cocktail party.

"Sad occasion, Mr. Haber, very sad for all of us," said Joe, with genuine sorrow written on his wrinkled black visage.

"Hard to believe he's not here to welcome us, Joe, isn't it?" responded Judd as he shook Joe's hand in greeting.

As they entered the massive living room the noise arising from animated conversation was louder. Judd noticed that a second bar he had never seen before was set up in front of the fireplace, and that at least twenty people were clustered around it while two grinning bartenders acceded to their requests with astonishing celerity. The main bar, all chrome and sparkling glass, had even more people besieging it.

The Ruttenberg house was one of Hollywood's most celebrated mansions; it had been built in the period of silent pictures when the cinema cornucopia seemed to be bottomless. As Judd looked around at the sterile modern decor, his memory flashed back to two other eras before Jackie Jason had become Mrs. Rudy Ruttenberg. When Mag had held that title the furnishings were all Victorian, quiet, subdued, old-fashioned, giving an air of tranquil gentility that charmingly reflected Mag's own retiring spirit and love of unobtrusive elegance. Judd remembered the enormous 19th-century dining room table, its graceful cabriole legs and the marquetry edging hugging the curved top; and a Victorian mahogany lounge with wicker sides, gold velvet tufted seat and tasseled bolsters. That had been years ago; with the coming of Janie the whole house had been transformed into a Mexican hacienda and that lasted just as long as Janie did.

Then it was Jackie's turn. The house was metamorphosed again, this time into a world of shining glass and steel and aluminum and chrome, a perfect extrapolation of Jackie's own brittle personality. During all these changes, only one room had remained the same—Rudy had been very stubborn about this although he had cheerfully paid for changes everywhere else—and this was Rudy's own study. It was a replica of the office he went to six days a week.

Although it was still day and the sunlight squeezed through the blue chrome blinds and laid brilliant stripes on the gleaming hardwood floor, all the lights in the house were on. As a result the faces of the milling guests took on a theatrical quality. It was as if everyone were in makeup for the occasion.

"How long do we have to stay, Dad?" asked Suz.

It was Milly who answered, not waiting for Judd's response. "About an hour, I would think; but be sure to talk to Jackie before you go."

"Of course," said Suz, and moved off toward the corner where Jackie sat, or was enthroned, on a high settee made of twisted wrought iron interlaced with dark strips of highly polished wood.

"I'd better say hello to some of the clients. I'll be right back; I won't be long," said Judd, starting to move away from Milly and Kerry.

"Of course. I'll be okay. Trot along," answered Milly.

As soon as Judd left, Kerry did the same thing, going directly to the main bar and shouldering his way to the front. He needed a drink.

Milly stood still for a moment observing the jostling masses. There were at least three hundred people in that room and she wondered how many of them really gave a damn for Rudy Ruttenberg, how many had even liked him, how many had really loathed and despised him, and how many of them had no emotional response to his death whatsoever, but had come to the condolence party—that's what is really was, a party—to sell or to buy from a group of people who spent their lives doing either one or the other.

"Champagne, Mrs. Haber?" It was Joe Rando, holding a square bamboo tray encrusted with silver on which sat two bottles of Piper Heidsieck (Rudy would have chuckled at that, said Milly to herself; he always disliked champagne) and a half-dozen glasses.

"Thanks, Joe. Yes." answered Milly, and Joe filled a glass for her and left with his tray to solicit other guests.

Judd was already in conversation with the Three Grandees, a rock group consisting of two men and a girl, whose names Milly could never remember. She knew it was something like Gary, Harry, and Mary, but she wasn't sure. She knew they'd been hot for the last two years and that Global did very well by them and for them. She also knew that Rudy had probably never spent more than fifteen minutes with them beyond the glad-to-have-you-with-us meeting after they'd been signed by the agency. Rudy never understood rock music, and never liked it; but he was glad to add rock people to his stable as long as one of his staff undertook the job of nursemaiding them.

"Too bad about the old guy," said one of the Three Grandees to Judd. "Here's to him wherever he is," and he drained his glass in one long gulp. "Who's taking over? You?"

Judd bit back his irritation at the summary question. "Don't worry, Gary; you'll be in good hands, I promise you. It'll take a little time, but Global will be in your corner whoever's the boss."

"All I want you to know, straight out front," said Mary, "and I'm speaking for all us Grandees, is that it better be somebody good. Our deal with Silver Records expires in about two months, and we don't want to be sold up the river to any schlock outfit. We're number three this week, and whoever's going to handle us better know it. We don't want any new guy."

"It'll probably still be Alex, don't worry. He's the rock guy. Here he comes now," said Judd and took the opportunity to walk away from the Grandees as Alex moved in, smiling and amiable. As Judd left he could hear Alex's ringing greeting, "Hi, how's our Three Grandees? That last thing of yours, "Solo Sunset," was fucking great! Congratulations!"

As Judd moved on, someone spun him around and threw his arm around his shoulders. It was Al Jackson.

"Too bad about the old man, really too bad; but it happens to all of us, eh, Judd?" said Al. "Maybe this isn't the time to talk, but what the hell, the ball has to go on rolling. I don't know what your plans are or what the shake will be, but National Agency could use you, and I'm National Agency. Give me a ring before you do anything you regret. I can offer you a hell of a sweet deal, and I mean *sweet*!"

Judd stepped back far enough to slide out of Al's encircling arm without insulting him, as if anyone could ever insult Al Jackson when money was the topic. "Thanks, Al, thanks very much. Maybe I'll do that. I mean give you a ring. I hadn't thought of anything like that yet."

"Do that," said Al. "It'll be worth it, I'm telling you."

Judd walked out to the terrace and lit a cigarette.

The lights of Los Angeles were beginning to dot the hills and valleys and the view of the city was breathtaking. Lousy son of a bitch, he said to himself, loudmouthed bastard. For Christ's sake, can't he wait? This is supposed to be Rudy's day. And as far as a job with National was concerned, he'd rather starve than work for Al Jackson. As a matter of fact Judd wondered how in hell Al had gotten an invitation to the house. Probably bummed it off some actor who was shooting and couldn't come anyway.

A heavy wash of perfume swept toward him out of the bright room behind him. It was Francoise Goulet being escorted by Jeb Marley. Judd knew what Francoise didn't know: that Jeb was going to be out on his can after he finished his direction on *Chapparal.* Once that happened he was sure that Jeb wouldn't be escorting Francoise anywhere.

"Hello, Fran. You look totally sensational, as always. Glad to see you, Jeb." He bent forward and kissed Francoise's cheek and shook hands with Jeb at the same time.

"Isn't it a lovely party? Have you tasted the caviare, and the paté? They're delicious," Francoise burbled. Seeing the gleam of rebuke in Judd's eyes, she added hastily, "I know it's a sad moment, and all that; but I'm sure Rudy would have wanted it to be the best party in town even if it was—I mean, even if it was on account of his death and all that."

Jeb patted her arm consolingly. "Judd knows what you mean, Fran."

Judd's face relaxed. What was the use? Francoise

was what she was: a fool whose whole career, or what there was of it, was accomplished by bedding various directors. Jeb was just another in what Judd knew to be a long line. Whatever brains she had, and they were not numerous to begin with, began and ended in bed. Why should he be angry at her?

"Sure, I know what you mean. And thanks for the tip. I'd better sample some of that caviare before it's all gone." He waved at both of them and stepped into the living room again.

The hubbub was unabated. The noise level had risen as the champagne bottles were uncorked one after the other, and the two bars were more crowded than ever. Judd looked around for Milly and finally found her listening to Ellie Schwartzman, the brassy, buxom wife of Sid Schwartzman, Paramount's current president. Nobody ever talked to Ellie; all you could do was listen. Even across the room he could see Milly's graven expression of fortitude as she faced the babbling Ellie. Judd waved at them, but Milly didn't see him; at least she didn't respond.

"My husband Sid" (Ellie always referred to her husband as my-husband-Sid) "has always told me that he knew for an absolute fact that the real brains behind Global wasn't Rudy Ruttenberg at all, not at all, but that the real brains belonged to your Judd. And my husband Sid said that if ever Judd wanted to get out of the agency business and go into the production end, Paramount would be lucky to get him. That's what my husband Sid said, 'lucky to get him,' and if you think I'm making this up, you're wrong,

Milly. My husband Sid had some great ideas for Judd.
Just you remember what my husband Sid said. He
means what he says." She paused for breath and
Milly, who had been waiting her chance to escape,
seized the opportune moment and said, as she started
away, "That's darling of you, Ellie; I'll be sure to tell
Judd. I know how much he likes Sid. And now if you'll
excuse me, I have to circulate," and she spun on her
heel and edged her way through the crowd.

As Milly departed, she could hear Ellie, shrill
above the crowd noise, "You just remember what my
husband Sid said and be sure you tell your Judd."

When Milly had gone, Ellie waved her left arm
high in the air until her husband Sid could see it. She
made a circle with the thumb and forefinger of her
right hand, and smiled smugly; Sid nodded and
smiled and made the same sign back.

The Paramount group were huddled together in a
corner and totally oblivious to the noise and chatter
swirling around them. Sid Schwartzman, a portly
man whose outstanding feature was his bald pate,
now gleaming in the electric light, was talking. The
others were listening intently and respectfully.

"I've said it before, Larry, and I'm saying it again. I
want to get rid of Ron Winner and fast. Why we signed
him in the first place, I'll never know, except that we
were conned by Judd Haber. Judd can sell anything to
a sucker, and that's what we were, suckers. As a matter of fact, I wish we had Judd on our team; but that's
another kettle of fish, and I'll get to that later. Right
now I'm talking about Winner. Get rid of him. Loan

him out even if we take a loss. There must be some schmuck independent who'd be glad to have him."

Larry Rudger, balding, pudgy, barrel-chested and nervous, nodding anxiously, answered him. "I'm working on it, chief; I know we have to unload him, and I'll do it. It ain't easy; he's a lousy actor and everyone in town knows it."

"Lousy or not, he's an actor and some dumb bastard can use him. I just don't want it to be us. We've taken enough of a beating."

"We're all working on it, Sid," said Mort Dorkas, the thin-faced and moustached casting director. "There's a guy in town right now from Brazil; wants to do some kind of samba Western. I'm taking him to the Springs this weekend and talking Winner to him. Maybe it'll work. I'll keep on it."

"You better. All of you better, is all I can say," said Sid.

The slap on his back was hearty and friendly. Sid Schwartzman turned around.

"Just talking about you, Ron. Good to see you. You're looking great, just great."

A small echoing chorus arose around Ron Winner, red-faced, smooth-shaven, blond hair neatly combed. "Good to see you, Ron . . . loved your job in *Night Rider* . . . never saw you looking better."

Ron Winner smiled a smile that had once ignited box-office fires. Now it was tired and drawn. He drew in his bulging stomach as tightly as he could.

"Thanks, fellows," he said. "Sad day, isn't it?"

Again the chorus functioned swiftly. "Sure

is . . . tough about old Rudy . . . happens to all of us . . . industry will never be the same again . . . rotten break, no matter how you look at it."

"I'd like to drop in tomorrow, Sid," said Ron, "and rap a little about my next assignment. I heard you just bought Sam Brennan's best-seller, *Ghost Desert*."

Sid Schwartzman's smile was frozen. All we need to do is put this putz into *Ghost Desert* and we got a bomb, he thought. "Sure, Ron, sure. Check me in the morning. We'll talk."

"Thanks, I will," responded Ron and waved at the group, happily relaxing his stomach as he moved out onto the crowded floor.

Jackie was holding court as guest after guest approached her to mumble condolences that could barely be heard above the noise. They queued up, some of them still holding their drinks. As each one came to his or her post in front of Jackie, he or she uttered some phrase of sympathy or greeting, bent forward to either pat or press her hand gently or to kiss her proffered cheek and walked away back into the crowd. To every one of them Jackie responded with the same acknowledgement. "How sweet of you. How very sweet of you." Now and again she would dab at her tearless eyes with the white handkerchief, during which the greeting and pressing of her hand were deferentially halted.

By this time Judd had joined her, together with Lettie and Alex; occasionally one of them leaned toward her and whispered the name of the person standing before her. Not that it mattered; she never acknowledged anyone by name. She only repeated again and again, "How sweet of you. How very sweet of you." It seemed to be effectual; none of the greeters seemed to feel that anything more appropriate was necessary in reply to their own sorrowful bromides.

Alex was whispering, "Ronald Wright, president of Warners . . . Saul Sidney, president of Columbia . . . Gabe Donner, he's the company's lawyer . . . Rudy Wharf, he's a client . . . Sara Rolfe, heads casting at NBC . . . Ellie Schwartzman, husband's Paramount's president . . . Ron Winner, he's a client . . . Al Jackson, an agent . . . " The list went on and on.

Jackie smiled and nodded and said, "How sweet of you. How very sweet of you." She was wondering when the hell this damn thing would be over. Her back ached; she loathed the varying odors emanating from the people who studiously brushed their lips across her cheek; her hand was sweating unpleasantly under the impact of the hundreds of handshakes.

Judd took over the litany when Alex stopped long enough to reach for the drink beside him.

"Jason Mordoe, former client . . . Ben Randolph, legal head at CBS . . . Tish Allen, *LA Times* reporter . . . Mary Wexell, heads makeup at CBS . . . Sonny Masters, Monarch Costumers . . . "

The line was growing thinner and the clamor in the room was diminishing as a number of guests who had made their obeisances to Jackie began to file past Joe Rando on the way to their waiting cars.

Judd excused himself to seek his family and Lettie went off to get her purse.

Alex seized the opportunity to lean forward and whisper to Jackie, "You were wonderful, Jackie, just wonderful; you carried it off beautifully."

"How sweet of you. How very sweet of you," said Jackie. Alex grinned.

Judd saw Milly at the end of the bar with Gabe Donner. He was making his way to them when there was a tap on his shoulder and someone grasped his right hand and shook it vigorously. It was Prompton Warwick.

"Just wanted to say hello, Judd, just hello," said Prompton, smiling broadly.

"And just what the hell are you doing here? Who invited you?" said Judd angrily, yanking his fingers from Prompton's clinging grasp.

"Now Judd, take it easy. After all, I'm the one who should be sore. I'm the one you threw out of your office. Remember?"

Judd had regained control by now. "Let's get something straight, Prompton. I consider you a slimy, filthy bastard not only because of my son, but because you're an insult to the whole industry, you and the others like you, and I don't want to have anything to do with you under any circumstances whatsoever. And now get the hell out of here."

Prompton Warwick continued to smile pleasantly. "You'll regret that, Judd. Nobody talks that way to Prompton Warwick."

"Too bad about Rudy, wasn't it? Too bad," he continued, in the same quiet, amiable tone.

Judd walked away without responding.

He was still furious by the time he reached Milly and Suz.

"Don't take it so hard, Judd," said Milly when she saw the taut expression on his face.

"Let's go, Milly. Where's Kerry?" answered Judd abruptly.

"Here I am. Are we leaving?" It was Kerry, a drink still in his hand. He'd come up behind them.

Milly looked inquiringly at him.

"Don't worry, Milly-Mom, I made the speech to Jackie. Let's go," said Kerry, setting his glass on a nearby table.

"I've just got to get my wrap. Be back in a minute." said Milly and disappeared into the crowd.

There was a tug on Judd's sleeve. It was Sid Schwartzman.

"Sad occasion, all right, eh, Judd? Must be especially tough on you. You've been with Rudy from the beginning, haven't you?" said Sid.

Judd, still fuming from his encounter with Prompton Warwick, nodded his head briefly. "From the very beginning," he responded.

Sid turned to Kerry and Suz. "You'll excuse me if I talk to your father for a minute, won't you? It's important."

"Don't mind a bit," said Kerry. "I could use another drink anyway. Let's go, Suz," and taking Suz's arm he walked her toward the bar.

"I'm leaving in a few minutes, Sid. Milly's coming right back. Can't it wait?" said Judd peremptorily.

"Sure it can wait, but I wanted you to think about

something, that's all. It's simple, Judd. I want you to consider joining us now that Rudy's gone. I've watched you for a lot of years and I've got a hell of an idea for you and for Paramount. You'll like it. I promise you, Judd, you'll like it."

Judd's smile was forced, his voice taut. "Jesus Christ, Sid. Do we have to talk business here? I asked you whether it could wait."

"This isn't business. It's something I wanted you to consider, that's all. I mean before anything happens at Global. I'll phone you in few days for lunch and explain what I mean," said Sid.

"There's Milly coming. I've got to go," said Judd, then realizing belatedly what Sid had been trying to say, he turned back and shook Sid's outstretched hand. "Thanks, Sid. I'm flattered, very. Phone me and we'll make a date. Say goodbye to Ellie for me, will you?"

Only Kerry seemed to be in a good humor when they finally reached the Haber home. He had been able to telephone Colette from the Ruttenberg library; there was plenty of time to get to her place.

Suz was fretting; she still didn't know whether Jake had gotten her message, but she'd phone again as soon as she got to her room.

Milly was so immersed in her own thoughts that she hadn't even commented on Judd's driving. She kept hearing Jackie's "How sweet of you. How very sweet of you," and she found herself filled with a surge of active hatred for this woman who had slept in Rudy's arms and never knew or understood him.

As Judd went to his study he was filled with conflicting emotions, anger at Prompton Warwick, anger at himself for being so uncontrolled in expressing his detestation, anger that such an event could have happened when he was sorrowing over Rudy's death. The presence of Prompton had somehow profaned what should have been a sacred occasion.

There was a message on his telephone pad, left there by the efficient Albert. All it said was "Call Mary Darrowitz." That was Mira's real name. He had forbidden her to call him at home, ever; it must be something terribly important for her to have done so.

He dialed the well-known number.

"Hello, this is Judd. I told you—"

"Judd, darling," she interrupted, "I know I shouldn't have; but this must have been such a horrible day for you, and I—"

This time he interrupted. "I told you not to call unless it was imperative."

"It is imperative, Judd. This call is to say love . . . you . . . very . . . much. That's all. 'Bye."

Judd held the receiver in his hand for some time before he put it back on its cradle. All the anger and turmoil of the day left him. What a lovely thing to do. How sweet. How very sweet. And then he began to smile as he realized he was mouthing Jackie's meaningless phrase. But it *was* sweet. He looked approvingly at the mirror, apostrophizing his image. "You're a lucky man, Judd Haber, a very lucky man."

He whistled as he unknotted his dark tie.

V

Mira lifted the oversized sponge, squeezed it gently into the scented bubbly water in her tub and then stroked it languorously and caressingly over her breasts. Once that was done, and she had admired her pouting pink-tipped nipples, she reached for the ever-present pack of cigarettes on the tray perched on the tub's edge, and nestled even deeper into the comforting water, throwing a discarded match onto the thick white carpet, where it looked like a faint pencil mark. She took a deep puff, and put her hand through the funnel of gray smoke as she exhaled. She glanced lazily at the clock on the wall. I have plenty of time, she thought. Judd won't be here for almost an hour. I'll wear the green outfit; it's clingy, especially around the ass, and Judd likes that. Funny how some men are ass-men, some go for tits, and some go right for the cunt with no preliminaries at all.

She could never forget the cunt-men she had to service at Grace's place. They were revolting; they hardly gave her time to lie down and spread her legs before they were on her, savaging her body, often biting her earlobes, her fingers, her breasts. She didn't cry out—

Grace had warned her never to do that—but she often bit her lips to stifle wrenching sobs of pain; instead of crying or struggling free, she moaned, simulating pleasure. That's what they paid for; that's what Grace expected of her girls; that's what Mira did with exemplary regularity. And the money was good, very good—far more than she earned modeling at the Whitestone & Harde fashion house.

Now it all seemed so far away. That was a lucky night when she took Danielle's place and went to the Plaza and met Judd. It didn't take her long to find that what he liked best was when she took his prick into her mouth. Not that he didn't like to fuck the regular way once in a while; but Mira always took care to suck him off at least once during their sessions, and she'd become pretty adept at that procedure. She liked the sixty-nine position for herself, but she realized that he didn't; once she found that out, she desisted. As a result she had very few climaxes with Judd, but the sacrifice was well worth it; she considered her present status to be eminently satisfactory.

Mira had never been one to take any chances; she had tasted poverty and found it bitter; she was determined not to taste it ever again. And the one sure weapon she had was her femaleness, a quality or a state that men were happy to pay to possess. Even as a little girl in Knoxville she had early realized that she would have to turn elsewhere than to her taxi-driver father and waitress mother for any luxuries.

It was in high school that her sexual talents began to reap calculable rewards. Never a serious student despite her parents' half-hearted injunctions to study, she found that if she encouraged the smart boys in her class to take her out in their cars and fuck her, they would write her term papers and help her cheat on exams. From that she progressed to small gifts, and then to larger ones, as her abilities expanded and her scope of activities widened. By the time she was nineteen and a salesgirl at Regan's Department Store she was thoroughly convinced that Knoxville offered her little she coveted. But she was also certain that her time would come if she were patient. It did come, in the person of a sex-starved dress salesman named Kirk Ruark who offered her a sweaty weekend in Atlantic City after his first taste of her talents. This was her chance to leave Tennessee forever, and she took immediate advantage of it. By going through his wallet while he slept she acquired the information she was seeking: to wit, the name and address of his firm in New York, and his address in Queens, where he lived with his wife and two children. She also learned (hardly a surprise to her) that his real name was Morris Eisen.

She removed the snapshots of his wife and children from the wallet as well as several credit cards. Armed with these documents, she woke him. She didn't find it overly difficult to persuade him to give her a check for $500 as a farewell gift. She promised to send him the evidence as soon as she had cashed the check. At first he was furious at her duplicity, but seeing he had little or no choice (she threatened to scream for help if he tried to wrest the papers from her by force), he sat down and wrote the check.

But that wasn't all she wanted. She insisted that he also write her a glowing recommendation to his company in New York—she wanted a job there as a model. Kirk Ruark/Morris Eisen balked at first, but she was adamant; he finally did what she requested, figuring she'd be fired in two weeks anyway if she got the job. After she had read the letter and placed it carefully in her purse, Mira thanked him profusely and cheerfully offered to go down on him one last time as a token of her gratitude. Eager though he was to get rid of her, he accepted her offer; he almost forgot her treachery, so expertly did she perform for his benefit.

She wished him good luck on his next sales stop in Boston, asked for his address there, and was on her way to New York and to Whitestone & Harde within hours. Armed with his letter, it took her just a half-hour's interview with Roger Whitestone to be hired as a part-time model. She had slipped off her dress to demonstrate her modeling values and had accepted his subsequent invitation for a quiet dinner that night "to get to know each other better." Forty-eight hours after that, Morris Eisen received his family pictures and credit cards at his hotel in Boston with a brief thank-you note written on Whitestone & Harde stationery.

By the time Morris Eisen got back to New York, Mira was an employee, and Morris was the recipient of hearty thanks from Roger Whitestone, who seemed extremely satisfied with Mira's abilities. Mira was very affable when she saw Morris again, but he steered clear of her. That was all right with Mira; she no longer needed him.

It was through one of her fellow-models in the office, Tina Marsh, that Mira first heard of Grace's establishment. They were at lunch one day and Mira was complaining about money: Her salary was small and living in New York was expensive. Tina listened and sympathized. When they were both sipping their coffee, Tina lit a cigarette and said, casually enough, "And all you get out of old Whitestone is some lousy dinners. Right?"

Mira didn't hesitate. "Right. But how'd you know, Tina?"

Tina patted her hand. "I've been there. Quite a few of us have," and she grinned.

Mira grinned back; both girls laughed, and Tina told her about the money she could make at Grace's if she were willing to turn a few tricks now and then. Mira warmed to the idea, and a few days later she became a member of Grace's stable. That's where she became Mira Dalloway instead of Mary Darrowitz, a name change instituted by Grace, who liked all her girls to have "lady names." And it was through Grace, of course, that she met Judd, and entered a new phase of life in Hollywood.

Although Mira had risen rapidly in the hierarchy of Grace's place (her services were frequently in demand), she consistently refused Grace's offers to become an in-house girl. She enjoyed her modeling job at Whitestone & Harde; it also gave her a respectable front. She once explained to Grace, "I like the money I make with you, but I wouldn't like it if I had to live here." Then she added as an afterthought, "Unless, of course, I was in a real jam." Grace assured her that she'd be welcome any time. The subject was never discussed again.

By now Roger's "quiet dinners" weren't as regular as they once were, a situation rendered explicable to Mira when she and Tina were asked to break in a new girl from Dallas, Jennifer Haller, tall, full-breasted and dark-eyed, who referred to Roger as "that sweet boss we have."

Despite the increasing liberation from Roger's "quiet dinners" and the sizeable income she now drew from her second profession at Grace's, Mira was restless and increasingly tired of the demands made on her body and spirit by her clients. She never knew when the phone call from Grace would bring her to some drunken or perverted lout whose idea of sex was pure sadism. Yet she needed the money she got. Her tastes had become sophisticated and sybaritic; the current setup with Judd fulfilled all these new cravings. She knew this arrangement could last for a very long time if she handled herself carefully, certainly long enough for her to collect enough jewels and other negotiable gifts to provide a sizeable nest-egg for whatever the uncertain future would hold. She also liked her job at Mirabelle Meredith's Salon de Couture; was glad to be a part of the normal working world, just as she had been at Whitestone & Harde in New York.

At this point Mira had no worries about her ability to keep Judd. She had developed extraordinary competence in bed and she knew how to employ her sexual skills to their best advantage. But she went beyond that. Clever and calculating, she had made every effort to learn as much about Judd as she could. She encouraged him to talk about Milly and to air his grievances about Kerry and his pride in Suz. She had learned how to mix his favorite drink, a martini with a dash of Pernod; the Sherman cigarettes he liked best were always awaiting him (she herself smoked Players); a duplicate of his imported electric razor was in the bathroom cabinet; an electric shoe-polisher was available; she had trained her discreet maid, Lottie, for the rare occasions when he dined with her, to season his food sparingly in deference to the occasional ulcer twinges he complained of; there was a duplicate pair of his sunglasses in the hall closet should he ever break the ones he carried (this had happened once and she had profited from the accident); his comb and brush were replicas of the ones he had at home; she had wheedled the name of his favorite after-shave lotion from him (Floris' Number 89) and it, too, was there.

There was even an exact reproduction of his blue silk dressing gown hanging in the closet. Judd had been as puzzled as he was delighted when she first presented this to him, and she admitted that she had wormed the name of the store in Hong Kong out of Josie, whom she had telephoned one day "on a woman-to-woman basis." Judd had been angry at this at first and had threatened to upbraid the faithful Josie; but by the time Mira had unzipped his fly and applied her agile fingers to his prick, he had promised to do nothing further about it.

It all worked for her. There was only one problem: she found Judd a profound bore. He almost never satisfied her sexually, although her mastery of the theatrical art of uncontrollable quivering during intercourse and her superb imitation of utter abandon when he was coming made him totally unaware of his ineptitude. But it was not only his lack of prowess as a lover; she was tired of his gripes about his office colleagues, about Milly, about Kerry, about his fatigue—his whole world bored her. Of course he never realized this.

What Mira yearned for was someone who could excite her, who could give her genuine fulfillment in bed, who really mattered to her. But she was far too smart to ever do anything about it. To cheat on Judd was to lose him; his jealousy and possessiveness had been made thoroughly clear to her when they had talked that night in the Plaza and he told her what he was going to do about getting her to the coast to be near him. "We've got to get one thing straight, Mira, and you'd better know it before you make the move," he had said. "I'll set you up; I'll pay the bills; I'll get you the job you want; but you have to know right up front that if I ever hear of your touching another man, I want you to understand that I couldn't handle it. I've never had anybody like you, and I'm not going to sit around and be double-crossed. I don't know what I'd do if it ever happened, but God help you if it does." His voice was grim; he leaned forward to kiss her and his lips were hard and bruising on her mouth.

She said, when he moved away from her, "I understand, Judd. Don't worry. I feel the same way about you. I'm crazy about you and being able to have you around is all I ask for. Nothing else. Just that."

Then she kissed him, her tongue flicking inside his mouth, her right hand clinging tightly to the tumescence at his crotch.

He wrapped his arms around her, then broke away from her, and they both laughed as he fondled the hand now tugging vigorously at his zipper.

"As long as that happens," he said, looking down at her busy fingers, "I'll be around." He grinned and took her hungrily into his arms gain, this time with unalloyed passion.

The water was losing its comforting warmth and Mira arose languidly from the tub. The bathroom mirrors that lined the ceiling and every available wall space reflected her exquisite body, now made more alluring by the rivulets of water dripping soundlessly onto the white carpet. She untied the ribbon and shook her head back and forth, releasing her long blonde hair, golden in the lights.

Mira ignored the multiple images in the mirrors and set about industriously drying herself, humming as she rubbed. Only when her swiftly moving towel invaded the genital area did she stop for a moment, drop the towel and begin to fondle her clitoris with slow, circular movements until she could feel its ardent swelling under her practiced finger. When she finally came her whole body quivered and she moaned

in an extremity of pleasure, pressing her legs together as tightly as she could as the spasms ceased.
Dipping a wash cloth into the scented tub water, she
wiped her pubic region carefully and proceeded to
complete the drying process with the giant bath towel
that she picked up from the floor.

She glanced at the clock; there was still plenty of
time before Judd was due. She knew by now that he
would never surprise her by coming early.

The slacks were new and fitted her flawlessly; she
was quite satisfied with the image in her dressing
room mirror, quite. Now she was ready.

She reached for a fresh cigarette, ignoring the half-
smoked one still smoldering on her dressing-table
ashtray, took a contented puff and threw the dead
match casually aside, missing the ashtray by inches.

As she smoked, waiting for the sound of Judd's key
in the door, she reached for her white telephone and
pushed the lever to the Off position. She did not want
any phone calls while Judd was present; Mira was a
very cautious woman and wanted nothing to imperil
her present status.

Judd was always careful to park his car several
blocks away from Mira's apartment, even though a
Mercedes was hardly unusual in that affluent neighborhood. But Judd was taking no chances.

There was little danger of discovery in the apartment itself; Judd had selected it with great care. It
was on the ground floor and could be entered either
through the main lobby—which Judd never used—-or
via a side alley where the garages were.

Judd braked to a halt, donned dark glasses, and began the three-block walk to where Mira was waiting. He glanced at his watch. He was just on time; impatiently he quickened his pace.

Judd was still turning the key in the apartment door when it was opened from the inside. There was Mira, redolent of the musky perfume he liked, both hands holding a small silver tray on which rested two martini glasses, a crystal bowl of caviare set in cracked ice and a dainty Limoges plate containing square biscuits. Judd admired these little theatrical "entrances" of Mira's; she seemed to have an infinite supply of them, each one as imaginative and entertaining as the one before. Sometimes she met him with a single rose that she placed in his lapel; sometimes with a lit cigarette—a Sherman, of course; sometimes with a beautifully wrapped miniature-sized bottle of his favorite scotch, sometimes with a sealed envelope with a note inside saying love . . . you . . . very . . . much, sometimes the door was opened only partially and her hand would reach out to grasp his and guide it to one of her bared breasts.

Mira curtsied coyly as she opened the door wide. "I've been waiting for you, Judd, as you can see. Is it cold enough?" referring to the martini that Judd took as he tried to kiss her despite the awkward encumbrance of the tray.

"Just right, and so are you," he responded, taking a quick sip of the martini and then leaving it on a nearby table as she did the same with the tray. He took her in his arms as she wound her body close to his and moved her pelvis around and in and out against his crotch.

She noticed his embrace was perfunctory. Slipping out of his arms, she walked with him to the couch, where she puffed up one of the oversized pillows for him. She brought their drinks over, and they toasted each other silently.

"What is it, Judd? What's wrong? . . . Of course, how stupid can I be? You're still grieving over Rudy, aren't you?"

"Of course I am, Mira. He was the closest friend I've ever had." He took her hand and traced the fingers with his own. "But it's not only that. I realize that every one of us has to die sometime and somewhere. It's always a shock when someone goes, but it wears off as time goes by. It's not that so much. It's wondering what's going to happen now."

"Nothing's going to happen, I'm sure. Global is too well organized and too big not to just keep rolling along. You told me only last week what the commission gross was—I forgot the figure, but it was a whopper."

"Twenty-four million six," he said.

"So what's bothering you then?" she said.

"Simple. There'll be no problem in keeping Global on top of the heap. What my problem will be is how the rest of the executives are going to react when I take over as head man in Rudy's place. You don't know these people the way I do; they're all cutthroats to differing degrees. Nobody's indispensable—I learned that early in the game—but I'd hate to have any of them try to fight me and maybe quit and go else-where."

"Are they all that good?" Mira asked.

"You're damn right they are. I don't like them all, but they can bring in the dough and none of them would have any trouble getting a spot in a rival agency in twenty minutes. The problem is this: How can I keep them under a new setup, taking orders from me?"

"You're probably just imagining things, Judd. I'll bet any one of them will be glad not to have to get in-volved in top-level decisions. Why don't you give them contracts as soon as you can?" Mira suggested.

Judd sat up slightly and said, "That's not so easy. None of us have contracts now; Rudy was against them. He always said, 'If I need to tie a man down with a contract it's because I'm afraid he'll leave or he's afraid I'm going to fire him. I want the people at Global to want to be here,' he said, 'and I want them to stay, but not because they have contracts. It's got to be a two-way street and if either one of us wants to get off the merry-go-round, he should have the right.'"

Mira had no answer to that. Neither of them spoke for a while, Judd lighting a cigarette, and Mira sip-ping her drink.

Mira was the first to break the silence. She knew there was nothing more she could offer on that sub-ject, and besides, she was completely uninterested in Judd's problems, domestic or business, although she had made an effort to indicate otherwise.

"Worrying about it isn't going to solve anything,

and you may be inventing a crisis that won't ever happen," she said. "Why don't you get undressed, take a hot shower, and join me in the bedroom. I've already had my bath," she continued, smiling, and pressing her body down on his on the couch.

He grinned, closed his eyes, and leaned back to enjoy her fragrance. "That's the best invitation I've had since I was here last week. Why not?"

"And if you'd rather not wait, why should you," she said, unzipping his trousers and extracting his prick, which began to swell in her hands. Swiftly she bent down and took the throbbing member in her mouth, gently biting it with her teeth, and began to move it up and down against her lips. Judd kept his eyes closed.

"Oh God, Mira, that's marvelous. Don't stop. But what about you?"

Mira was too busy to answer; he didn't expect or want a response.

She continued her efforts and was rewarded with a sudden spasm and swift ejaculation, which she had foreseen. She removed her lips and replaced them with her ready handkerchief at precisely the moment of the discharge.

Judd sighed, a sigh of total satisfaction, and turned his face against the pillow.

"Rest now, Judd. We'll talk more about it later. Just rest," said Mira.

She got up, crumpled the handkerchief in her hand and threw it into the nearby wastebasket. Then she lit a cigarette and watched. It was only a matter of moments before Judd was asleep.

Mira looked down at the sleeping man, his fly still open, his trousers in disarray, his clean-shaven face heavy and pale against the puffed pillow. Thank God that's over, she thought, it's getting harder to do every time, harder to fake desire of any kind.

VI

This was the day scheduled for the first staff conference without Rudy at the head of the long oak table. All the executives would be there (all but Rudy), each with his own private thoughts and public voice: Judd, Alex, Lettie, Jim, Josie to take notes and, for the first time, a newcomer, Jackie, who would probably sit in the heavy leather chair at the head of the table: Rudy's chair.

The people who would attend this morning's meeting were all contemplating it at various highly personalized levels as the hour for it approached.

When Judd came down to the breakfast room that morning to the table set for three, Suz was already at her place, a book propped in front of her as she ate hurriedly and without expression.

"Good morning, Suz," said Judd as he took his accustomed chair and pressed the buzzer under the table for Albert.

"Morning, Dad," answered Suz, without looking up from her book.

"I suppose Kerry's sleeping as usual, eh?" commented Judd as he contemplated the empty third chair.

"No idea; I imagine so," said Suz, gulping her coffee and turning a page.

Judd realized there was no point in attempting any further conversation and turned to Albert, who had entered in the meantime and had placed copies of the *Hollywood Reporter, Variety,* and the *Los Angeles Times* at the right side of his plate, with the Calendar section of the *Times* open at the Film Clips page.

"What have we got this morning, Albert?" questioned Judd.

"Scrambled eggs, bacon, those crescent rolls you like and guava jelly," said Albert.

"Perfect," said Judd, reaching for the newspapers with one hand and the coffee cup Albert had filled with the other.

There was nothing in either of the trade papers that arrested his attention beyond a single item in the *Hollywood Reporter* gossip column that said, "It will be interesting to see who comes out on top for the head man's spot now open at Global. Whoever gets it has a job ahead of him filling Rudy Ruttenberg's shoes. They were big ones. He wasn't called Mr. Hollywood for nothing."

Albert was back with his eggs and bacon. "Excuse me, Mr. Haber, but Mrs. Haber asked if you'd come to her room before you leave. She wants to see you."

"Thanks, Albert. I won't forget," said Judd and wondered for a passing second what Milly wanted to talk to him about. She invariably breakfasted in her room and he never saw her until the evening when he came home. It had been many years since he'd abandoned the custom of coming into her room and kissing her good morning before leaving for the office.

Judd read again, "They were big ones." Of course they were, he thought to himself, but that doesn't mean he couldn't fit them. After all, he'd practically started with Rudy and had learned every trick in the business. Let's see, how many years was it? Almost thirty, a long time, anyway, and Judd felt that there wasn't much that he hadn't mastered by now. It would be exciting and very pleasant. Not only would he get a bigger cut of the profits, but all of Hollywood would have to reckon with him. Maybe no one would ever call him Mr. Hollywood, but he knew that with all the resources of Global Talent at his command he would be Mr. Hollywood with or without the title.

He knew perfectly well that no immediate decision would be made about the presidency; after all, Jackie would want to talk it over with him before she made an official pronouncement. With Rudy's death she was actually the boss. She owned the ninety percent of the stock that Rudy had retained for himself after giving away the remaining ten percent to various charities. He wondered how his colleagues really felt about him; he realized that some of them probably hated his guts, for good or bad reasons.

As he sipped his coffee, he thought about them. There was Alex. He had no real fondness for Alex. In fact, if Alex didn't toe the the line he was perfectly willing to let him go. Rudy had hired him while Judd was away, and Judd had never respected him as a man. He smiled wryly as he recalled the one time he had complained about Alex to Rudy. Rudy had listened and then said quietly, "Nobody asked you to love Alex, but he brings in the clients and they bring in the commissions and the commissions are what keeps Global on top." "But he's such a slimy bastard," said Judd, unconvinced. Rudy smiled, tapped the ash from his ever-present cigar, and said, "His clients don't seem to think so and they're the ones who pay ten percent." Rudy was right, of course, but Rudy wasn't there any more. No. he'd have to make it quite clear to Alex that he, Judd Haber, was the boss and no one else, and that if Alex didn't like it that way, the exit door was always open.

The others? Lettie wouldn't be any problem; she was a damn good agent and almost her only fault was her foul language. She liked her job, and she'd take orders from him the same way she took them from Rudy.

There wouldn't be any trouble with Jim, either. He was a first-rate man with the figures and knew the contents of every deal ever made at Global; perhaps a raise might not be a bad idea for Jim. As office manager he worked hard and had been a loyal and faithful employee. Judd knew Rudy had enormous faith in Jim, and while Judd didn't feel that Jim was a dynamo, he recognized that Jim's sense of organization and order had contributed significantly to Global's growth. Yes. Jim deserved a raise and he'd give it to him as soon as possible.

He hadn't noticed that Suz was standing beside him, ready to leave.

"Daydreaming, Dad?" she said, and leaned forward to kiss him on the cheek. "I'm off. Got an exam at ten in French. Wish me luck. Probably won't see you till tomorrow. Got a date tonight for dinner."

Judd rose and hugged her. "Okay, luck with the exam. By the way, you've been out to dinner a lot these last few months." He smiled and continued, "Same fellow? That Isaacs boy you told us about?"

Suz stopped at the door. "Same fellow." She started to say more, but decided against it.

"When are we going to meet him?" asked Judd.

Suz hesitated for a second or two before she responded. "One of these days I'll bring him around. I promise."

Judd gave her an inquiring look as he said, "Is it serious, Suz? Anything you want to tell me?"

Suz hesitated for a long moment and then said, "Nope. Not yet anyway. But I'll let you know when there's anything to tell."

Judd blew her a kiss and said, "That's fair enough. We'd like to meet him, whoever he is, whenever you're ready."

"You will, Dad, you will. I'm not ready yet," answered Suz as she almost ran out of the room, banging the door as she went. He could hear the roar of her Porsche as she pulled out of the driveway into the street.

The coffee was cold. Judd buzzed and Albert appeared with coffee pot in hand.

Judd sipped the hot coffee, put the cup down, and lit a cigarette.

It would be an interesting meeting, very, he continued to muse to himself, interesting and enjoyable. He patted his mouth with his napkin, extinguished his cigarette, and started toward the door, calling out as he went, "Albert. My briefcase. It's on the mantel in the bedroom. Will you get it for me, please?"

"Of course, Mr. Haber," came Albert's voice from the kitchen, "And Mrs. Haber. Remember she wanted to see you."

Judd had completely forgotten about Milly's request. He hurried up the staircase to her bedroom, knocked perfunctorily, and entered even as he heard her "Come in."

Milly took off her reading glasses as he came into the room, put the paper to one side, and smiled up at him from her bed with its breakfast tray on the covers beside her.

"You look very nice this morning, Judd. I like that blue pinstripe tie. Never noticed it before. Where did you get it?"

"Saks," answered Judd, and leaned uncomfortably against the door. He didn't want to be late, and he was nonplussed at her question about his tie. It was one Mira had bought him, one of the entrance-presents she had given him.

"Anything wrong, Milly? What did Kerry do now?"

Milly smiled broadly. "Nothing this time, but I hardly blame you for asking. It just occurred to me that this must be a very special morning for you—I know this is the staff meeting time—without Rudy, and I thought I'd like to wish you luck. That's all."

Judd was surprised at her sensitivity to the importance of the occasion—he so rarely discussed office matters with her anymore— but he concealed it with an answering smile.

"That's nice of you, Milly. Very. It'll be some weeks, maybe longer, before anything happens, but I'm grateful for your good wishes."

Milly looked up at him. "Anyway, good luck, Judd. It's not every woman's husband who's going to be president of Global Talent Associates."

"Don't be premature, Milly. But thanks, just the same. I'll let you know what happens."

"Do. I'd like to know."

As Judd closed the door behind him, he couldn't see that Milly kept looking at the closed door, and that she shook her head and murmured, "Poor Judd. He doesn't realize how much he wants it."

Then she turned back to her newspaper, putting on her glasses as she did so.

The shower was intense, invigorating; Alex soaped himself slowly, turned the indicator cold for a few seconds, then stepped briskly out onto the thick-piled carpeting, looking around the room for what he wanted. He shouted through the closed door, "Fran! Where the hell are the bath towels? I can't find any and I'm soaking wet."

Francoise Goulet stirred uneasily in her sleep, lifted her silk eye mask, raised herself on one elbow and shouted to the door. "They're in the closet. The one next to the john." Then she sank back into her pillow and closed her eyes again.

"I found 'em. Thanks," came Alex's answering voice.

The towel was soft and luxurious. He rubbed himself vigorously, slipped into the toweling robe hanging behind the door, wondered for a second or two whether it belonged to Jeb Marley or any of a dozen other people he could think of, opened the medicine cabinet door and found the electric razor he was certain would be there. He shaved carefully and methodically. Once finished, he searched in the closet for a small scissors and clipped his moustache with the same care. Not finding any after-shave lotion, he used witch hazel, splashing it generously onto his gleaming cheeks.

This would be an interesting day, he thought to himself, very interesting indeed. For once the old bastard wouldn't be there with his lousy jokes and his probing questions. He wondered whether it was politic to phone Jackie and wish her well at the first meeting of Global Talent Associates over which she would preside. Preside! What the hell does she know about the agency business? Nothing. But as Mrs. Rudy she'd be the new boss, so to speak, that is until she got around to giving him the job. He wanted it fiercely and he knew she was going to give it to him. Alex Deming, President of Global Talent Associates. It had a nice resonance, and he addressed himself to the closest mirror and said it aloud: Alex Deming, President of Global Talent Associates. Or would it sound better if he used his full name, Alexander Charles Deming, President of Global Talent Associates? No, he'd keep the Alex. After all, no one had ever thought of Rudy as Rudolph.

Since this was the first meeting without the old bastard he was sure that no announcement would be made. It would have been in poor taste, at least that's what he had told Jackie over the phone last night when he had called to say goodnight. What he'd recommended to her, and he was sure she would do it, was to appoint Jim Banton to be in charge of all office procedures for a month or so until things were sorted out a little bit. After all, Jim had been office manager for some time now and he could handle all the details. No one paid much attention to Jim, but they had all followed the system of sending copies of progress reports and deal-memos to Jim for years now, a system Rudy had initiated, and no harm would be done in continuing that method.

Yes, a month or so would be fine. Then Jackie would announce him president and that would be that. He grinned at the thought of that moment of triumph. It would be nice to see Judd Haber's ears pinned back as Jackie would make the statement and ask Jim to send out the announcement to the press. He knew damn well Judd didn't like him, and he also knew (which gave him great satisfaction) that Judd was assuming he'd get the job. Not that Judd was a bad agent; he wasn't bad at all, but he'd have to be even better if he wanted to stay with Global. No more of those long

trips abroad; Alex was going to take those over himself. And the top clients would have to know immediately that they would be serviced by the president
himself. Also (and Alex grinned even more at this
thought) the president would get a bigger cut of the
commissions and Judd would get less.

As for the other staff members, none of them really
mattered. He had no intention of making any
changes, at least for the time being, as long as they
kept on their toes. Lettie was okay; she handled people pretty well, and he knew she loved her job and
would do anything asked of her to keep it. And Jim
Banton was Jim Banton; he was good figure-man and
nothing more.

He walked back into the bedroom. Francoise was
asleep again, one breast out of the coverlet, one hand
flung across her face.

He dressed quickly, leaned down and touched the
exposed nipple gently, a caress she didn't feel, and
opened and closed the door behind him as quietly as
possible. That was a good fuck last night, he reflected,
as he pressed the elevator button and awaited the red
flash of the Down sign. However, now that he was to be
president, he'd better save himself for Jackie. Come to
think of it, maybe he'd marry Jackie. That would
clinch the deal beautifully, make it legal, so to speak.
He was whistling cheerfully as the elevator door
opened.

"They were big ones," repeated Lettie to herself
aloud as she sipped her orange juice, her eyes glued to

the *Hollywood Reporter.* "Too big for anyone else at Global," she apostrophized the paper as she reached for a cigarette with her other hand. Nevertheless, I suppose it's a toss-up between Judd and Alex, she reflected, the smoke curling slowly in front of her. Neither of them have one-tenth of what Rudy had, but what business was it of hers? That'll be Jackie's decision; she controls the whole show now and she's the one who'll be calling the shots.

Either way, it won't affect me, she thought to herself. I've got my own stable of clients; I know my job and everyone at Global knows I do. Rudy gave me a break when I didn't know what the hell I was doing, but I've proved myself a dozen different ways since then and the books show it. Jim Banton knows; he knows which deals have my initials and which are marked JH or AD.

There was the sound of a drawer being opened in the adjoining room and Lettie rose casually to her feet, stubbed out her cigarette in the coffee cup saucer and went into the bedroom.

The girl in the room looked barely eighteen; she was struggling into a pair of blue jeans, her torso still naked, her small breasts bobbing as she bent to twitch at the jeans.

"Eve," said Lettie, her voice flat, "I want you out of here in ten minutes. Understand me?"

The girl had finally succeeded in getting her pants on. She came over to Lettie, her arms outstretched, smiling mischievously. "Aw, come on, Lettie. You're not throwing me out, are you? Not after last night."

Lettie stepped away from the outstretched arms.
"Last night's over, baby. There's fifty bucks in a envelope on the dining room table. Ten minutes. And I
mean it."

The girl turned her back sulkily. "Okay, if that's
the way you want it."

"That's the way I want it," said Lettie.

The girl walked past Lettie as if on her way to the
bathroom.

Lettie started to protest, but the girl kept moving
into the dining room and said over her shoulder,
"Don't get nervous, honey, I'm just getting the envelope. I'll be out in time. Don't worry." She giggled as
she disappeared through the doorway.

"That's just like you, never pushing yourself, never
letting anyone know how good you are at the job. You
know damn well you know more about what makes
Global tick than anybody in the whole office. You're an
idiot, Jim, a soft-headed fool. All you've got to do is ask
to see that bitch, Jackie Ruttenberg. Just ask her, that's
all I want." Margie's voice became shrill as she leaned
toward her husband at the breakfast table, her stained
housecoat half-open, her scrawny breasts revealed.

Jim Banton put down the paper, took off his thick
bifocals, and said as quietly as he could, "Lay off me,
Margie, will you? I've got a good job and I want to keep
it. I'm not the man to run the shop, and I'm not going
to ask for the job, and I've told you ten times to leave
me alone."

"You're a fool, Jim, you've always been a fool and

you'll never change. You wouldn't even be there except for me. You'd still be pushing pencils at Penney's."
Margie got up from the table, walked over to the stove
and poured herself another cup of coffee. Then she sat
down heavily opposite her husband and he knew she
was going to start all over again. God, he hated her,
her rasping tongue, her sloppy dress, her thick lips.
Jesus Christ, why couldn't she let him alone? All he
asked of life was to be let alone.

"None of the others know a thing about running
the place, and you know it. You've told me often
enough how you have to correct their deal memos.
Sure, Judd and Alex may be good agents, and Lettie,
too, for that matter; but when it comes to actually but-
toning up the deal and drawing the contract who did
Rudy call in for advice? You, Jim Banton, that's who."

Jim got up wearily from the table. His back ached;
it always did when she started bedeviling him about
something he didn't want to do. It was his weak spot,
he'd got it in a car accident years before.

"Listen, Margie," he said as he headed for the door,
"I don't want the job; I haven't got a right to the job;
I'm not going to ask for the job, and that's final. I'll see
you tonight," and he was out in the hall.

Even as he hurried to the elevator he could hear her
voice, raised stridently now so that he would be sure to
hear her. "You're a damn fool, Jim Banton, a prize idiot,
and you'll never get anywhere in the world. Never!"

Josie held the half-empty bottle of bourbon in her
trembling hand. "Oh, Martin, not again. You prom-

ised me you wouldn't. You promised."

Martin looked up at her sheepishly from the couch. "Come on, Josie, don't start that again. A guy has to have a drink now and then."

"There's no now and then for you, Martin, and we both know it. I bet you never went to the AA meeting last night. You lied to me, didn't you?"

"That's right, Josie. I lied," said Martin, running his thick fingers through his tangled black hair. "I only said I'd go to shut you up."

Josie began to cry. She sank down into the over-stuffed armchair as sobs shook her whole body.

Martin didn't make a move to comfort her. He waited, saying nothing. He was used to these scenes. By now they made no impression on him. He knew if he waited long enough she'd stop crying, come over to kiss him goodbye, and go off to her job.

The sound of the sobs began to trail off. Josie dabbed at her eyes, walked over to the couch, bent down and held Martin tight in her arms for a moment. "I guess there's no use, is there? I have to go now. Goodbye, Martin."

"Bye," he said extricating himself from her embrace and watching her as she took her purse in one hand and the bottle in the other.

As soon as the door closed behind her Martin got up from the couch, rummaged underneath it, and pulled out a second bottle, this one unopened. He fumbled with the cap, took a long drink from the bottle and returned to the couch, the bottle propped against a pillow close to his right hand.

VII

The staff meeting was at 10:00 that morning. The traditional meeting time had been 8:30 for years; but Alex had phoned everyone to say that Jackie wanted it at 10:00.

As usual Josie was there a half hour before to lay out the thick yellow legal pads, the freshly sharpened pencils, the three ashtrays, and the giant-sized carafe of coffee sitting on its silver tray surrounded by the cups and saucers. Josie had always been the one secretary in the office who had recorded the meeting notes, even though the normal procedure would have been to use Rita Jensen, Rudy's own secretary. It had all started years ago when Rita was hospitalized for a number of weeks with a broken foot and Judd had offered Josie's services as a replacement. It wasn't long before Rudy was telling Judd that she reminded him in many ways of Milly, and that as far as he was concerned, he'd like to have her take over the post of conference secretary permanently, if it didn't disturb Judd's schedule. Judd talked it over with Josie, who was delighted to do anything that would please Judd. By the time Rita returned to her desk, Josie had become an official attendant at the conferences; and since Rita was more than happy not to have to come to work at such an early hour, there were no problems of hurt dignity involved.

As Josie was arranging the pads and other paraphernalia on the long oak table, she hesitated for a moment as she placed a pad and pencil in front of what had always been Rudy's chair. A little uncertain what to do on this momentous occasion, she first removed the pad and pencil, held them for a second, and then replaced them. Perhaps Mrs. R would use them. It was better not to risk not having them there, although privately and secretly Josie felt that the very presence of Mrs. R at this Monday morning conference was bizarre, even a little intrusive somehow.

Josie rearranged the coffee cups for the second time, then sat down at the end of the table with her steno pad and a pencil in her lap waiting for the first arrivals. She glanced around the empty room as if checking all the details, her eyes lingering longest on Rudy's chair. She could see him, one hand drumming on the table, the other holding his cigar, now and again interrupting someone's report. "Did you get that, Josie?" Her answer through the years: "Yes, I did, Mr. R."

Then the image vanished and she thought about Martin and the way she had left him this morning. She and he both knew he was a confirmed and incurable alcoholic, incurable because he would do nothing to help himself. She remembered the day she had learned the scalding truth; that her Martin was not only an alcoholic but had deliberately married her in order to feed his indulgence. She learned then that he had lied to her about many things. That was years ago; Josie now knew he would never change and she also knew that she would never leave him, try though she might and sensible though it would be.

Their first meeting was a bizarre one; she had been shopping at the Broadway in Hollywood and had come out to find that she had left the keys of her locked car in the ignition. Martin was a parking attendant then—he later explained that it was only a temporary job—and he had been most gallant and helpful in extricating her keys, securing a coat hanger from the dress department to do so. She had been grateful; he had been charming and attractive, with shining coal-black eyes, slim of body and grace-ful of movement. It seemed only natural for her to ac-cept his invitation to have a cup of coffee—he explained that he was just about to go off duty any-way. (It was months later that she learned he had been fired for being drunk that very afternoon.)

The cup of coffee turned into lunch, and he told her that he had been a salesman in Bullock's, that there had been a cutback in employees, and that he was temporarily out of work, which was why he'd accepted the parking attendant job.

There had been meetings after that. Once he had taken her to the race track, where he seemed to be well known, but she thought nothing of it, clinging af-fectionately to his arm and drinking in his knowl-edgeable chatter about the horses and jockeys. She hadn't even noticed that he drank a good deal wherever they went; it all seemed part of his charm and sophistication.

Then the day came when he told her that he had landed a job as a salesman at Ohrbach's, to start in one week. That same day, when she congratulated him on his new position and the glowing future he told her it assured, he asked her to marry him and she had said yes.

Their four-day honeymoon in Maine was marked by his passionate sexual ardor, to which her virginal body responded with total joy. After they moved into her apartment, he threw off all pretense.

She could still remember that half-hour of revelation. She came home from the office, a bag of groceries in either arm, and had knocked vainly at the apartment door while fumbling for her key. When she eventually got the door open he was sprawled on the couch, two empty bottles of whiskey beside him, sound asleep.

Totally unprepared for this sight and not knowing what else to do, she first shook him into wakefulness and then ran to the bathroom, wet a towel, and dabbed at his face and forehead with it.

He grinned sleepily up at her and tried to embrace her; but she repulsed him and began to cry out of fright and bewilderment. He looked at her blankly, closed his eyes, turned away, and went to back to sleep.

Josie didn't try again to wake him. She went into the bedroom, undressed mechanically, and fought sleeplessness most of the night.

She started to tiptoe by his still-recumbent form the next morning when he suddenly awoke as if he had been waiting for her. He was apparently sober; he spoke thickly and he told her what she never expected to hear. Martin spared her nothing. He told her he had been a drunk for years and had dried out repeatedly, that he hadn't had a regular job since he was 22, that both the Bullock's and Ohrbach jobs were lies, that he got along with occasional work like the parking attendant job, that he lived on those and his infrequent winnings at the track, and that he had no intention of ever working again now that they were married and she had a regular salary that was enough to support them both.

He told her all this in a monotone, his black eyes focused on her mesmerically as he spoke. Too horrified to talk, Josie turned away from him toward the door; but he grabbed her arms before she could reach it, and he bent her back while he kissed her hard and brutally, silencing all comment. And to her utter horror and despair, as his body pressed against hers and he fumbled with her skirt, she felt her own body responding all on its own, and her hands clung to his shoulders with fierce, unexpected passion.

It had been that way ever since. Martin was drunk most of the time, but now and again when he was sober he made love to Josie, and she lived for those moments when she gasped in ecstasy as he drove his penis in and out of her willing body. She lived in shame at her weakness, but knew she would never leave him.

No one at the office knew anything about Martin. There had been no occasion to mention his name. Even Judd never questioned her about her domestic life; he had asked casually about her husband and had been satisfied with her response that Martin was a salesman who was out of town a great deal.

The conference room door opened. It was Jim Banton, the first of the executives to arrive, bearing as he always did his big ledger books and various manila folders with the names of agents on their covers. It had long been Rudy's custom to ask Jim to report on the status of all pending deals and those consummated during the week. This enabled Rudy to direct sharp, probing questions at the people around the table, although he always ameliorated criticism with praise for transactions already concluded.

"Morning, Josie, all set up as usual, eh?"

"Yes, Mr. B."

Jim set down his ledgers and folders, meticulously straightened the yellow pad that didn't need straightening, sat down, and then turned to Josie. He gestured at the material in front of him. "Guess you wonder why I brought all this stuff: I wasn't sure myself; but I don't know what Mrs. Ruttenberg will want to know and I thought I'd better be prepared. It'll be a strange meeting, won't it? I mean without Rudy up there at the other end of the table."

"I know how you feel, Mr. B. I'm sure all the other executives feel a little odd, too. I know I do."

"Well, whatever happens, it can't affect Global in the long run." He slapped his books affectionately.

"We're way ahead of the game and I've got the figures to prove it. And whoever sits in that chair won't change much." He paused, then said apologetically, "I don't mean that any one of them, even your Mr. Haber, couldn't ever be as good as Rudy, though I doubt it. I just mean Global is too big by now to do anything but just keep rolling along. That was Rudy's doing, of course." He suddenly looked very forlorn and solemn. "I'll miss him a hell of a lot. He was damn good to me."

"I understand, Mr. B. All of us feel the same way," said Josie.

Jim poured himself a cup of coffee and sipped it meditatively. Neither of them spoke again; they were waiting.

The door opened noisily and a brusque Alex Deming entered, carrying a bulging attache case with a prominent gold A D. He flung the case carelessly onto the table at the chair he usually occupied and then came over to slap Jim cheerfully on the back.

"Early as usual, eh, Jim?" he said, reaching for the carafe and a cup and saucer. "Odd without the old boy, isn't it?" He poured the coffee into his cup, took a long sip, and sat down. "And you, Josie, don't look so glum. Global's going to carry on, and you know it."

"Mr. B and I were just commenting on how strange it is without Mr. R there at the head of the table," said Josie.

"Don't worry, Josie," answered Alex, laughing pleasantly. "Someone will be there eventually. Can't have an empty chair forever, can we?" He glanced at his watch. "Where's Judd? Ought to be here by now; or is my watch fast?"

Jim started to say something when the door opened and Judd appeared. He, too, had a briefcase in one hand and he smiled affably as he entered the room.

"Morning, Jim, Alex, Josie. Lovely morning, isn't it?"

"It *is* a beautiful day, Mr. H," said Josie, smiling up at him.

"I think I saw Jackie's car go into the parking lot as I came in. It was a blue Rolls headed straight for Rudy's stall, so I figured it must be her. We ought to be able to start as soon as she gets here," Judd concluded.

There was a sound of female voices in the corridor and a male voice interrupting. Everyone in the room looked up inquiringly as the door opened and Jackie entered, flanked by Lettie and Gabe Donner.

Jim and Judd rose; Alex did the same, more slowly.

"Good morning, everybody," said Jackie, and looked uncertainly around the room. "Is that where Rudy usually sat?" she asked, indicating the empty armchair at the head of the table.

It was Lettie who answered over a chorus of "Good mornings" from the assembled executives and Josie. "That's right, Jackie, that's the one."

Gabe waved a greeting at everyone in the room and drew up a chair so that he sat next to Jackie.

"Thanks, Lettie," said Jackie, seating herself firmly in Rudy's chair. She squirmed a little. "It's too big for me, but I'm not going to be in it very often so I don't suppose it really matters."

"I think it suits you perfectly, Jackie," said Alex

gallantly.

Gabe tapped on the table with a pencil. "I don't know how your meetings were conducted and neither does Mrs. Ruttenberg; but I know all you people have things to do and clients to see and we want to make this meeting short. The only reason I'm here is because I'm the company attorney, as you know. There may be questions I can answer."

"Glad to have you with us," said Judd.

"We usually start with Jim here," volunteered Alex, indicating Jim Banton, "going over what's still on the back burner and then each of us makes an individual report on what we're up to at the moment."

"We can handle it any way that's convenient for you, however," said Lettie.

"By the way, Josie here," said Judd, indicating Josie with her pencil poised over her pad, "usually takes all the conference notes."

"Since this isn't a regular meeting, let's dispense with that this time, shall we?" said Gabe amiably.

"I agree," said Alex as if the question had been addressed to him. Everyone in the room nodded in assent.

Jackie leaned as far back as she could in the capacious leather chair and fumbled for a cigarette in her purse, while Gabe leaned forward and offered his lighter. She puffed nervously for a few seconds, then moved forward and put both her elbows on the table.

"All of you know me and if any of you are wondering whether I intend to sit in this chair for keeps, stop wondering. That's not my intention. I'm better at spending money than making it. Isn't that right, Gabe?"

Gabe grinned, patted her hand, and said, "Much better, Jackie. Much." They both chuckled.

"I like money, I always have, lots of it, and I don't much care where it comes from," said Jackie. "I haven't the vaguest idea how Global runs," she continued, "but Gabe here tells me there's one of you who does, and that's you, Jim Banton. Am I wrong?"

Jim flushed. "If you mean do I know the status of all the deals, the income and the expenses, I guess I do know that. But I couldn't fit that chair, Mrs. Ruttenberg, I really couldn't, and if—"

Jackie interrupted Jim by raising her hand. "I never said anything about anybody fitting Rudy's chair. All I want to say is that until I make up my mind what I'm going to do about Global, I want you, Jim, to sit in as a sort of temporary clearing station of what goes on. You can report to Gabe once or twice a week, and then Gabe can tell me whatever I should know. Okay with you? Any objections, anybody?"

I don't get it, thought Judd. Does that mean she's grooming Jim Banton for the presidency? He's a nice guy, but what the hell does he know about Global except the figures? Jackie knows damn well I'm the only man in the room Rudy really trusted. Even as he thought these things, he got up and shook Jim's unprotesting hand.

"I think that's a darn good notion," he said. "I like working with Jim." He then returned to his chair.

"Excellent idea, Jackie," said Alex. "That'll give

you time to figure things out without making any hasty decisions. Jim and I have always gotten along. I'm delighted for you, Jim." He smiled at Jackie and she smiled back.

"What about you, Lettie?" asked Jackie.

"I'm all for it if that's what you mean," answered Lettie.

Gabe tapped his pencil again. "We haven't heard from you, Jim. Okay? You understand it's just a temporary arrangement, nothing more."

Jim cleared his throat before he spoke. "Sure, sure. I understand it's only temporary, and that's dandy with me. I'll call you tomorrow morning, Gabe, if that's okay with you, and we can make a date to go over the books so you can see how we operate. And thanks, Mrs. Ruttenberg; I won't—"

"You can call me Jackie."

Jim flushed and continued. "Thanks, Jackie. I will. I was going to say that I won't let you or Global down." He started to gather his ledgers together into a neat pile. "And like I said, I understand it's only temporary, and that's fine as far as I'm concerned. I wouldn't want it any other way."

"Good," said Jackie, snuffing her cigarette in the ashtray. "That's all I've got to say right now and you'd better all get going and start making some money for Global—and me. I'll make up my mind on the next move in a month or so." She turned to Lettie. "I saw you getting out of a cab when I came in this morning. Car trouble? Can I drop you anywhere, Lettie?"

"That would be nice, Jackie. Thanks. If you could

take me to Slaven's Garage on Sunset—that's where the car is—-I'd appreciate it. It's right on your way."

Jackie rose and snapped her purse shut. "No problem. Let's get out of here." She strode purposefully to the door with Lettie following her. "Good luck to all of you and to Global," and she was gone with Lettie.

Gabe got up, slapped Jim jovially on the back, and said, as he headed for the door, "I'll expect your call, Jim. So long, everybody."

The silence that ensued was finally broken by Josie, who gathered up her unused notebook and pencil. "If you'll excuse me, Mr. H, I still have that long letter to our London office to transcribe, and I guess I'd better get at it."

"Sure, sure. Of course, Josie," answered Judd absent-mindedly, rolling his pencil back and forth on the table as he spoke.

Jim took a firm grasp of the ledgers and manila folders he had brought to the meeting, stood up, and announced awkwardly, "Me, too; I've got a lot to clean up for Gabe before I call him." He bumped his chair out and lurched to the door, then stood there clumsily balancing the stuff in his hands, shuffling his feet a little as he stood there. "I'm sure you both know I hadn't the vaguest idea this would happen; but as Gabe and Mrs. Ruttenberg both said, it's only temporary. I don't want either of you to think I consider it any more than just that—temporary. I know as well as you do that I'm not the man for that job and that everybody at Global knows it. I guess Mrs. Ruttenberg—Jackie—doesn't want to make any big changes for a while. I can't think of any other reason, can you?"

Alex smiled and said, "For God's sake, Jim, don't be so modest; we're both delighted. Aren't we delighted, Judd?"

"Absolutely. Delighted, as Alex says," answered Judd.

"As far as I'm concerned," continued Alex affably, "it could be permanent. I know what a hell of a job you do for Global and how responsible you are. Hell, I think you'd make a great president for keeps."

Judd smiled and shook his head in affirmation. "I agree with Alex there. As far as I can see Global couldn't be in better hands."

Jim was deeply pleased and looked it. His grin was boyish. "Thanks for that. But I don't want the job and I'm only taking it because that's the way Jackie wants it for now. I'll be seeing you. So long," and he was gone.

Instantly both Judd and Alex got up as if Jim's leaving was some sort of signal.

"I'd better get to work," said Judd.

"Me, too," said Alex.

Alex ambled down the hall to his office whistling softly and feeling a little dance step just under the surface of his walk. Well, that's done; Jackie handled it very well, he reflected, and Jim will hold down the fort for a month or so. At the end of that time Jackie would make her move to put him, Alex Deming, in as president and that would be that. He was sure Judd was a bit nonplussed, to put it gently, at Jim's interim appointment, but he'll be a lot more astonished when he gets the news that he, Alex, will have the job. He must remember to send Jackie some flowers. He'd phone her first, though, and congratulate her on what she did. Yes, that would be a smart thing to do. He quickened his step and entered his office.

Judd, too, was thinking of the meeting and the unexpected selection of Jim to head the office for the time being. Judd did not like it. Not that Jim could ever really handle the complex affairs of Global. He did not like that there had ever been any thought whatsoever in anybody's mind that he, Judd, would not take over the reins immediately. It was only a temporary postponement, of course, but what was the point? It seemed such an unnecessary step. But it would be impolitic, if not downright foolish, to indicate anything but wholehearted approval of Jim's brief tenancy. He'd just have to be a little more patient, that's all.

Jim Banton sat at his paper-strewn desk and put his head in his hands. He knew that he should be phoning Margie to tell her what had happened; she'd made him promise to let her know as soon as he came out of the conference. But he knew just what she'd say. She'd tell him that this was just the beginning; that he should keep the job, that he deserved it, that he'd be good at it, and that he should worm himself into Gabe's confidence and flatter Jackie as much as possible. He knew it would be hopeless for him to tell Margie, as he had before, that he didn't want the job, that he wished Jackie had never given it to him even on this provisional basis, and that he wished they would let him go on doing exactly what he had been doing for years.

He reached glumly for the phone and dialed his home number.

It was late that afternoon, almost 6:30, when Josie came into Judd's office after her discreet knock. This had become an unofficial ritual, established through the years, a brief period of relaxation when the employer-employee relationship was disregarded and the formality they observed in the outer office was eliminated. By now Josie was aware of every element in Judd's life, and that included his deteriorating relationship with Milly, although Josie would never mention that to him unless he brought it up. She also shared his growing distress about Kerry and the life he was leading.

Judd was certain that Josie knew of his affair with Mira ever since that first time when she had brought in Mira's bills and he had approved their payment. Now and again, he had even asked for her advice when seeking a gift for Mira—always referred to as Miss D—and her counsel was always sound and useful. He had nothing to fear from Josie; he knew he could trust her loyalty and judgement one hundred percent.

These late afternoon conferences—they were really just friendly chats—were a welcome hiatus in the strains and stresses of the day, and they talked openly as old friends, which indeed they were by this time, in many ways.

It was a curiously one-sided relationship. Although

Josie knew almost everything that could be known about Judd and his affairs, both business and personal, Judd knew very little about Josie. He had politely tried to question her on her private life, but all he really knew was that she was married to a man named Martin. It wasn't that Josie didn't trust Judd; she simply felt such intense shame over her relationship with her husband that she could never bring herself to talk about him. Judd sensed her reluctance to speak of this part of her life. Respecting her reticence, he had refrained from many questions.

Invariably the meeting began with Judd taking a small glass of scotch from his liquor cabinet while Josie sipped contentedly on a Coca-Cola. Judd had long since stopped offering her anything stronger. She always declined. Her rejection of liquor had become a standard joke between them. Judd never knew why Josie refused to drink anything stronger than Coke; that was part of her private world, the world of Martin, that made any form of alcohol anathema. Judd assumed that her Calvinist upbringing was the source of her abstinence.

This particular day duplicated others. "Just wanted to say good night, Mr. H," Josie said as she entered. "Anything I can do before I leave?"

"Not tonight, Josie," said Judd, his back to her, pouring out the two drinks and offering her the Coke.

Judd raised his glass. "Well, Josie, let's drink this one to Global and the future. Shall we?"

"Gladly," Josie answered. They both smiled as they clicked glasses ceremoniously.

Judd toyed with the glass on his desk. "What did you think of the meeting?"

"Frankly, Mr. H, I think Mrs. R did a smart thing. It's only been a matter of days since Mr. R's funeral and she needs time to figure out what she wants to do. My guess is that she'll wait to make the official appointment in a few weeks after she confers with Gabe Donner. After all, there may be salary adjustments and bonuses to discuss, maybe even stock options even though Mr. R never believed in them."

"I guess you're right, Josie, although I confess I don't know why she has to wait. Any of those things could be handled afterwards just as well, don't you think?"

"They could, of course; but maybe Mrs. R doesn't want to be boxed in until she knows all the figures." She smiled. "Remember she said she likes money, lots of it, and before she gives any of it away, I guess she wants to know how much there really is."

"You make a lot of sense, Josie. I'm sure there's nothing to be concerned about. It's just that I'd like to get it over with. There are a few things I'd like to start doing immediately. And one of them, Josie, would be to make you my assistant. Assistant to the president of Global Talent Associates. How would you like that?" Judd lifted his glass in a silent toast to her as he said this.

"Oh, Mr. H! That's nice of you, but you know, I don't really care what my title is. I love working for you, and that's all that matters to me. In any case, let's not count our chickens before they're hatched. But thank you, Mr. H. Thank you very much," said Josie.

"You're right again, Josie. I'm sure it will only be a couple of weeks at the most, and then everything will be settled. In the meantime Jim will do a good job; he always has."

"I know that Mr. B doesn't want the job for keeps. He said so at the meeting and I believe him. He's great just where he is and that's where he wants to stay." She glanced at her wristwatch. "I'm sure you want to get home and tell Mrs. Milly about the meeting. She must be waiting to hear. Or did you already phone her?"

Although Josie always referred to the staff members by the first initial of their last names, she broke this custom when it came to Judd's family. Following his lead she called them by their first names, as if they had become part of her own family. In a sense this was true. The only concession she made to propriety was to refer to them as Mrs. Milly, Mr. Kerry and Miss Suz.

Her mention of Milly caused a flicker of consternation on Judd's face. "No, I haven't phoned her yet. I got busy with other things and frankly I forgot. I'll do it before I leave."

Josie took a sip of her Coca-Cola. "Does Mrs. Milly still like her class at UCLA? You haven't mentioned it lately," she said.

Judd looked up from the papers he was arranging on his desk. "Oh, sure," he said. "I mean, I guess so. Actually we haven't discussed it for some time." He suddenly realized what he was revealing about his relationship with Milly and added hastily, "You know I've been up to my ears getting things in order after Rudy's death and I guess I've neglected a lot of things I should have been doing."

Josie's response was reassuring. "Of course, I understand. These have been busy days for all of us. What about Miss Suz, Mr. H.? All well there?" said Josie.

"Suz is fine; as a matter of fact I think she's interested in some youngster at school. She won't talk about him, but I bet I'm right."

"Miss Suz is quite a girl, Mr. H. You're lucky to have her as a daughter, but I'm certain you know that, don't you?"

"You know I'm crazy about Suz and there's nothing in the world I wouldn't do for her," answered Judd, smiling.

Josie rose to her feet, reaching for her purse on the chair. She felt intuitively that it was highly inadvisable to talk about Kerry; she knew about Kerry and Prompton Warwick and the porn films and she realized that this was one subject that Judd didn't want to discuss. It was too inflammatory.

"Well, I guess I'll be going now, Mr. H. You're sure there's nothing I can do?" she said, turning toward the door.

"Not a thing, Josie. Good night. See you in the morning."

"Good night, Mr. H," said Josie, as she closed the door behind her.

Almost as soon as the door clicked shut, Judd

reached for his private phone. He hesitated, his finger on the dial, and then dialed Mira Dalloway's number.

VIII

The Polo Lounge was crowded as usual; Hollywood was lunching and contacting as vigorously as ever and the buzz of social conversation was larded at almost every table with bursts of business talk. "Make it against the net and you've got a deal..." "For Christ's sake, Jerry, I've been with you for seven months and you haven't come up with a single offer..." "Okay, okay, okay; but a percentage against what; you know the picture is going to be a flop, let's get the money up front; the hell with a percentage of nothing..." "I told the son of a bitch not to shoot me from the right side; but he paid no attention. I look like Grandma Moses, the bastard..." "Look here, Lenny, I've been in this town a hell of a long time and I've done over 35 pictures; I'm simply not going to work for peanuts. Tell CBS to shove it as far as I'm concerned. Who needs them?" "If we can sell the paperback rights—and we will, I'm betting on that—we can hold out for two-fifty, maybe three. Why take the first stinking offer we get? Let's play it cool..." "I know you don't like to work for nothing, but everybody in town will be there; it's a big charity and it'll do your image a lot of good . . . " "It's not that I don't think you've got talent, hell, you're loaded with it; but maybe I'm not the guy to handle you. Look, I've tried, but I've struck out and I don't want to hold you back. Anyway that's how I see it. I'm sorry."

The chair opposite Prompton Warwick was empty, but Prompton didn't seem to mind in the least. He sipped his cocktail and gazed around the noisy room. Kerry was late as usual, but it didn't matter.

As Prompton looked about him he could recognize at least a half-dozen of his clients; but he made no effort to attract their attention. None of them indicated they knew him, as one or two accidentally met his roving glance. It was an unwritten agreement in Hollywood that people who worked in porn pictures did so as unobtrusively as possible. They rarely used their own names on the screen; they demanded and received payment in cash, thus avoiding any check record of the source of their incomes; and they never publicly acknowledged that their agent for these jobs was Prompton Warwick.

At first Prompton had been infuriated with this conspiracy of silence, but as his reputation grew and more and more out-of-work actors and actresses and directors sought his aid, his anger had simmered down to an accepting resentment. By now it amused him to see his clients avoid him in public places. He and they both knew the truth and as long as his agency continued to flourish, he was perfectly willing to abide by the rules of nonrecognition. Besides, he would not always be a porn agent; Prompton had his dreams, too, and someday he knew they would be realized, though he didn't know quite how. In the meantime his net worth was increasing markedly every year, a fact that gave him considerable satisfaction.

The maitre d' was ushering two women to a table. The dim lights made it difficult to see them well, but he thought he knew one of them. They both turned around at that moment and Prompton recognized Mirabelle Meredith, the designer; he'd seen her picture in the advertisements for her clothes. He could not see the face of the other woman behind the huge dark sunglasses she affected.

At that moment Kerry entered and looked around the room for Prompton. Prompton started to rise and wave, but Mirabelle saw him standing uncertainly at the door, raised her hand in greeting, and Kerry went to her table for a polite handshake in acknowledgement. Prompton couldn't hear the conversation, but apparently Mirabelle was introducing Kerry to her companion. The woman took off her glasses, and even at that distance Prompton could see that she was strikingly beautiful. Kerry said something; the woman laughed, and at that instant Prompton knew who she was. He smiled at the recollection.

She was Mira, Mira Dalloway, and Prompton knew her very well, though he doubted whether she would want to remember him. Prompton Warwick had been one of Grace's customers back in New York. He remembered how terrific Mira had been in bed and wondered idly what she was doing with Mirabelle. She must have changed her profession, he mused, grinning. So many people in Hollywood didn't want their pasts discussed.

"Sorry. I know I'm late; forgive me, Prompton. Got caught in traffic on Sunset," said Kerry, sitting down and clapping Prompton on the shoulder.

"No problem. I only just got here myself." Prompton signaled to their waiter and pointed to Kerry. "Our waiter will bring your martini in a minute. I told him to wait until you got here. Who's the dame with Mirabelle? The one you just said hello to."

Kerry glanced up at the table where Mirabelle and Mira were engaged in conversation. "Oh, her name's Mira Dalloway and she's one of Mirabelle's models. Isn't she a knockout? What makes you ask? Know her?"

The waiter had brought Kerry's drink by then and he started sipping it.

"Do I know her? I sure do. I've been there many times and she's one hell of a lay—when you ball her you know damn well you've been laid."

Kerry laughed, then looked again at the table where Mira and Mirabelle were chatting. Mira caught his inquiring gaze and smiled back at him.

"Where did you know her?"

"New York. Some years ago. She worked in a place on 55th Street then. I don't know what she's doing out here; maybe she's reformed. Too bad if she has, it would be a waste; as I said, you got the works when you had her."

Kerry unfolded his napkin and took up the menu. "Maybe I'll find out for myself and report back. I'll let you know if I do."

"I'd be interested. But if you make the grade, better not mention my name. I doubt if she wants to remember old clients if she's got a spot with Mirabelle."

"Okay, I promise."

"And now let's order. Meantime we can go over the new script if you want to," said Prompton.

Kerry grinned. "Aren't they all the same? Fucking international style."

Prompton grinned back. "Sure. But this time you do it with mirrors. You gotta admit that's a twist."

"Is he any relation to the Global executive, Judd Haber?" asked Mira, stubbing out her cigarette.

"He's his son. Good-looking, isn't he?" responded Mirabelle.

"Terrific," said Mira, replacing her sunglasses and looking at Kerry across the room.

"I've heard that he's a bit of a problem to his family," said Mirabelle.

"With a body like that he wouldn't be a problem to me," said Mira.

The two women laughed and Mirabelle drew out a sheaf of papers.

"I want to go over these ad proofs with you, Mira, since some of them involve you and next month's showings at Magnin's."

"Sure. Let's do it," said Mira, turning her gaze back to Mirabelle. "By the way, who's the man with him? I thought I knew him for a minute."

Mirabelle extracted her glasses from her purse and

looked where Mira pointed. "No idea. Never saw him before."

Mira kept looking at Prompton, now gesticulating forcefully to Kerry. "I think I have, but I'm not sure." She paused. "Okay, let's look at what you have."

The two women busied themselves with the ad proofs.

Sid Schwartzman was leaning forward in his chair, his face close to Judd's, his eggs Benedict neglected, his voice earnest and emphatic. "You can write your own ticket, Judd, and may the stockholders strike me dead for saying that, but I mean it," he said.

"That's very nice of you." Judd answered, "very nice, indeed; but you know my heart's with Global and always has been."

"Okay, so you'll be president. Big deal! I'm not knocking you, Judd; how could I be when I'm offering you such a job? But a Rudy you're not and maybe never will be. There was only one Mr. Hollywood and that was Rudy. Besides, wouldn't you like to be on the other side of the fence for a change? Buying is more fun than selling, believe me, and with you in a top spot—and I mean top!—we'd go places. Paramount could use you. I could use you. I'm still figuring the details of how it will work; but I can tell you right now that it's going to work because I want it to work. All I want to be sure of is that you're interested. That's all I'm asking now."

Judd smiled affably. "I know you mean what you say, Sid. It's just that I can't make any commitments right now. Not for a while, anyway."

"Will you promise me not to do anything until I get back to you with the whole schmear put together? Promise me that much, Judd. Will you?"

Judd put out his hand and Sid grasped it. "Okay. I promise not to do anything until I hear from you. Is that okay for now?"

"That's good enough for me, Judd. Just don't shelve it till you hear what I've got to say. This is Sid Schwartzman talking, not any schmuck in town. We're having a board meeting next week; I've got to clear away a few things first; but there won't be any problem, I promise you. What Sid Schwartzman wants, Sid Schwartzman gets."

"Your eggs are getting cold, Sid. Better eat them."

Sid grinned and picked up his fork. "Who needs eggs; it's you I need, not eggs."

"Hello, Dad. Nice to see you, Sid." It was Kerry's voice. He was standing beside the table on the way out. "Sid Schwartzman, Prompton Warwick." He smiled mischievously at Judd. "You know Prompton."

"Hello, Kerry," said Judd. Barely looking at Prompton, he added, "Yes. I do."

Sid Schwartzman acknowledged Prompton's presence with a perfunctory wave and Prompton smiled at him. "Be seeing you," said Kerry, and he and Prompton were gone.

"What's your son doing with that shit, Prompton Warwick?" asked Sid Schwartzman.

"How do I know?" said Judd, hardly concealing his irritation. "He's my son, but he picks his own friends."

"Sure, sure, sure," said Sid, not really interested. "So think it over, Judd; that's all I ask before you make any commitment to Global. Hell, you'll be president all right; but who in hell wants to work for Jackie Ruttenberg? Put that in your pipe and smoke it a little."

"Okay, I'll let you know. I promise." said Judd. "And now, let's get out of here. I'm still working for Global and I've got a lot to do this afternoon."

As the two men waited for their cars to be brought, Mirabelle and Mira came down the carpeted sidewalk.

Mirabelle went up to Judd and Sid. "Hi, Sid, Judd. Nice to bump into you." She turned to Mira, indicating her with a sweep of her hand. "Mira Dalloway, Judd Haber, Sid Schwartzman."

"Hi, Mirabelle. Nice to meet you, Miss Dalloway," said Sid, signaling to the attendant who was opening the door of his car in the driveway.

"You're looking well, Mirabelle. Hello, Miss Dalloway," said Judd, smiling pleasantly.

"Nice to meet both of you," said Mira, also smiling.

The two men moved off to their respective cars and Mirabelle called after them, "Just ran into Kerry, Judd. He's getting handsomer every day."

"That he is," said Judd noncommittally and got into his car.

"You're right about Mr. Haber's son. He really is handsome," said Mira, deliberately turning her gaze away from Judd's departing car.

IX

Milly hated the motel room; she hated everything about it, the peeling wallpaper, the gurgling sound of the leaking faucet, the shabby, thick pseudo-velvet curtains always tightly drawn, the dented bed-lamp, the black carpet splotched with white, and the cracked bathroom mirror.

Jerry knew how much she disliked coming here for their rendezvous—it was called the Romancero; she had shuddered when she first heard the name—but he'd once explained to her why he'd chosen this run-down motel in the most unattractive section of Culver City.

"Can't you understand, Milly," he had said, "this is precisely the kind of place where none of my errant colleagues would dream of going for their extra-curricular romances, and Lord knows, the people you go with wouldn't even know such a place exists. It took me a long time to find; I did a lot of discreet scouting, and you have to admit it has its advantages. We don't have to go through the front entrance ever, and besides, once we're here and in bed, what's the difference? Neither of us are meeting for an aesthetic experience," he concluded, grinning.

To her own chagrin, Milly knew he was right, but she also knew that wasn't how it had been in the beginning. In fact, there were moments when she could not believe that their relationship had changed (or degenerated) from an exchange of intellectual viewpoints to this sexual joust on Wednesday afternoons from four to five. Now there was very little conversation, intellectual or otherwise. The ritual, or rather the routine, was always the same. Jerry was to arrive first in his green Plymouth to sign the register with some phony names (Milly never knew what names he used and didn't ask), go to the room, undress, and wait for her. She was to arrive ten minutes afterwards, check to see that his green Plymouth was in its expected parking space, and then proceed directly to the room. It was usually the same room, number 189, and it was understood that if through some mischance Jerry could not obtain 189, there would be a note taped to the windshield of the green Plymouth which would tell her what the number of the new room would be. That had happened only once, which was why Milly knew room 189 so thoroughly and hated it so thoroughly.

Their lovemaking was swift, prosaic, untender. As she entered the already curtain-darkened room, Jerry's arms went around her. His right hand sought her hand and brought it down to enclose his stiffened penis while his other hand tugged at the zipper in the back of her dress. It was only a matter of minutes before she was as naked as he; and not many minutes later the swift foreplay of kissing her stiff nipples was over and he had entered her and she was arching her body to meet the rapidly increasing tempo of his thrusts. The whole process sometimes took less than ten minutes from the time Milly entered room 189 to the time Jerry lifted his body away from hers and rolled away, his left hand seeking a cigarette from the pack placed carefully on the chair beside the bed.

This occasion was no different from the preceding ones. Jerry lit his cigarette, puffed deeply and with pleasure, then turned to Milly with the inquiry that may once have been motivated by affection and solicitude: "How was it for you, dear?"

"Fine. Just fine," answered Milly, her fingers fumbling for the grimy coverlet to conceal her nakedness.

Jerry tamped out his cigarette, propped himself on an elbow, and said, "Mind if I just close my eyes for a few minutes? I'd like to savor what just happened. How about you?"

"Go ahead. I'll have a cigarette in the meantime."

As Jerry turned away from her to burrow deeper into the blankets, she looked at the mass of his form under the covers, remembering his heavy body pressing down on hers, the disturbing irritation of his unkempt moustache, the too-small brown eyes.

She stabbed out her cigarette and took another from her purse on the bedside table. Poor, dear, frightened Jerry, she thought. He smiled in his sleep and she could see the repulsive tobacco-stain on his teeth. She had never even noticed it when they had first been meeting each other.

It had been over a year ago when she had first registered in Jerry Horton's American Lit course as part of her curriculum when she had enrolled at UCLA as a mature student, as they called it. Desolate at the impasse in her relationship with Judd and his total disinterest in anything but his business, she had listened eagerly to the lectures Jerry had given on Faulkner and Hemingway and Fitzgerald. To her they were food she desperately craved, food she could never find at home.

At first their relationship had been markedly formal, teacher and student, each playing his or her expected and traditional role. She remembered the day it had begun to change. It was in the parking lot at the close of class. Her car had refused to start, and Jerry, having noticed her dilemma, offered to help by calling the Auto Club. When he came back from the phone call saying it would be at least an hour before they could come to her aid, he had gallantly suggested they have a drink together in the Faculty Center bar. She found herself telling him how she was starved for knowledge, and how much his class meant to her, a compliment he accepted with grace and charm. It was on this first occasion that he had suggested she call him Jerry and he would call her Milly, that is, he had added cautiously, when they were not in class together.

There had been other meetings after that, most of them concerned with her class work, where again and again he had brilliantly clarified a number of puzzling points for her. Her gratitude grew apace. At last she had someone to talk to about things that she valued. Soon their meetings became longer, and Jerry suggested that they avoid the Faculty Center and meet in rather obscure bars on Westwood Boulevard. She recalled his exact phrase when he had proposed this: "After all, no use starting any rumors about a fire when there are no flames—as yet," and he had leaned over and kissed her cheek.

It was not a quantum leap from the bars to the Romancero Motel. At first Milly had guilty twinges; but when he told her that his wife had been a nurse, had never gone to college, and that he had married her when she became pregnant after a youthful affair, she had believed that he, too, was seeking something besides sexual satisfaction. (By the time—after one of their increasingly frequent quarrels—he had also told her that his wife had worked for seven years so he could get his doctorate, his relation to his wife no longer mattered).

The affair—she smiled wryly; the word hardly described the emotionless coupling they engaged in once a week—had swiftly deteriorated into merely this tawdry sex romp. Less and less did they talk at all. It had become a rueful version of "Wham! Bam! Thank you, ma'am!" Milly puffed nervously at her cigarette as she remembered the words.

Jerry stirred uneasily in his sleep, but did not wake. How she wished he were Judd; not the Judd who would be coming home tonight from the office, but the Judd she used to know, the one with rapture and excitement in his eyes, the young man of so many years ago, the young man who did not exist any more at all.

There was the shrill sound of an alarm, and Jerry sat up abruptly. It was his wristwatch. "I must have dropped off," he said. "We'd better get going; Martha expects me in thirty minutes. We have some problems to settle about the kids. Seems Morey wants permission to be in the school play and Martha says he should first get better grades."

Milly found herself pleased at the interruption. "Then we'd better get moving, as you say," and she reached for her stockings.

Jerry always left the room ahead of her, first cracking the door and peering out to see whether any other tenants of the Romancero Motel were in evidence, then turning back for a swift farewell kiss before hurrying to his car. Then it was Milly's turn, once his car had started and disappeared.

Going down Sepulveda Boulevard on the way home, Milly found herself wondering why she did not terminate this now almost pointless relationship with Jerry. She knew the answer, but she didn't like it. It was all she had, even though what was once an excitingly surreptitious, dynamic encounter had been reduced to an empty grinding of two bodies. She knew that she would probably continue coming every Wednesday to the Romancero Motel until the Judd she still loved became the man he once was, a concept that she clung to stubbornly and forlornly, one she would never admit seemed nothing but a desolate hope. As for Jerry, she knew what kept him faithful to their Wednesday rendezvous; he really enjoyed the brief sexual contact. He always had an orgasm whereas Milly rarely reached a climax. And knowing what he knew about Milly, he was certain that she would be as careful as he was never to be discovered. This certainty fed into his cowardice, a vital part of his psyche. No, Jerry would never be the one to call it quits. Not as long as she continued to humor his paranoia.

He would have been astonished and terror-stricken to learn that Milly occasionally indulged in the fantasy of wondering what Judd would have done if she ever told him about Jerry. Would it have meant anything more to him than an invasion of his proprietary rights? She doubted it.

The two bodies were as one, Jake's suntanned skin in sharp contrast to Suz's whiteness, as they moved rhythmically in sexual rhapsody. She felt waves of delightful dizziness engulf her as the tempo of their movement increased until they both attained orgasm at the same moment. Jake didn't move as their muscles relaxed; he looked deep into her wide-open eyes and kissed her open mouth tenderly again and again. She entwined her arms around his naked shoulders and hugged him to her breasts with all her strength. Only when she released her hold did he roll away from her to the other side of the bed.

She leaned on her elbow and yanked at the blanket so that they were both completely uncovered. Jake's lithe body glistened with a thin layer of sweat and she bent down to kiss his neck, while he fondled her breasts with gentle, sweeping movements.

"Wasn't it marvelous, Jake? It was for me," she said.

He smiled and ran his hand down her leg. "It's always marvelous with you, Suz. But it was especially wonderful here in a real bed, wasn't it?"

"God, yes. As soon as Amy mentioned she was going to visit her parents for the weekend, I asked about this place."

Jake looked around the sunlit room with its Degas and Rousseau reproductions and the big Giacometti poster on the back of the door. It was a very cheerful room, the dominant color being a light, dancing blue that prevailed even in the bed covers. Amy Goodell was an art major and a friend of Suz. Jake had never met her; he wished he could tell her "thank you" for the glory of this afternoon with Suz.

"Does Amy know about me—I mean about us?" he asked.

"No. Nobody does," answered Suz promptly. "All she knows is that I wanted the apartment. She's smart enough to realize I didn't want it to play solitaire in, but she never asked. It's a lot better than the back of my car, isn't it?" And they both laughed aloud.

Suz got up from the bed. "How would you like a drink in honor of the occasion? Amy always keeps some scotch in the kitchen, at least she used to."

"I'd love it," said Jake.

He watched her lovingly as she walked out of the

room, her taut teasing breasts, firm buttocks, and her now-disheveled hair tumbling about her head. God, she was beautiful.

Jake could hear the rattle of ice in the kitchen; he shouted across the room. "I forgot to tell you how beautiful you are and how much I love you, Suz."

She shouted back. "So are you, and I love you too, Jake Isaacs."

They touched glasses; each took an initial sip and then they kissed each other again.

Suz picked up her wristwatch lying on the bedside table. "You know what, Jake, I have almost four full hours before I have to get home again. What about you?"

"Me too. I've got the whole afternoon off with nothing to do but love you," and he reached for her hand to kiss it.

Suz set her empty glass down on the bedside table, came back to the bed, and sat on its edge. "I've got a great idea. I know I've asked you before and you always said no, but I'm going to try again."

"Try again for what?" asked Jake.

"I want to meet your family, your father and mother and brothers." She leaned across the bed and caressed his cheek. "Please, Jake. I really mean it."

Jake dropped her hand he had been fondling; his brown eyes half closed and his mien became serious. "Suz, we've been through this before. You wouldn't like what you'd see, and I've told you that before when you asked me. You don't have any idea how we live, and you wouldn't like it. We don't live in Bel Air, you know, the way you do."

Suz drew back from him and retorted, "I'm tired of that Bel Air bit, Jake, and you know it. I don't think everyone in the world lives in Bel Air, but at least you know where I live and that's more than I can say about you." She rolled away from him to the other side of the bed.

He put his hand on her shoulder. "What's the point, Suz? You'd hate what you'd find and you might even hate me, for all I know."

Suz straightened up in bed. "That's as silly a thing as you've said in your life, Jake, and you ought to be ashamed of yourself. You're just a reverse snob, that's all. They're your family and if they're related to you, I want to know them."

Jake took her chin in both hands and looked deep into her eyes. "You want the truth, Suz?"

"Of course, Jake; we've never lied to each other about anything."

Still holding on to her chin, he said, "You know I love you, Suz, and—"

She interrupted him in mid-sentence with a deep, loving kiss, and then said, "I love you, too, Jake, and that's what really counts. Nothing else."

"But you don't understand, Suz. I come from a totally different background than you do. You've probably never even seen the kind of world I'm part of. And I don't want to lose you," he said.

Suz leaned forward and hugged him as tightly as she could. "Jake Isaacs," she said, "I love you for what you are, not for where you come from, and I give you my solemn word that nothing on earth can change that. Ever! Now let's stop talking about it and go. Okay?" She got up and started for the bathroom.

He arose and went to her, and their kiss was long and passionate. When their bodies separated, he was the first to speak. "Okay. You win. But remember what I said. I'll phone and tell them we're coming."

Jake walked to the desk phone and dialed while Suz watched him with a pleased smile.

"Hello. Pop? This is Jake; let me speak to Mom."

"Hello, Mom. Listen, I'd like to come down in about an hour or so. I want you to meet somebody. Yes, a girl. Is it okay? . . . Thanks. See you soon. Bye."

As he cradled the phone, his face unsmiling, Sue kissed his cheek and then disappeared into the bathroom. He could hear her through the closed door. "I'll bet I'm ready before you are," she shouted cheerfully.

Jake reached for his clothes on the chair beside the bed and began to dress, his movements slow and irresolute.

The ride downtown from the west side was a long one. When Jake parried Suz's inquiries as to where they were going with a repetitive "You'll see," she knew he was deeply concerned about this visit. Had she been wrong to be so insistent? Was Jake right? Would it have been better if she had never asked him to do this? She looked at his grim profile as he drove with eyes straight ahead and her whole body ached for him. She encircled his waist with her arm and squeezed. He flashed her a quick smile of gratitude and retreated into silence again. She was respectful of

Jake's mood, and was determined not to show any disapproval no matter what she encountered. All she
knew—and she was certain of this—was that she loved
Jake and that Jake loved her, and that no relatives, no
matter how or where they lived, could possibly break
up that reality.

As they approached Fairfax Avenue Jake wondered
whether this journey might be the end of their relationship, and his throat constricted. She would be horrified, he knew; she would compare what she was
going to see with her elegant home life. But at least
she would understand something of his origin, and
why he had been fearful of exposing her to it.

As the car threaded its way along Fairfax Avenue,
Suz felt as if she were in a foreign city. The day was
warm; as they stopped at lights she could hear the ba-
bel of foreign tongues through the open car window.
She wasn't sure what languages were spoken, but she
thought some of them might be Russian or Hebrew or
perhaps Polish.

The street was crowded with people, many carrying
packages. Suz was about to tell Jake how colorful it
all seemed, but she thought better of it when she observed the stubborn angle of his chin as he continued
to look rigidly ahead, never turning to glance at her.

Jake made a sudden right turn and stopped in front
of a storefront whose grimy window bore the legend
SAM ISAACS—FINE TAILORING in chipped gold
lettering. Next door was a shoemaker shop and the
other side was flanked by a laundromat. In front of the
Isaacs store was a low dirty-white fence with flaking

paint, with many slats broken, guarding a tiny un-
tended square of dirt varied by occasional clumps of
overgrown grass. It was obvious that the shop, like the
others, had once been a house that now served as a
store. A rickety wooden bench on the sidewalk in front
of the laundry was occupied by a gray-haired man
with a scraggly beard who was reading a book and
mumbling the words aloud as he turned the pages.
Seated next to him was a stout woman, her hair un-
combed, her heavy jowls wet with perspiration while
she plied her knitting needles assiduously. There was
also a boy of about fourteen busily engaged in carving
what seemed to be his initials on the front door of the
tailor shop. When he heard the sound of Jake's car
coming to a halt, he stopped his work long enough to
look at Suz and whistle in admiration. Seeing that
they intended to enter the shop, he closed and pock-
eted his knife and strolled slowly away down the
street.

Jake opened the car door for Suz and said, "Well,
this is it. They live behind the store."

When Jake and Suz entered the shop, they encountered a stoop-shouldered man with thick eyebrows
and piercing black eyes who was busy plying an iron
under the light of a bare bulb. His face broke into a
happy smile as he recognized Jake.

"Hi, Jake," he said. He motioned toward the back of
the store. "They're in there. They're waiting for you."

Jake gestured towards Suz. "Fyodor, this is Miss
Haber. My cousin, Fyodor."

Fyodor put down his iron, wiped his hand carefully

with a nearby cloth, and then extended his hand to Suz and shook hers. "Nice to know you, Miss Haber. Any friend of Jake's a friend of mine," and he grinned at her cheerfully.

"Thank you, Fyodor," said Suz. "I'm very glad to meet you."

As they walked toward the rear of the shop, separated from the store's activities by a green velvet curtain, Jake explained, "Fyodor's been with us for almost five years now. My father brought him over from Odessa." He looked at Suz almost belligerently. "He's a good man. I like him," he said, somewhat sharply, as if he expected Suz to disagree.

Suz was about to reply when the curtain was swept aside and a heavy-set man, with pendulous stomach that almost concealed the belt holding up his baggy khaki trousers, appeared in the opening. He embraced Jake with a hearty bear hug and kissed him on both cheeks. When he released him, he turned to Suz and exclaimed admiringly to his son, "Well, well, Jake, so this is your girl. She's a looker all right, a real looker."

"My father, Sam Isaacs. This is Susan Haber," said Jake.

Sam's huge hand almost engulfed Suz's smaller one. He shook it several times ceremoniously.

"Susan Haber. That's a nice name. I like it," said Sam, releasing her hand and propelling Jake and Suz further into the room. "Come in, come in. Becky will be right out." He turned his head toward a swinging door that led to the kitchen. "Becky! It's Jake. Jake and his girl; come in and say hello."

The swinging door opened and Jake's mother appeared, wiping her hands on a white apron adorned with a design of small red arrows. Twinkling eyes, robust, brown hair flecked with gray and tied in a tidy bun, she rushed to the group at the curtain and spoke directly to Suz. "I knew you'd be pretty. Jake has wonderful taste. I just knew it. I'm Becky, Jake's mother, and I'm glad to see you." She took Susan's hand in hers and shook it vigorously while Suz said, "I'm Susan Haber, and I'm very glad to meet you, Mrs. Isaacs."

Becky turned to Jake and kissed him, just as Sam had, on both his cheeks. "And you, Jake. How have you been? You don't come as often as you used to; but I know how busy you must be studying all the time. Anyway, I'm glad you're here. Now everybody sit down, and I'll be back in a minute." She turned on her heel and returned to the kitchen.

The room where they were—Suz surmised it was the living room—was small and sparsely furnished. An oblong table covered with a green tablecloth and places set for six people occupied the central section. As the two small windows in the room gave scant light, the green-and-red-flecked glass ceiling fixture had been turned on. The stainless-steel cutlery set beside each plate reflected a dull sheen. Suz noticed the white paper napkins neatly folded on the left of each setting. The furniture consisted of an old black leather sofa, much the worse for wear and age, against one of the walls, a somewhat decrepit-looking

Morris chair that Suz instantly knew was Sam's special seat, and six straight cane-back chairs now grouped around the table. The carpet had evidently once been blue, but age and use had taken their toll and only occasional blotches remained of the original color. The walls were gray and showed evidence of having been repainted many times. One of them bore a large calendar advertising *DAVE'S FISH MARKET—FRESH AND TASTY* juxtaposed to at least a half-dozen photographs of Jake at various ages. Suz recognized the one that was snapped when Jake had been made captain of the basketball team; but when she evinced interest in the others, Jake discouraged her so summarily that she asked no further questions.

The opposite wall had a single photograph, faded by time, which was evidently a picture of Sam and Becky dressed in their wedding clothes. Even from across the room Suz could see what a pretty woman Becky had been when she was young. Directly below the wedding photograph was a small American flag fastened to a copy of the Declaration of Independence. Suz wondered why it was given such prominence, but did not think it was polite to ask about it.

Sam motioned to the Morris chair, and when Suz had seated herself, Jake and he sat in the straight chairs. The curtain parted and two small boys appeared, each carrying books in a leather strap. These were Jake's younger brothers, Eddie and Alvin, aged ten and twelve respectively. They were curious about Suz, and when Jake introduced them they both mumbled something that sounded like, "Glad to know ya," and disappeared, only to reappear less than a moment later, traces of water still on their hands.

Jake maintained a strained silence, leaving most of the conversation to Suz and his father. Sam seemed to be quite pleased to answer Suz's questions, and Suz learned for the first time that Jake had been born in Odessa and had left Russia with his parents when he was three years old. She also learned that Sam had mastered the craft of tailoring by working for below-scale wages as an apprentice for some years, often for ten and twelve hours a day, and had gone to night school at the same time to learn English. He was very proud of being the proprietor of *SAM ISAACS—FINE TAILORING*, which he had started about six years ago. Suz also learned that Becky worked, too, as a seamstress, at least that's what Suz assumed when Sam said that she "sewed for very fine people." Suz questioned him about Fyodor and Sam told her that he and Becky had paid for Fyodor's passage to America. This last bit of information was extracted from Sam with some difficulty and prodding from Suz; he seemed embarrassed to discuss it. During this interchange Eddie and Alvin sat straight upright in their chairs, saying nothing, and never taking their eyes off Suz, apparently fascinated by her novelty.

When the conversation faltered, Suz decided to ask about the flag and the Declaration of Independence. Sam seemed very pleased that she had noticed it. "That's easy. You see America has been very good to us; I love America. I'm proud to be an American citizen. That's all it means," explained Sam.

"That's a nice thing to say, Mr. Isaacs. We don't hear that very often," said Suz. She glanced at Jake, who was still silent, and finally said, "Isn't that true, Jake?"

"Suz is right; we don't hear it very often," responded Jake noncommittally.

At this point Becky returned with an unwieldy wooden tray holding six glasses of tea and what Suz thought were crepes suzettes. When she said that to Jake, telling him how much she liked them, he unsmilingly corrected her and told her they were blintzes. Suz was embarrassed, but Becky brushed her discomfort aside. "So what's the difference if they taste good. Right, Sam?" To which the affable Sam responded, "Becky's blintzes are the best. I ought to know, I've been eating them for over thirty years and I'm still alive." Then he laughed and Eddie and Alvin laughed too, as did Suz. Only Jake remained silent.

Becky fluttered around Suz, refilling her glass with tea before she had even half-emptied it, urging her to eat more blintzes, and in general treating her as a guest of honor.

During the visit, Suz found herself babbling almost pointlessly to keep the conversation going. Sam and Becky contributed what they could, but it was obviously hard for them, and Jake made no effort to come to Suz's aid. The two small boys said almost nothing except to ask for further helpings of blintzes and more tea.

Suz rattled on about college and how popular Jake

was with everyone. Becky would occasionally interject with a "Jake, he's a good boy, our Jake," while Sam nodded his head appreciatively, and now and again would echo Becky's remarks and pat Jake on the shoulder lovingly.

When Jake and Suz finally got up to leave, Sam shook hands once again with Suz, and Becky started to do the same thing, but changed her mind, leaned forward and suddenly kissed her on the cheek. "You were very nice to come to see us, Susan, very nice. I'm grateful and so is Sam. And you," turning to Jake, "you're just a lucky fellow, that's what you are, son."

Jake flushed and said laconically, "I know I'm lucky, Mom. I know."

Eddie and Alvin each said, "Good-bye. Nice to meet you," and scurried out of the room.

As Jake and Suz went through the shop to the street, Fyodor, still wielding his iron, stopped long enough to smile warmly at them. "Glad you came, Miss Haber," he said. "Be seeing you, Jake."

"Thanks, Fyodor," said Suz.

"Bye, Fyodor," said Jake.

When they reached the car, Jake was still silent. He started the engine and they began the drive back toward Suz's home. They drove for a few minutes until Jake finally said, "Well, now you've seen where I live and where I come from. Let's not do it again. Once is enough. But don't say I didn't warn you, Suz. Different from Bel Air and your family, I imagine, isn't it?"

Suz did not respond instantly and Jake continued, "Well, what do you think? I was right, wasn't I?"

Suz turned sharply and, barely restraining her anger, said, "Jake Isaacs, you're a jerk, but luckily you're a jerk I love. Now listen to me and don't interrupt. I don't want to hear what you've got to say until I finish. Okay?"

Jake's answer was a terse, "Okay. I'm listening."

"In the first place, I'm ashamed of you, Jake, because you're ashamed of your father and mother. I like Sam and Becky. I like them very much. Sure they're not college graduates, sure they don't live in Bel Air which you're so fond of reminding me about. But they're decent, warm, loving, hard-working people, the kind of people that came to this country and are glad to be here. When your father said, 'I love America,' I could have hugged him. And they're so proud of you, it sticks out all over them. I'm ashamed of you. I love you, but I'm also ashamed of you and I want you to know both things. Now it's your turn. What have you got to say for yourself? I'm listening."

Jake's face was a study in conflicting emotions, surprise, relief, humiliation, chagrin. He saw an empty parking space and swerved the car against the curb.

Suz was astonished. "What are you doing, Jake? Going to make me get out and walk, or what?"

Jake smiled, a warm, loving, tender smile. "No, Suz; but I can't tell you what I want to tell you and concentrate on my driving."

Suz was still angry. "Okay. I'm listening."

Jake took one of her hands in his. She started to withdraw it, but thought better of it. "Suz Haber, first, second, and third, I love you and I'll always love you. Fourth, or was it third, I'm not ashamed of my parents. I was afraid that you'd be and if that happened I knew we couldn't go on together. I knew—"

Suz interrupted, "But how could you think that! You're crazy, Jake."

"No matter how, but I did, and I was wrong, one hundred percent wrong. I guess what worried me all the time was that you'd compare the way I live with the way you live; but now I see that was as crazy as you say it is. I should have trusted you more, Suz, much more."

Suz squeezed the hand that held hers. "The way I live and the way you live have nothing to do with us. We love each other, that's the only thing that counts. You may not like my parents at all; they may not even like you—though I don't know how that could ever happen. But even if it does, what's that got to do with how we feel about each other?"

Jake leaned toward her and began to kiss her eyes. "Nothing, Suz, nothing. You're right. Will you ever forgive me?" He sat back in his seat and looked deep into her eyes, his own eyes misting.

Suz threw her arms around him, held him close and whispered, "I love you, Jake. I've told you that before and I'm telling it to you now. Just because you were a jerk for a little while doesn't change that. Nothing can change it. Nothing."

Their kiss was long and intense, and when they finally broke apart, both were smiling.

"And now," said Suz, "you've got to do something for me."

"Anything you say," said Jake, happily.

"This time when you take me home, you're to drop me in front of my house, not a block away."

"It's a deal," answered Jake.

He started the car and they proceeded into the traffic. He drove with his left hand, his other hand squeezing hers as hard as he could, both of them grinning with new joy.

X

Mira looked around her living room with satisfaction. Even though it had originally been a furnished apartment, Mira had been able to store some of the stodgier pieces and replace them with new ones. It had been easy to persuade Judd to agree to the substitutions, especially since some of them—the carved teakwood footstool and the leather Barca Lounger— had been selected for his comfort. The pale-blue pleated draperies were beautiful with the white carpet, and the polished cherrywood mantel gleamed as the sunlight struck it. Mira had a good eye and Judd had been delighted to comply with all her suggestions. He told her once, when she showed him a tole lamp she'd found in an antique shop on Melrose, "You're got marvelous taste, Mira, just marvelous." To which she'd responded, "That's why I selected you, Judd." They'd both laughed.

She looked at her watch. He ought to be here any minute now. She settled down on the pillow-strewn couch and lit a cigarette. At that moment the doorbell rang. She tamped her cigarette out with deliberate slowness and then rose for a final approving look in

the Venetian mirror over the fireplace before ambling
toward the door. The bell rang again.

Mira opened the door. Kerry stood there, his hand
still on the bell.

"Come in," said Mira. "My, you're an impatient
man."

Kerry's smile was inviting as he shook her proffered hand and then bent down to kiss it. "I am that,
at least when it comes to you. I haven't been able to
get you out of my mind since I first met you at the Polo
Lounge. And before you ask me, yes, I'd love a drink."

Mira put her arm through his and walked with him
to the couch. "Make yourself at home," she said. "If
you want to take off your coat and tie, please do. I like
my guests to be comfortable. Be with you in a minute." She turned on her heel and went through the
swinging doors into the kitchen.

Kerry took off his coat, loosened his tie, and took a
cigarette from the small silver box on the side table.

Mira's voice was muffled as the rattle of ice cubes
being dislodged was heard. "What'll it be? Name it."

"Martini, if you don't mind. And if you have any
Pernod, I'd like a dash of that in it."

As Mira mixed the martini and reached for the
Pernod, she suddenly found herself unaccountably
frightened. It was the mention of the Pernod—the
same thing Judd liked—that did it. She wondered if
she was being a reckless fool to start anything with
Kerry. After all, he was Judd's son. She could still
hear Judd's voice that night in the Plaza: "I'm not going to sit around and be double-crossed. As I said, I

don't know what I'd do if it ever happened, but God help you if it does." Mira shuddered slightly at the memory. And this wouldn't be just anybody; it would be Kerry.

Kerry was calling from the living room. "Hey, how's with that drink? I've got a hunch we've got a lot to cover this afternoon."

Mira was forced to smile at his brashness, but she knew he was right. She'd never met a more attractive man; he oozed sexuality from every pore. She'd known that when he'd phoned and asked to see her and she'd instantly assented. Maybe it would work out all right. Maybe Judd would never find out. Maybe. She set the cocktail glasses and the pitcher of martinis on a small ebony tray and returned to the living room.

Kerry was sprawled full-length on the couch, but rose when she entered. "Now you're talking," he said, downing the drink. Then he took her shoulders in his hands, held her out at full arm's length, looked deep into her eyes and said, "Jesus Christ, Mira, you're the most beautiful girl I've ever seen, and I've seen a lot of beautiful women. You wouldn't slap my face if I kissed you, would you?" Suiting the action to the words, he took her glass from her hand, put it on the table and kissed her, his tongue forcing its way past her teeth deep into her mouth.

Mira gasped for breath and pushed him away. "My God, Kerry. You are impatient. I was right. Now sit down. Want another drink?"

"No. Another kiss, but I can wait," he answered with a slow, boyish grin.

Mira retrieved her drink; she sipped it slowly as she sat next to him on the couch. She could see the ripple of his muscles through the thin silk of his shirt, and the slim tapering lines of his torso. She knew how the afternoon would end and she didn't mind in the least. He'd probably be sensational in bed.

"First things first," she said. "How'd you get my number? I'm not listed."

He smiled, again that boyish smile. "I found that out right away. Then I just asked Mirabelle; she gave it to me."

"Very enterprising of you, Kerry," Mira said. "What made you think I'd want to see you?"

For an instant of reflection Kerry thought he would tell her about Prompton, but he remembered his promise. "Two things. One, the way you looked at me across the room in the Polo Lounge; and two, I got the impression from Mirabelle when I asked for your number that you wouldn't exactly not take the call."

This time it was Mira's turn to smile. "Touché," she said. "Touché on both accounts."

She found herself genuinely amused at his self-satisfied grin.

Kerry reached for her, but she shook her head and skillfully removed his searching fingers from her waist. "Let's talk. Shall we?" she said.

"Why not? What do you want to know?" he responded.

"I don't know a thing about you except that you're a hell of a hunk. What do you do? Anything?" she asked.

Kerry was pleased at the way things were going and he was absolutely certain that Prompton was right when he had said that Mira was a hell of a lay. This would be a great afternoon, he thought complacently.

Mira settled herself more comfortably against the pillows. "Well, I repeat: What do you do?"

Kerry unbuttoned his shirt and leaned back so that he was directly opposite her. "I'm an actor. Surprised?"

"No. Not really," she answered.

"Now ask me where I act?" he queried.

"All right. I will. Where do you act?"

Kerry got up, bowed to an imaginary audience and then said, "I'm a porn actor. I act in pictures and I'm damn good, if I do say so myself. That shock you?"

Mira started to laugh. "Hardly."

"I don't use my own name, of course," Kerry said, sitting down again. "My old man's pretty well known in this town. He's a big shot with Global Talent— that's an agency—and it wouldn't be a good idea."

Mira smiled conspiratorially to herself and did not answer. She wondered what Kerry would say if he knew his "old man" had been in her bed all yesterday afternoon. She could see herself writhing and moaning in pretended ecstasy when Judd finally ejaculated, and suddenly, to her surprise, she began to laugh aloud at the absurdity of the situation.

Kerry looked perplexed. "What's so funny?" he asked petulantly.

She stroked his cheek. "Nothing. Nothing to do

with you. Something just struck me funny, that's all," she said soothingly.

"Okay. That's enough about me. I know what you do; you model for Mirabelle. Right?"

"Right," she said.

"That settles that," said Kerry. "Now I'll have another drink, if it's okay with you."

Mira poured the martini from the small pitcher on the tray and again he downed it with a single gulp. He reached for the pitcher himself and filled his glass again.

Mira reached for a cigarette and as she put it in her mouth Kerry whipped out his lighter. She took one puff and Kerry removed the cigarette from her lips, placed it on the ashtray to smolder, put his arms around her and kissed her for the second time that afternoon. This time his kiss was long and filled with passion while he pressed his body against hers. Again his tongue explored her mouth and this time her own tongue darted forward to meet his.

Mira could feel his erection pressing against her; her head began to swim; she clutched him tightly with both arms and ground her body against his. He rolled over on top of her, holding her with one hand while he slipped off one shoulder of her low-cut dress and caressed the curve of her breasts with fingertip gentleness. Her eyes closed in the enjoyment of his roving fingers; she knew that her nipples were stiff and demanding. Kerry slid down from her mouth and began to kiss her nipples, rolling his wet lips back and forth. Mira had never experienced such lovemaking

in all her years of sex. She finally opened her eyes and
fondled Kerry's hair with one hand, stroking and
twisting it between her fingers.

The shrill sound of the telephone was like a fire
alarm.

Kerry rolled away from her, his face red, his eyes
angry at the interruption. "Oh, shit," he said. "It's
the goddamn phone. Are you going to answer it?"

Mira sat up, her body still quivering with unful-
filled desire, adjusted her dress and answered, "No.
Probably a wrong number. We'll never know, will
we?" She then got up, walked to the offending telephone, clicked it off and said to Kerry, "Won't happen
again." Then pointing to a hallway, she said. "That's
the bedroom. First on the left. I'll be waiting for you."
She came close to him, bent down, squeezed his bulging crotch while she kissed him, and then strode into
the bedroom.

When the naked Kerry entered the bedroom some
moments later he saw Mira lying on the huge bed,
her nude form streaked with the sunlight slipping between the slats of the wooden shutters. Mira had
closed them, wanting dim light. She held out her
arms without saying a word and he lowered himself
slowly onto her willing body.

Their union was rhythmic. By now they were both
glistening with sweat, and as Mira arched her hips to
meet the increasing speed of Kerry's thrusts, fireflies
seemed to dance before her closed eyes. Kerry, too,
kept his eyes closed; Mira held his shoulders in a vise-
like grip, her fingernails digging deeply into his

flesh. They both reached the climax simultaneously, their breath rasping, their legs and arms locked in what seemed like a single mass, an inextricable tangle.

Still panting, Kerry moved to one side of the bed, and leaned on his elbow. "Mira, Mira, Mira—you are incredible. You really are, you know." He put his hand on her forehead and traced a line with his fingers past her face and all the way down to her curling pubic hair, saying as he moved his hand, "From here to there, you are incredible."

Mira reached down to clasp his hand. "You, too, Kerry. It's been wonderful. The best I've ever had." She smiled. "Did I say you were impatient? Well, so was I. And now you know it."

Kerry kissed her shoulder and stood up beside the bed. Mira regarded his young, beautifully proportioned body, so alive, so different from the paunchy, middle-aged Judd, so marvelously different. Judd. She knew she needed Judd; but she also knew she needed—she wanted—Kerry, too. She knew that this afternoon was only the first of many. She closed her eyes to relive the pulsating oblivion that had overwhelmed her as she had reached orgasm with Kerry.

"Hey, don't go to sleep on me. Not yet, anyway. Where's the bathroom?" It was Kerry's voice; she opened her eyes and smiled up at him. "Right there. The door on the left. The other one's mine. I think you'll find everything you'll need."

When Mira returned to the living room after donning a lace negligee, she straightened the couch pillows, emptied the ashtray into the desk wastebasket, looked again with satisfaction into the Venetian mirror, hesitated for a second and then poured herself another drink from the martini pitcher. She could hear the sound of the shower running in the bathroom as she settled herself back against the pillows, drink in hand, smiling to herself.

He was young, she thought, so magnificently young, and so unbelievably handsome. If he only weren't Judd's son; but he was, and there was nothing she could do about it. She knew she was taking extraordinary risks, but she felt certain she could handle it somehow; she must, that's all. Kerry was simply too good to lose. She could still feel his distended prick moving with inexorable force into her moist, receptive cunt and the delirious ecstasy that had overwhelmed her. She pressed her hand between her legs and closed her eyes.

The rattle of the bathroom door handle disturbed her reverie and she opened her eyes to see Kerry emerging, fully dressed except for his tie and jacket. Mira patted the place next to her on the couch invitingly; but Kerry did not move. There was an enigmatic smile on his face as he looked down at her.

"Find everything you want, Kerry?" she asked. "If not, just ask and I'll get it for you. This place is well supplied."

He continued to smile. "So I noticed," he said. "In fact, more than I needed. I'll show you what I mean. Excuse me a minute." He turned on his heel and disappeared into the bathroom once more, returning this time with a blue silk dressing gown on his arm and one hand held behind his back. He was still smiling.

He held up the robe admiringly. "I found this in the closet; the door was open. It's a beauty. Looks Chinese." nese."

Mira sucked in her breath. She sat straight up on the couch, her drink in her hand. "It is. I keep a lot of men's things in there. They're my brother's. My brother, Andy—he lives in New York—but he comes out here a lot. He's in textiles, you know, and he hates hotels. Travels so much, you know. So he stays here whenever he comes through." Mira could feel a film of perspiration forming on her lip. Her hand clenched tighter on the glass.

Kerry held the robe up and twirled it around. "Funny. How come your brother Andy has a robe with the initials J.H. on the pocket?" By now Kerry's smile had become a wide grin. He took his hand from behind his back; it was holding a bottle. "And I see he uses Floris number 89 for his after-shave lotion."

The glass slipped from Mira's hand and fell soundlessly onto the thick carpet.

Suddenly Kerry began to laugh, louder and louder. He came over to Mira, sat down beside her, laughing uncontrollably. Then he dropped the bottle and the robe onto the couch, still laughing, hooting, howling, subsiding into hiccups and giggles.

He took her hand in his. "I said you were incredible, Mira, and you are. So Andy is my old man." He stopped laughing long enough to drop her hand; but almost as he did so, he started again.

Mira picked up the fallen glass; her first impulse

was to lie, to offer denials, to explain everything away; but Kerry's laughter became so contagious that she, too, started to laugh as she put her hand on his shoulder, both of them utterly convulsed.

Kerry patted her on the back and between giggles, he said, "The after-shave lotion. It's my father's favorite. But the robe. It's a dead give-away. It's the same robe Milly-Mom bought him in Hong Kong. The very same one, isn't it?"

"Of course," answered Mira. "I forgot it was in the closet and that you might see it. That was dumb of me, real dumb."

By now their laughter had subsided. Kerry was the first to speak. "I think it's the funniest thing that ever happened to me in my whole life. My old man! The big shot! I wish he could have seen me in your bed," and he began to laugh again.

Mira smiled and caressed his cheek. "Let's hope he never does, Kerry. Let's make it our secret, shall we?"

Kerry bent over and kissed the tip of her nose. "It's a deal; but you've got to admit it's funny."

"I do. I do. And you're not sore at me?"

"Hell, no. I think you're wonderful, and I wouldn't have missed this for the world. They say a son should follow in his father's footsteps, don't they?" He grinned a wide, triumphant grin. "Well, that's what I'm doing and loving it, too." He put his face close to hers and then said, "Tell me. Tell me honestly, Mira. Is the old man any good?"

Mira kissed him gently, smiled and said "You're infinitely better. Infinitely."

Kerry held her for a long time in his arms and murmured into her ear, "If you think I'm surprised at that, I'm not." He released her, smiling, waved his arms around the room and said, "What's in it then for you? All this?"

Mira imitated his sweeping gesture and answered, "All this. Not bad, is it?"

"Mira Dalloway, you're sensational. I knew it the first time I saw you; but I never counted on this. This makes it all the better," and he began to laugh again, laughter in which she soon joined.

"Nobody would believe this, nobody," said Kerry. "And I wouldn't blame them. I can hardly believe it myself."

"Now that we have our little secret together, I think we both deserve another drink, don't you?" said Mira. "I'll make another batch." She got up with pitcher in hand and went to the kitchen, followed by the sound of Kerry's chuckles.

"Don't forget the Pernod, Mira. By the way, I picked that habit up from my old man," said Kerry as she left the room.

"I thought so," answered Mira's voice from the kitchen, and Kerry began to chuckle once more as he savored the absurdity of the situation.

When Mira returned from the kitchen with the pitcher and two clean glasses she found Kerry had donned his coat and tie. He glanced at his watch and said. "Gotta go now. Got a date at the Beverly Wilshire. Business, believe it or not."

"I believe it," said Mira, and they clicked glasses together.

"To us," said Kerry. He grinned. "And to the old man. What he doesn't know won't hurt him. Right?"

"Right," said Mira, and they both drained their glasses.

Kerry stood up and Mira rose at the same time. They walked together to the apartment door, his arm around her waist.

"Thursday at three," she said.

"Thursday at three it is," was his response. "I'll be here." Then he laughed again. He crushed her in his arms and she held him tightly against her body. "The old man. Jesus! The old son of a bitch!" And the door closed behind him. Mira could hear his muffled laughter in the hallway.

As Kerry drove along Wilshire Boulevard he found himself grinning to himself; laughter rose up again. The idea that both he and his old man were fucking Mira struck him as the funniest coincidence of all time. And the best part of it all, he reflected, was that the old man was keeping Mira and he, Kerry, was double-crossing him! Too bad he couldn't tell the old son of a bitch what was really going on. But it was going to be wonderful, he thought as he remembered the taste of Mira's nipple in his mouth. Kerry knew Mira wanted him, he was dead sure of that. Hell, after the old man, who probably couldn't get it up at all, he must have been a godsend to her. And he knew he wanted Mira; she was the best lay he'd ever had anywhere, even better than Colette. Thursday was only two days away. He laughed so hard he almost ran a red light.

When Kerry left, Mira went into her dressing room and sat down in front of her mirror. It could have been ghastly, she reflected, looking at her face in the glass; but Kerry was right. It was funny, that's what it was, just plain funny. Judd would never have to know. He always arranged his appointments with her well in advance, and now with Rudy's death he'd probably have so much to do that she'd have plenty of free time for Kerry. And she knew Kerry wanted her. She was positive of that. She also knew she wanted Kerry more than any man she'd ever had in her life.

She smiled into the mirror. Thursday was only two days away.

XI

Kerry was at the bar of the Bistro, sipping his drink and smiling to himself. He was waiting for Prompton; they were to have dinner together. He hardly listened to the buzz of conversation around him as he savored the two hours he had just spent with Mira, another in the series of afternoons that had become such an extremely enjoyable part of his life. He was very pleased with himself and with the whole situation; in fact, his newly found private joy and subsequent public good humor had even elicited flattering comments at home from Milly-Mom and even from Judd. When Judd had asked him jokingly what seemed to have made him so mellow and agreeable, he answered with a disarming pleasantry, but had been almost unable to resist the temptation to remark casually, "Nothing unusual; it just so happens I'm laying a new girl. She's sensational in bed. Name's Mira something-or-other. Maybe you know her?" He never did say it; but even the thought of what would have happened had he done so gratified him enormously. He motioned to the bartender for a refill.

The tap on his shoulder was from Sid Schwartzman

passing by with his wife, Ellie.

"Hi, Kerry. Good to see you. What's new?" said Sid jovially. "Judd here tonight?"

"Hello, Sid," answered Kerry. "Hello, Ellie. No, he's not. Will I do?"

Sid laughed and slapped him on the back. "You'll do, Kerry; but not for what I want. When you see your father tell him you ran into me and that I'll call him in a few days." He started to move away as Ellie tugged at his arm. "He'll know what I mean," he continued, looking over his shoulder at Kerry. "You won't forget now, will you?"

Kerry smiled. There's something I'd like to tell the old man, all right, but it's not about Sid Schwartzman, he thought to himself, and chuckled.

"So there you are. Just where I figured you'd be." It was Prompton and accompanying him was a tall, thin man in a blue suit and no smile.

"I ran into Ed Garrell here and asked him to join us for a drink at the table. You remember him, don't you, Kerry? Last time you two saw each other was in a sauna. Remember?"

"Nice to see you again, Mr. Garrell," said Kerry.

"Same here," responded Garrell. The two men shook hands. "I'm meeting someone for dinner, but he left word he'll be late and Prompton insisted I say hello to you while I was waiting."

Kerry was impatient to be alone with Prompton, but he concealed his irritation and followed the two men to a table where an attentive waiter stood.

"What'll it be?" queried Prompton.

"Martini and a dash of Pernod for me," said Kerry.

"Martini, no Pernod," said Prompton. "And you?" He turned to Ed Garrell.

"Orange juice, please," answered Garrell.

Kerry and Prompton lit cigarettes; Prompton waved aside Kerry's gold lighter.

Prompton was all amiability as he leaned back in his chair. "I'm glad I ran into Ed," he said to Kerry. "You two have something in common. Ed, here, is a partner in Warwick Artists Representatives. We've been in a few other things together, too, back in Vegas. Right, Ed?"

"That's right, Prompton," answered Garrell laconically.

"Ed loves the entertainment business and especially anything to do with pictures and now that you're a star, Kerry, I thought you two ought to know each other better."

"I'm not really a star yet," protested Kerry.

"I'm the one who sees the grosses, and if I say you're a star, you're a star," said Prompton.

The waiter arrived with the drinks.

Prompton lifted his glass. "Here's to Warwick Artists Representatives, to one of its client stars, and to its principal stockholder. Bottoms up, guys." They all emptied their glasses, except for Garrell, who took a perfunctory sip of his orange juice.

"I hope you're happy with Warwick," said Garrell. "Prompton runs a damn good company, at least from where I sit."

"Thanks, Ed," said Prompton.

"No complaints from my end, either," said Kerry, wondering when Garrell would leave so that he could tell his news to Prompton.

Ed Garrell now turned to Kerry. "How's your father? Must be pretty busy these days what with the boss's death, I imagine. Global's a great outfit. They made me a bundle some years back and as a matter of fact I've still got a small sum invested with them."

"My father's fine, thank you," said Kerry curtly.

"Well, he's with the best firm in the agency racket as far as I'm concerned. I've only met your father a few times—my dealings were with Rudy Ruttenberg—but from all I've heard he's one of the top men in that company."

Prompton's face was unsmiling. "I'm with you, Ed, about Global being the best in the business; but I'm not very fond of Judd Haber, as Kerry here knows."

"As I said before," remarked Garrell, "I don't know him well at all; I'm just quoting what I've heard." A waiter tapped Garrell on the shoulder and said, "Pardon me; but there's a gentleman asking for you."

Garrell got up. "Must be my dinner partner. Excuse me. Glad to have seen you again, Mr. Haber. Thanks for the drink, Prompton."

"Good to see you, Ed," said Prompton as Garrell walked away to shake hands with a gray-haired man who moved forward to greet him.

Kerry looked after him. "That's Gabe Donner he's with, isn't it?"

Prompton looked after the retreating figures of the two men as they were conducted to a table.

"Yeah. That's Gabe all right. Best entertainment lawyer in the industry, they tell me. You know him?"

"Not very well," said Kerry. "Global's one of his clients, is all I know."

Prompton beckoned to the waiter, who answered his signal immediately and arrived at their table with the menus. Prompton studied his while Kerry tapped impatiently with his fingers on the table. "Let's see; what'll we have? For me, the prosciutto and melon, then the swordfish and a small green salad with the house dressing. And a bottle of Chardonnay, your best. What about you, Kerry?"

Kerry crushed out a cigarette he'd just lit and said sharply, "Fine with me. Anything you say."

Surprised at the asperity in Kerry's tone, Prompton said, "Anything the matter, Kerry? Maybe you're just hungry."

The waiter, pencil in hand, turned his attention to Kerry. "And you, sir, what would you like?"

"I'll take whatever Mr. Warwick ordered," said Kerry, waving the waiter away. The waiter shrugged his shoulders almost imperceptibly and moved away.

Prompton leaned his elbows on the table and stared straight into Kerry's eyes. "There's something eating you, Kerry. What is it? Didn't you like Ed Garrell; he's—"

"Garrell's fine," interrupted Kerry, "but I've got something very important to talk to you about and I didn't want anyone around, that's all."

Prompton took one of the cigarettes Kerry offered him, lit it carefully, blew an almost perfect smoke ring, smiled, and then settled back in his chair. "Okay. Shoot. I'm all ears. I'll bet I know what it is, too. Your old man's been made president of Global. Is that it?"

Kerry started to laugh; he was completely relaxed by now and was contemplating his impending news with delight.

"In a way, it's about my old man, all right; but nothing like that. You're way off base." He dissolved in giggles.

"Must be something funny. Speak up," said Prompton.

"Your prosciutto and melon, gentlemen." It was the waiter. He served them and then showed Prompton the bottle of Chardonnay. By now Prompton was genuinely curious, and he spoke curtly to the waiter. "Fine. Thank you very much. You can pour the wine now."

Both men maintained a complete silence while the waiter filled the glasses, a silence not broken until the waiter had moved out of earshot.

"Okay, Kerry, let's have it. What's up?" said Prompton.

Kerry, savoring every moment of the announcement he was about to make, delayed responding until he had taken a long sip of the wine. He put down his glass and said, "Remember that good-looker with Mirabelle at the Polo Lounge when we lunched there?"

Prompton's eyes began to twinkle. "Sure, of course. Mira Dalloway. But what about her?"

"Remember you said you knew her back in New York and that she was a sensational lay. Remember?"

"Sure, sure; but so what?"

"Well, Prompton, you were right! She is just that—a sensational lay!"

Prompton's face broke into a jovial grin as he saw Kerry's self-satisfied smile. "So that's it. Congratulations, my boy."

He clapped Kerry heartily on the shoulder. "That calls for a toast." He lifted his glass, smiling. "To you and Mira."

Kerry caught his arm so that Prompton spilled his untasted wine. "But that's not all, Prompton, not by a long shot."

Now Kerry lifted his own wine glass. "That's not all. This will kill you! The guy who's keeping her and fucking her when I'm not around is my old man! How would you like to drink to that?"

Prompton's reaction to Kerry's words was an explosive one. He slammed his hand down on the table; people at the next banquette were startled, but neither Kerry nor Prompton were aware of their polite but puzzled looks. Then Prompton began to laugh, and it soon became uncontrollable. His whole body shook; Kerry joined him, and the two of them started clapping each other on the shoulders, laughing with unbridled glee. Kerry put down his glass just as it began to spill, and his voice was triumphant as he sputtered, between howls of laughter, "I told you it was important, didn't I?"

Prompton wiped his eyes with his napkin. "You

mean to tell me that you're fucking Mira while the old man pays the bills and he doesn't know it?" Prompton's fat face was purple with hilarity.

"That's exactly it."

"How'd you find out? Don't tell me she told you!"

"Well, after I discovered a duplicate of a blue dressing gown my old man got from Hong Kong and a bottle of Floris' after-shave lotion that he fancies, I put two and two together. That's when Mira 'fessed up. I caught her with her pants down!"

"I'll be goddamned," said Prompton. "That's the funniest thing I've ever heard in my whole fucking life. The great Judd Haber being double-crossed in bed by his own son! Kerry, you've made my day. Now you really deserve a toast." He refilled their wine, and they touched glasses.

"You're a bloody genius, Kerry. I knew you had the longest prick in town when I saw you in that sauna, but I never knew it was long enough to reach into your father's bed!"

"I'd give a fortune to see my old man's face if he ever found out."

"So would I," answered Prompton, "so would I."

Then laughter caught them both again with resounding shouts; the people at the next table looked severely askance.

When they both stopped long enough to talk, Prompton said, almost to himself, "Judd Haber. The high-and-mighty mogul of Global Talent. It's just too good to be true."

Kerry nodded solemnly. "It's true. You can take my

word for it." They broke into howls of laughter again.

XII

Judd had finished his dictation and Josie was closing her pad and gathering her pencils together preparing to leave.

"Anything else, Mr. H?"

Judd leaned back. "Yes, Josie. There's one thing more. You won't need to take this down. You'll remember it, I'm sure."

"Yes, Mr. H. What is it?"

"I just told Jim Banton that starting next Monday you're to get a twenty percent salary increase. Is that okay with you?"

Josie half rose from her chair and then sat down again. "Oh, Mr. H! That's marvelous. I couldn't be more grateful. Thank you very much. That's just wonderful of you."

Judd smiled affably, leaned forward and patted her hand. "I meant to do this weeks ago; but what with Rudy's death I just never got around to it. And you'll be pleased to know that when I mentioned it to Lettie and Alex and Jim, they all agreed it was long overdue. So go out and buy yourself a new dress or something to celebrate and surprise your husband."

Josie had a swift flashing picture of her husband, stretched out on the couch, his bottle near at hand. Martin wouldn't care one bit, she thought bitterly. He'd never notice whether or not she wore a new dress.

She got up and walked to the door. Judd rose and followed her. As she started to open the door, he put both his hands on her shoulders and kissed her on the cheek. "That's for good luck, Josie. Only don't tell your husband I kissed you." His eyes twinkled and he grinned. "He might misunderstand. Husbands can be funny that way."

Josie felt herself blushing. "Oh, Mr. H! You're the nicest man I've ever known. Thank you again," and the door closed behind her.

Judd returned to his desk, a complacent smile on his face. He looked idly at his pad and then pressed his buzzer.

"Josie? I was so busy giving you a raise that I forgot to ask you. Any appointments today?"

"Just Sid Schwartzman. Remember, he called last week, and I stalled him like you wanted me to; but he kept phoning and you said it would be okay sometime this week. He's coming in about 3:30. Want me to cancel it?"

Judd drummed his fingers on the desk. "No. It's okay. I think I know what he wants. Might as well get it over with. That's not for another twenty minutes anyway. Thanks, Josie."

Judd glanced at the beautiful onyx desk clock Milly had given him for one of their anniversaries. He really ought to pay a little more attention to Milly, he thought to himself. He ought to ask her how she's getting along at UCLA. Probably finding it a little on the dull side, he imagined. Then the image of Suz swam into his consciousness. Suz, too. He hadn't really talked to her in days. She seemed very preoccupied the few times he'd seen her recently and even when she was home for dinner he'd noticed that her thoughts were elsewhere. Must be that new boy she likes, that Isaacs fellow at Occidental. Wonder if she was really serious about him? Couldn't tell nowadays with kids. Maybe he should have a father-daughter talk with her one of these days. Might not be a bad idea. . . . Then he thought about Kerry, and his good humor vanished. He wished Kerry had never come back to the house, had gone off on his own. An actor in porn pictures. His son, Kerry Haber. The thought enraged him and he clenched his fist. He certainly didn't want any father-son talk with him! Let Milly handle that end of it, since she always seemed to be on Kerry's side no matter what the boy did. . . . Anyway, he knew they must all understand that there was a lot of tension at the office following Rudy's death and the decision on the presidency still up in the air. It was almost four weeks now since Jackie had put Jim in as a sort of temporary coordinator; but it would probably happen any day now. Any day, and he would be the president of Global Talent Associates. Any day . . . Wonder what Mira would say when he told her? She'd probably reach for his prick and whisper into his ear "love . . . you . . . very . . . much . . . Mr.

President." He was sure that's how she'd respond. At the thought of Mira he sensed the beginnings of an erection and he laughed aloud as he saw the bulge in his trousers. God, he was lucky to have found her. And when he was president he could invent trips out of town and she could meet him and they could spend hours and hours in bed together. The image of her naked, glistening body entwined with his made him close his eyes with delight. He reached for his private phone, dialed her number, and finally put the receiver down in disappointment. Maybe she was working today at Mirabelle's or shopping or something. Too bad; he wanted to hear her love . . . you . . . very . . . much.

The intercom buzzed. It was Josie's voice. "Mr. Schwartzman is here, Mr. H. Shall I send him in?"

"Sure, send him right in," answered Judd, feeling his erection subsiding as he replaced the phone on its cradle.

There was a knock on the door.

"Come in, Sid. Come right in. I've been expecting you," said Judd.

When Sid entered, Judd waved him to the leather chair opposite his desk. "Hi, Sid. How've you been? Haven't seen you since we lunched together at the Polo Lounge."

Sid sat down slowly, reached across the desk, and the two men shook hands.

"That's not my fault, Judd; God knows I've been trying to see you, but your secretary won't let me through. I even sent you a message through Kerry when I saw him a few nights ago at the Bistro. Didn't he tell you what I said?"

"As a matter of fact, he didn't. Maybe he forgot," said Judd.

Sid waved his hands in dismissal. "Doesn't matter. I'm here now, and that's what counts. I've got a few things to say to you and I want you to listen. You remember that day at lunch, I talked to you about Paramount. You haven't forgotten, have you?"

Judd smiled. "No. Of course I haven't forgotten. I was very flattered, but—"

Sid interrupted, saying, "I know. I know. You've probably been up to your ass straightening things out after Rudy conked out. But that's over now, and I'm here to talk real business with you. I want you to know that I meant every word I said that day in the Polo Lounge."

"I'm sure you did, Sid. You know I've always respected you as a man who means what he says," answered Judd.

"Okay, okay. Now let's get down to what I really meant. Are you ready?"

"Go ahead. I'm listening," Judd answered.

Sid put both elbows on the desk, propped his head on his hands, and looked straight into Judd's eyes. "Okay. This is it. Straight. No shit. Paramount needs you, Judd; I need you. It's a great job; you can do anything you want with it. It'll all be up to you. Interested?"

"I don't know yet. What is it?" queried Judd.

"I haven't even got a title for it yet; but what I want you to do is come in as the head of all the talent departments, the casting, the writers, the directors—all of 'em. I guess you could be called creative administrator or chief coordinator or something like that. You're better with words than I am. Invent your own title, but that's the job. And this is the deal. Are you listening?"

Judd nodded his head in assent.

Sid held out his left hand and started to tick off items on it with his right, bending down finger after finger as he proceeded. "One, I'm offering you a five year deal—straight with no options. Two, you get a new company car every year; we got an arrangement with Mercedes; you'll get the top of the line. Three, a weekly expense account—you name the amount you want and you got it. Four, I don't know your salary here, but whatever it is, I'll pay you fifty percent more. Five, I've no idea what your commission draw is at Global, but I'm giving you stock options instead to make up for it." Sid now changed hands, seizing his right hand with his left and continuing to bend down finger after finger. "Six, you're to be in complete charge, like I told you. Seven, you'll have all the help you need, and anybody you think isn't making the grade, out he'll go. I'll take your word for it. I want you to be happy. Eight, if you want to write and produce one picture a year on your own—I heard you like writing—you've got it. That's the deal, Judd. The board went along with everything in it, and this is Sid Schwartzman of Paramount talking. Did you hear me?"

Judd did not respond immediately and Sid must

have felt that he had left something unsaid. Acting on that impulse, he leaned back in his chair and said, "If you want to know why I'm offering you such a sweet deal, it's simple—you're worth it. You're the best damn agent in town. You can sell anybody. Hell, you sold us Ron Winner and even I'm a better actor than he is. But to hell with that. It's done. I know you like talent and you know how to pick 'em. I want to make Paramount the best and the biggest in the industry and with you on my team, we can do it. I know you like stories; I've watched you when you brought in package deals and we went over the script together. You've discovered and sold more actors and writers and directors than anybody in the business—sure, some of them were lemons, but most of them made it. And you picked 'em, Judd. You're creative, whatever the hell that is, and no matter what you say, being president of Global—I know that's in the bag—you're still nothing but an agent, a salesman, a high-class peddler. I'm offering you a chance to do something you can do better than anyone else in this town and enjoy doing it. You don't have to make up your mind today. Nobody's got this job; I just invented it. And nobody else is in line for it. Nobody but you, Judd. You've got everything I want. And this is Sid Schwartzman of Paramount talking, like I said before. What do you say, Judd?"

Judd finally broke his silence. "As an agent, Sid, I've got to tell you that's one hell of a deal; but—"

"But what?" interjected Sid. "What don't you like about it? Speak up and we'll talk about it. Right now if you want to."

"No. It's not the deal, Sid. It sounds terrific; but there's a lot to think about. A lot."

"You mean Global, don't you? That's up to you; but you know this town. An agent is shit in this town, even the best of them and that means you, even if they call you Mr. Hollywood—which they won't." Sid got up from his chair and put out his hand.

"That's my spiel, Judd. Kick it around. Talk it over with your wife. Ellie says you're got a hell of wife in Milly. Ask her what she thinks. Take your time."

Sid's remarks about asking Milly brought a flood of memories to Judd. It was true; Milly was indeed "a hell of a wife"; Judd could recall at least a half-dozen times early in his career when he and Milly had sat up together late into the night talking the pros and cons of various negotiations he was involved in. How much he had relied on Milly's sage advice! Funny, he hadn't talked to her about his business affairs in years, many years. In fact, he hadn't talked to her about much of anything.

He shook Sid's hand vigorously. "It's a hell of a deal. Let me think about it."

Sid pumped Judd's hand up and down. "Think. Think all you want. Just remember what I said, Sid Schwartzman of Paramount. I'll wait to hear from you, Judd. You know my home number in case you can't reach me at the studio. So long, Judd."

"Goodbye, Sid. I'll call you one way or the other."

It was lunchtime and the campus was crowded with jostling students as Suz waited for Jake. She swung her book bag back and forth, and rearranged her hair as the light breeze played havoc with it. She lit her second cigarette and puffed at it nervously.

Several passing students greeted her cheerfully as she stood there and she returned their salutations with a perfunctory "Hi."

Then she saw him, and she darted forward. "Hi, Jake. What kept you? I've been waiting ten minutes."

"Hi, darling. I'm very sorry. Old Streeter got going on one of his anecdotes and wouldn't let us leave till he finished. Forgive me?"

She ran her fingers up and down his arm lovingly. "Of course. It's just that I have something to talk to you about." Her smile was infectious and he grinned back at her.

"Same here; but we can't talk now," he said.

"I'm parked in the lot. Let's go to my car. Okay?" said Suz, propelling him in the direction of the parking lot.

They walked slowly to the parking lot. She shifted her book bag awkwardly to her left hand. Jake started to take the bag from her, but she shook her head. "Thanks, Jake; but it's not heavy. I'm used to it," she said, reaching out to squeeze his fingers. He responded with an answering pressure.

Once in the car, Jake took her into his arms. "Oh, Suz, my darling Suz. I'm the luckiest man in the whole world." He released her, took her chin in his hands and said, looking deep into her eyes, "That's what Mom said, remember? And she was right."

Suz brushed his cheek with a kiss and said, "I'm

lucky too, Jake. You were certainly silly about that visit, weren't you? Say it, Jake. Say, I was silly," she said, pulling playfully at his ear.

"I was silly," said Jake, continuing to cup her chin in his hand.

"That settles that," answered Suz. "And now what I wanted to say to you. I want to make a date and take you home to meet my family. After all, I've met yours. Now it's my turn."

Jake's face stiffened, but he answered, "I'd like that, Suz. I'd like it very much, but you can't blame me if I'm a little nervous about the idea. I've never seen how you live but I can guess. And your parents and your brother—they're probably miles apart from my family. You've seen them now; you know what I'm talking about."

Suz didn't answer immediately, but when she did her voice was breaking. "So what if they are—miles apart, I mean. You're being a jerk again, Jake Isaacs, and I just won't have it!"

Jake leaned forward and kissed her tenderly; at first she did not respond but, overcome by his nearness, she took his head in her hands and held her lips to his for a long moment.

When they released each other, Jake said, "You're right, Suz, I am a jerk and twice in two weeks is too much." They both laughed at his sheepish admission.

"Oh, Jake, you're such a baby; sure, my home is kind of grand compared to yours, but what's that got to do with us? Nothing, and you haven't even met my parents yet. My father's an agent, as you know; and all he thinks of is his business. We hardly see each other even though we live in the same house and my mother—well, she's okay; but she's kind of dead inside, if you know what I mean. I suppose she and my father had something going when they first married, but by now they're just polite to each other and that's about all. As far as my brother Kerry is concerned, I don't even like him very much. He's just a spoiled brat."

Jake started to laugh and then checked himself. "I must say, Suz, the way you describe your family they don't sound exactly adorable."

"Oh, they're all right enough, and I love my mother and father; but I've got my own life to lead and what I do with it is up to me, not to them. You'll understand better when you meet them," said Suz. "And," she continued, "I want that to be soon."

"But suppose they don't like me," said Jake jokingly.

"That's their bad luck," said Suz, and leaned forward to kiss him. "They don't have to love you. I do. Isn't that enough?"

"It's enough for me," said Jake.

"Good. Then that's settled. You'll come?" said Suz.

"I'm ready anytime you say," answered Jake.

"It's about time you said that. You're the most stubborn guy I've ever met. I don't know how I keep loving you, but I do," said Suz, her eyes brimming with happiness. "Right now my father's involved with a big change in the office—the big boss died some weeks ago—and he's waiting to be moved up; but as soon as that's over and done with you're coming to dinner at the Haber house. Agreed?"

Jake kissed both her hands, one at a time, and said simply, "Agreed," and then continued, filled with suppressed excitement. "And now I have something to tell you. I was going to tell you before, but it just came through."

"What?" questioned Suz.

"Well, you know I'm getting my degree this June, and—"

"Of course I know that; but what's that got to do with us?" said Suz. Then she looked anxiously into his eyes. "Or are you trying to tell me you're leaving town or something? I thought we had agreed that you were staying on for graduate work. Changed your mind?"

Jake smiled and patted her hand. "No. Nothing like that. Just the opposite, in fact. I've been offered a job, a real job, right here at Occidental, and it won't interfere with my graduate work at all. You're looking at the new assistant basketball coach of Occidental College. Be impressed!" His grin was wide and contagious.

Suz threw her arms around him. "Oh, Jake! That's wonderful! I'm so proud of you. When did all this happen?"

"I told you. The final word came through this morning," he answered.

"That's just terrific!" she responded.

"And that, my darling Suz, brings up another point," said Jake.

"What's that?" queried Suz.

Jake's tone was very serious. "This one involves you," he said.

"Well, what is it?" asked Suz.

"I'm not sure this is the right time to bring it up," said Jake. "It's really a question." He cast his eyes down and seemed to be examining his shoes.

Now it was Suz's tone that became serious, belying the twinkle in her eyes. "Jake Isaacs. Look at me." She took his chin in her hand so their faces were very close together. Then she said very gravely, "Are you trying to ask me to marry you?"

"How'd you guess?" he said, astonished.

"Ask me," she responded promptly.

"Okay. I will. Will you marry me?" said Jake, his voice trembling.

"The answer is yes. A thousand times yes. I love you, Jake Isaacs, and I wondered when you'd ask," said Suz, her face suffused with joy.

This time when they kissed it was with rising passion, their arms locking their bodies together in a tight embrace of sheer delight.

The sound of bells announcing the start of the next class rang through the quiet afternoon.

They broke apart at the sound, smiling.

"You know what, Jake," said Suz.

"What?" he responded.

"We're engaged," said Suz solemnly. "That's what."

"And I'm your fiancé," said Jake playfully.

"And I'm yours," said Suz, her face radiating the happiness she felt. "And," she continued, foraging in her book bag, "we ought to celebrate. How'd you like a glass of champagne? I hope it's still cold!" From out of the bag she extracted a bottle and two styrofoam cups, her eyes brimming with merriment at his amazement.

"Where did that come from? Moet Chandon. Wow! How'd you know we were going to be engaged?" queried Jake, totally astonished.

Suz began to twist the cork from the bottle, but stopped long enough to kiss him on both cheeks and say, "I wanted it to happen, that's why. I was determined to make it happen today and I got prepared. Besides, Dad will never miss this bottle."

Jake started to laugh. "I should have known, Suz. You're wonderful and I love you."

"I love you, too, Jake Isaacs. Now here's to us," said Suz, pouring the champagne into the two cups, one of which she held out to him.

XIII

Judd finished signing the last of the letters in the folder labeled *Mr. Haber—To Do* and put it on top of the second folder, an unmarked one, that Josie had brought in to him some fifteen minutes before. He flicked on his digital watch; it was a few minutes after three. He saw that his desk calendar (another gift from Milly, he remembered) said October 19. It was exactly five weeks since Rudy's funeral and about four weeks from that Monday morning office meeting when Jackie had appointed Jim Banton as provisional head of the company.

He thought back over the intervening weeks. There had been other weekly meetings since then, of course, but they were routine and perfunctory in every way. Lettie and Alex and he reported on deal progress; Jim read aloud memos from the branch offices and asked for volunteers to follow up in individual instances, requests to which Alex or Lettie or he always responded instantly; Josie took notes and that was about it. The meetings rarely lasted more than a half-hour. The big chair at the end of the table—Rudy's chair—remained unoccupied and no one commented;

but he felt, and he was sure the others must have felt it, too, that there was no life in the room. He missed Rudy's booming voice and his astute, often acerbic interruptions of the droning reports. Once, a week ago, during the course of a meeting, Judd asked Jim casually if he had any word as yet from Jackie, and Alex responded before Jim could reply. He could still hear Alex's cheerful voice saying, "I think I can answer that one better than Jim. Last time Jackie and I talked she told me she would be out of town for a couple of weeks." That's all Alex said, but Judd felt in his bones that Alex knew more than he was saying. And yet maybe Alex was telling the truth and that's all there was to it. What was the matter with Jackie? he thought to himself. What is she waiting for? She'd said she'd clear up everything in a month or so.

He had once talked privately to Jim Banton about it. He knew that Jim was uncomfortable in his post and was eager to have someone else take over. All Jim could tell him then was that he had weekly meetings with Gabe Donner, and that while Gabe was always polite and pleasant, the subject of the presidency had never been mentioned. Judd knew Jim was a completely honest man and was telling the exact truth.

Lettie seemed almost indifferent to the outcome; at least she never brought it up either privately with Judd or at the weekly meetings. The only thing she'd requested since Rudy's death was to promote Jenny from the switchboard to the receptionist's desk. Jim Banton had approved this. Judd didn't know whether she had other things on her mind or just didn't give a damn. Alex, likewise, appeared to manifest no impatience or even curiosity, and went out of his way to praise Jim extravagantly for the way he handled the office procedures. If he did have any inside information, he kept it to his perpetually smiling self. Judd himself was too able a politician to call Jackie and ask directly what was going on. He was certain of the ultimate resolution, of course. That wasn't the point. It was simply that he couldn't understand the delay.

Judd tapped his fingers on the desk and then pressed the button twice for Josie to come in. She entered almost immediately.

"All signed, Josie. Send them on their merry way," he said pleasantly.

Josie took up the bulging folders. "Thank you, Mr. H. Anything else?" she said, standing at the door.

"Just wanted to know what your husband said when you told him about the raise," said Judd, smiling.

"Oh, he was delighted, just delighted," answered Josie with no hesitation.

"That makes me happy, Josie. Why don't you bring him around the office one of these days and I'll buy you both an expensive lunch." He smiled and chuckled. "That is, if you don't tell Jim Banton I'll be putting it on my expense account."

"Oh, Mr. H! As if you would ever do that," said Josie. "Martin can't get away for lunch that easily; but I'll be sure to tell him and I know he'll be pleased at the invitation."

"Anytime, Josie, anytime. Just tell me when."

"I will, Mr. H. I will. I promise," said Josie.

The door closed softly behind her. Once outside his office the tears began to well up in Josie's eyes and she dabbed at them angrily with her handkerchief. How could she tell Mr. H that she never even mentioned the raise to Martin, that all it would have meant to him was more money for liquor? She thought of the two men, her Martin and Mr. H. How different they were! What a wonderful, understanding man Mr. H was, how generous and kind! By this time she was back at her desk and had put the two folders down in front of her, the one marked *Mr. Haber—To Do* and the unmarked folder with the bills from Mira Dalloway. What was the matter with Mr. H? Why was he doing this to Mrs. Milly? It was somehow betraying himself as well as his wife. She shook her head in disapproval and started on the task of putting the letters and checks in their respective envelopes, ready for mailing.

Judd settled back in his chair, reflecting again on the events succeeding Rudy's death. He didn't hear the knock on the door until it came again.

"Come in," he said.

It was Josie again, bearing a letter. She handed it to him. "Sorry to bother you, Mr. H, but you forgot to sign this one. It must have been clipped to another letter. It's the one terminating our contract with Jeb Marley."

Judd smiled as he reached for his pen. "Guess I just didn't want to sign it, Josie. It's always hard when we send one of those out. Poor Jeb. I hope he gets another agent."

Josie did not respond. As he started to sign the letter his private phone rang. Judd picked it up. It was Mira.

Josie stood uncertainly in front of the desk. Judd's voice was very formal and businesslike. "Yes . . . yes, a little . . . okay, enjoy yourself. . . . Good. I'll try you then . . . Thank you very much . . . me too," and then he put down the phone and completed signing the letter, which he handed to Josie. As she picked it up, she said, "You have a funny message. From Sid Schwartzman. He didn't even ask to speak to you. He just said to tell you that Sid Schwartzman of Paramount said 'Nu?'"

Judd chuckled. "I'm sure you know what that means by now, don't you, Josie?"

Josie smiled. "Yes, I do, Mr. H. Any answer?"

"If he calls again, and I'm not in, just tell him you gave me the message and I said not yet. Got it? Not yet."

"I'll tell him what you said," answered Josie, leaving the room.

When the door had closed behind her Judd thought briefly of Sid's message. He was an odd guy, Sid; but Judd knew he meant what he had said when he offered Judd the new spot at Paramount. It was really quite a job; Judd envisioned the headlines in *Variety* and *The Hollywood Reporter:* Haber of Global New Creative Boss of Paramount. At least that's the way he'd write it if he was a reporter. It would make quite a stir in the industry.

Judd dismissed his musings about Paramount and concentrated instead on Mira's phone call. That was nice of Mira. Just like her, too, to phone and ask whether he had tried to reach her and that she was going out for a couple of hours on a modeling stint for Mirabelle. He savored once again her "love . . . you . . . very . . . much," uttered just before she'd hung up.

What a lucky man he was, to have Mira Dalloway in his life. As he thought of her he could smell the pungent odor of her perfume and feel her fingers on his prick, up and down, up and down, and then the soft fullness of her lips as she took it in her mouth. He could see his hand reaching down to caress her long, blonde hair. God, she was wonderful. He especially loved her hair, the glowing sheen of it as it cascaded down her naked back.

A sudden whirring noise disturbed him. It was that damned watch of his, the one Milly had given him. He must have pressed the alarm button accidentally. Irritated, he shut it off and tried to resume his musing about Mira. But something strange happened. The hair was no longer golden blonde; it was red, a flaming auburn red, and her face when she looked up at him wasn't Mira's face, it was Milly's. And Milly's eyes, brimming with love and solicitude; Milly's arms cradling his body; it was Milly in his bed, not Mira, a young, beautiful, adoring Milly; it was Milly in his arms; it was Milly's lips seeking his; it was Milly's body moving rhythmically with his own; it was Milly stroking his cheeks with gentle, searching fingers, Milly's breasts, round and full, that he was fondling with loving tenderness.

Judd tried desperately to erase her image and replace it with Mira's; but no matter how hard he tried,
he could not succeed. It was no use.

He arose abruptly from his desk and opened the liquor cabinet. Maybe a drink would help. What was the
matter with him? He hadn't thought of Milly that way
for years. He poured himself a half glass of scotch and
relished the sharp sting in his throat.

Returning to his desk, he felt strangely uncomfortable. He couldn't understand what was happening to
him. He wanted to exorcise Milly from his consciousness, but she refused to leave. He forced himself to
think of Mira; it was Mira he wanted, not Milly. But
despite every effort he made, it was Milly who dominated his visions and to his utter surprise he found
himself regarding this dream-Milly, this intruder
into his innermost thoughts, with affection. Memories of the times they had been together flooded his
mind: the time he had brought her roses, yellow roses,
that wonderful night in Santa Barbara, when they
had walked on the beach together, arm in arm like
young lovers; her birthday party at Chasen's when he
had stood up and toasted her as "the most beautiful
woman in this or any other room," and the deafening
applause from all their friends that followed; that
wonderful evening when they had dined together at
Gaddis's in Hong Kong and had toasted each other at
the candlelit table; that night on the pier at Malibu,
serenaded by the crashing of the waves and the wind's
whistling, when she had kissed him full on the lips

and said, "Judd Haber. You know why I'm a lucky woman? It's because I love you and you're my husband. That's why."

The intercom buzzed, shattering Judd's reveries, and when he picked up the phone he found that he was sweating. His hand shook as he answered. "Yes, Josie. What is it?"

Josie's voice sounded agitated. "I'm sorry to bother you again, Mr. H. May I come in? It's important."

Judd could not conceal his irritation. "What's so important? Come on in, of course."

Josie seemed flustered when she entered. "It's that Mr. Warwick. Prompton Warwick. He wouldn't let me announce him. He insisted that I come in and tell you personally that he's here. He said it was very important."

Judd clenched his hand in anger. "You know I don't want to see that swine. Tell him I'm busy; tell him anything, but get rid of him. And let me know when he's gone."

"Yes, Mr. H. I'll do the best I can."

The thought of Prompton Warwick daring to come to see him after their last conversation angered Judd beyond reason. Just because Warwick was Kerry's porn agent—the son of a bitch, said Judd aloud.

Again there was the shrill sound of the intercom. Judd picked up the phone. "Did you get rid of him, Josie?" "I tried, Mr. H. He wouldn't listen. He gave me something to give to you. He says you'll see him as soon as you get it. Shall I bring it in?" said Josie.

Judd's face was a study in repressed irritation

when Josie reappeared, now more nervous than ever. She held out an office envelope and Judd snatched it from her hand. He tore it open immediately, saying as he did so, "The gall of that bastard. The gall!" and then his face crumbled as he looked at the two words scrawled on the back of an interoffice memo sheet: Mira Dalloway. That's all there was on the page. The muscles in his stomach tightened.

"Okay, Josie. Send the bastard in. I'll get rid of him myself," he announced to the astonished Josie.

"Yes, Mr. H. Of course. I'll send him right in," said Josie, turning toward the door. She hesitated at the threshold. "Would you like me to call you in few minutes, you know, saying Jim needs you immediately, like we always do?" Her words were fumbling, uncertain. She had never seen Judd change his mind this way.

"No. Never mind, Josie. He'll be out of here as fast as he came in. Don't worry," answered Judd reassuringly.

As the door closed behind Josie, Judd tried to organize his thoughts. He knew what had happened, of course. Warwick had found out about Mira. Blackmail—that's what the scum wanted. Blackmail.

As the door opened and the smiling Prompton appeared in the opening he could hear Josie's voice behind him. "He's waiting for you, Mr. Warwick."

Prompton was dressed impeccably. His well-tailored gray flannel suit fit perfectly; the blue tie with tiny white dots complemented the white silk shirt and the sapphire cufflinks. He walked briskly toward the desk, his hand outstretched in greeting, his grin amiable and disarming.

"Hi, Judd. Glad you could see me. Thought you might," he said affably, still holding out his hand.

Judd did not rise from his chair nor did he extend his hand to meet Prompton's. In a flat, controlled voice he said, "Don't bother to sit down, Prompton. You won't be here that long, I promise you."

Totally undismayed by Judd's rebuff, Prompton withdrew his hand, reached in his pocket for his cigarette case, drew a cigarette out, tapped it on the case, lit it with a gold lighter he pulled from his side pocket, and drew the ashtray near the edge of the desk. He did all this without saying a word.

Judd could hardly believe what he was seeing. He half rose from his chair and said threateningly, "Prompton, I'm warning you. If you don't get the hell out of here in two minutes, I'm going to throw you out myself. And I mean it."

Prompton exhaled a puff of smoke. "Sorry you feel that way, Judd. But don't worry. I won't be long. This is just a friendly call." He drew up the chair opposite the desk and sat down. "Mind if I sit? You got my note, I imagine."

Judd reclined once more in his chair. "Yes. What about it?"

Prompton ashed his cigarette. "You mean what about her, don't you?" Prompton asked pleasantly. "Quite a doll, isn't she?" he concluded in the same agreeable tone.

Judd fingered the heavy metal ruler on his desk,

trying to mask his emotions. "I don't know what you're talking about, Prompton. Come to the point."

"Okay, I will," said Prompton, crushing his cigarette in the ashtray. "Mira Dalloway. You know her, of course?" said Prompton.

"I've met her, if that's what you mean," answered Judd abruptly.

"That's not what I mean. I'm sure we're talking about the same person, aren't we? The one who lives at 747 Spalding Drive in Beverly Hills and works as a model for Mirabelle Meredith and originally was one of the girls at Grace's in New York on 55th Street. Or maybe you don't know her that well?"

"I told you I've met her. That's all I know," said Judd, clutching the ruler tightly in his right hand.

"Come, come, Judd, let's level with each other, shall we?" Prompton leaned forward and put his hand over Judd's, patting it. "You've not only met her, Judd. You're fucking her and quite regularly, too, for some time now. You really should be more careful, Judd, when you're keeping a dame. Leaving Chinese silk dressing gowns around with your initials, and that fancy English after-shave lotion you use, that isn't smart. Right?" He withdrew his hand from Judd's still smiling.

It was what he had thought might happen someday, what he had most dreaded, that someone, somehow, would discover his liaison with Mira. That someone would blackmail him, or Milly would be informed. The thought of Milly, trusting, loyal, loving Milly facing Prompton while he told her about Mira and their afternoons together made the veins in his forehead swell with anger. As he envisioned Prompton sitting in their living room talking to Milly, the thought enraged him; he lifted the heavy ruler as if to strike, but Prompton caught his hand and pushed it down again on the desk.

"Take it easy, Judd. We've all been caught in the wrong bed now and then." He smiled agreeably.

The image of Prompton in Mira's apartment, in her bed, his body in her arms, was so humiliating to Judd that his face flamed with fury. The bitch! The bitch with her "love . . . you . . . very . . . much." His face twisted in disgust, and he closed his eyes to eradicate the vision. Reason returned, and he realized he must not let Prompton see the depth of his repugnance and he must not discuss Mira with him. He opened his eyes and could feel a sense of control flowing back into his tense body.

"Okay, Prompton. Let's get this over with. What do you want? How much?" Judd said brusquely.

To Judd's complete surprise, Prompton relaxed in his chair and began to laugh; he laughed as if unable to stop himself. When he finally subsided, he smiled his amiable smile and said, "What do I want? Nothing, Judd. Nothing at all. Surprised?"

"Very," said Judd succinctly. There was something wrong. If it wasn't blackmail, what was it? What did Prompton want if not money?

Now Prompton repeated the elaborate ceremony of extracting another cigarette from his case and lighting it slowly. Looking directly into Judd's eyes he said, "If you're thinking that I'm going to tell your old lady, forget it. That's not what it's all about, Judd. Besides I don't think it will be necessary. I really don't think so. It's you I'm interested in, Judd, you and nobody else."

"For God's sake, Prompton, what do you want?" said Judd, his voice choked with anguish.

"I'm not through yet, Judd, not by a long shot, so just listen. You'll soon get the idea," said Prompton quietly.

Prompton ashed his cigarette, leaned back affably in his chair and gazed at the ceiling as if he were trying to remember something accurately. "You've got a son, Kerry, a nice kid who I like a lot and who I represent for films. Well, it seems—"

"What's Kerry got to do with this?" interrupted Judd.

"What's Kerry got to do with this?" said Prompton mockingly. "That's a good question and I'm going to answer it."

There was tense silence in the room as the two men looked at each other, Prompton in complete control of himself, smiling pleasantly, Judd, his eyes narrowed, his blood racing, angry, bewildered, a man at bay.

"Are you ready, Judd?" Then, not waiting for a response, Prompton continued, his eyes never leaving Judd's gaze. "This is the best part of it, so pay attention." Prompton was still smiling, but his voice became biting and rancorous. "Your Mira Dalloway is not only double-crossing you, Judd; but she's doing it with your own son, with Kerry. Every Tuesday and

Thursday, the days you're not there, Kerry is fucking Mira. Today is Tuesday and he's doing it right now. How do I know? I got it from the horse's mouth, Judd, from Kerry himself. Ask him if you don't believe me." He smiled his widest smile. "But I don't think you will, Judd. I really don't think you will."

For a paralyzed second, Judd sat immobile in his chair, stunned. Then he suddenly reached across the desk, his eyes flashing with fury, grasped Prompton by the throat with both hands and shouted, "You're a goddamn liar! There's not a word of truth in what you're saying! Now get the hell out of here!"

Prompton reached up with both hands, wrested himself free of Judd's grip, and rose unaffected from his chair, looking down at Judd, who sat back crumpled and somehow shrunken.

"I'll pretend you never did that, Judd; and now before I leave I want to tell you a few things that I've been wanting to say for a long time. You asked me what I wanted and I told you nothing. That's not quite true. You're an arrogant son of a bitch, Judd; you act as if I'm shit; you threw me out of your office; you won't greet me when we meet, and I'm not a guy who forgets those things. Not me. I wanted to see you squirm, Judd, I wanted to see you hurt; I wanted to see the big shot at Global kicked right in the balls, I wanted to see you the way you are now, Judd, with your guts ripped out of you. And it was worth it. I said I wasn't going to tell your old lady, and I won't. But you won't believe that, Judd, and you'll be living with wondering when I'll tell her. That'll be hard on you. And there's more to come, a lot more; but that can wait. That's all, Judd. Thanks for seeing me." With that Prompton Warwick turned and left the room, adjusting his rumpled tie as he did so.

Judd sat motionless at his desk after the door had closed behind Prompton. Anger churned in him. He clenched and unclenched his fist. The scum, the slimy bastard, the shit. For a wild moment he felt that it couldn't be true, it couldn't. With Kerry, his own son. But he knew it was. He struck at his desk with his open hand and sobs wracked his dry throat. He put his head on the desk, cradling it with his arms, his shoulders convulsing.

His first instinct was rage, at Mira, at Kerry, at Prompton, at the whole world he had so carefully contrived, now in shambles. Slowly his sobs decreased; he brushed his reddened eyes with his sleeve, dazed. Mechanically, he noticed the two cigarette stubs in his ashtray. He picked them up and dropped them in his wastebasket.

He sat very still for a few seconds. Then he rang Josie's phone.

"Josie," he said, crushing the quaver in his voice, "What's the name of that detective agency? You know, the man we used when Francoise Goulet was in a jam with that Mafia guy? Remember?"

"It's in the files, Mr. H. Shall I get it for you? I think the man we used was Darnton, Charles Darnton."

"Whoever it was, phone him. If he's not in find out where he is and leave word for him to phone me immediately. It's important. And don't take any other calls.

From anybody. Got it?"

"Of course, Mr. H."

Judd sat very still at his desk, clasping and unclasping his hands again and again. He was sweating. He glanced at his private phone and clicked the Off button in place.

XIV

Milly reached automatically for her perfume atomizer and then remembered how insistent Jerry was
that she never wear any perfume. He had explained,
quite seriously, that the scent might cling to his
clothes and his wife Martha might become suspi-
cious. When he told her this, Milly was annoyed at his
excessive caution—it reduced their meetings at the
Romancero Motel to a cheap, sordid level—but by now
she was accustomed to his persistent fears. She also
admitted to herself that his paranoid procedures to
avoid discovery were becoming a growing irritation
and that she could no longer look forward to their
weekly encounters with her earlier elation.

She returned the unused atomizer to her purse and
snapped it shut as she walked down the hall. She
passed Judd's room. That reminded her that he
seemed more and more tense as the weeks went by
with no word from Jackie about the presidency of
Global. Poor Judd, she thought, as she approached
her car waiting in the driveway, it must be horrible for
him not to have the announcement made. For a fleet-
ing moment, she was tempted to stop and phone him

at his office.

Even though Judd had long since stopped confiding in her about his business problems, Milly knew that he was going through a disturbing and troubling time. She wanted to put her arms around him, comfort him as she had done many times before during crises. If Judd could only realize that Global was not the end of the world, that there were more important things in life for him—for both of them together—than any presidency could ever offer!

By now Culver City was passing by the car windows, and the Romancero Motel was only a few blocks away. In a few minutes she would park in a far corner of the motel lot—Jerry cautioned her never to park next to his car—she would see the green Plymouth; she would look at the dashboard for any change of room; she would enter the room in semi-darkness and Jerry's nude form would embrace her. The prospect dismayed her. It had all become so mechanized, so devoid of any real emotion. What was it she felt for Jerry? she thought to herself. Was it anything deeper than pity? It certainly was never love, ever. True, she confessed to herself, it had once been sheer lust, a release denied her body for such a long time, but even that was gone now. Actually, neither of them had ever used the word *love* to each other. She corrected herself. Once Jerry had said it when he was leaving the motel, but evidently regretting the possible consequences, he had never repeated it since. As far as she was concerned, she knew that she had loved only once in her life. That had been Judd. It was a word she still reserved in her innermost mind for him. A shocking recognition of her disloyalty to Judd overwhelmed her. She had always known that she still loved Judd; granted, it was another Judd, the man who had once brought her yellow roses; but she knew that that same Judd was still inside the stress-ridden executive waiting to become president of Global Talent. He didn't know it, but what she was doing at this moment made her feel degraded, defiled, unclean in his eyes. It was humiliating and shameful for Judd as well as for her.

The entrance to the Romancero Motel loomed in front of her. She turned into the driveway, rolled to an empty parking space on the far side for the lot, locked the car and hurried past the parked green Plymouth. She looked at the windshield; there was no note on it. She knocked twice on the door of room 189—another of Jerry's protective rituals—and Jerry opened the door.

It was all just as it had always been: his naked body, his groping for her hand to embrace his penis; his other hand seeking her zipper; his quick, welcoming kiss and his "right on time, Milly, right on time."

Their love-making—she thought to herself what a travesty the word *love-making* was—finally was concluded with a shuddering gasp from Jerry and a sigh of simulated satisfaction from Milly.

Jerry rolled to one side, reached for a cigarette, lit it, and then said, "That was a good one. How was it for you, dear?"

"Fine, very good," said Milly, lighting her own cigarette, her feigning wearing thin.

Milly knew the remainder of their meeting almost by heart. Jerry would discuss the internecine conflicts in his department, excoriate his department head, touch briefly on the absence of understanding manifested by his wife Martha, inquire politely into the state of Milly's daily patterns, and conclude questioning: Did she think anyone who might recognize them had observed them at the Romancero Motel? By now Milly was able to contribute a series of short one or two-word responses. Jerry never noticed her lack of interest. Ultimately, Jerry would glance at his watch, comment on the swift passage of time, kiss her as he arose to shower and dress, edge open the door to peer outside when he had finished, return for a final hurried embrace, and be gone, leaving her to dress and leave at her convenience.

But today was different. This time Jerry crushed his cigarette in the battered tin ashtray, lit another, leaned on his elbow, and said, "I'm so glad this was a particularly good one, dear," he said. "I wanted this one to be especially good."

Milly had come to hate his euphemistic "one," but all she said was, "It was very good, Jerry. Very good."

"I'm so glad, Milly, so very glad. And I'll tell you why." His voice became clipped, precise, the voice he employed when lecturing. "You see, Milly, I've got news for you. For both of us. I hope it won't upset you too much."

Milly lacked curiosity about Jerry's news. She was sure it was something trivial: changing their meeting day, something like that. She knew that any departure from routine was a momentous event to Jerry.

"What is it, Jerry? What do you want to tell me?" she finally asked.

Jerry stood up, cigarette still in hand, and paced around the little room. Milly saw—as if for the first time—his bony body and hirsute legs. "This will be hard on us, on you, I'm sure; but I may as well get it over with. I haven't told you, but I've been in correspondence with Northwestern about a job—there's an opening in Twentieth Century Lit there—and yesterday they phoned and accepted me. I'm getting a three thousand dollar increase. I start this fall, but—and this is what I mean when I said it'll be hard on us— Martha wants to get settled, find a house and all that as soon as possible, and we're leaving with the kids right after the quarter ends, which, as you know, is only about two weeks away."

Milly sat up in bed, not troubling to cover her breasts, and looked up at Jerry. "You mean this is our last time together? Is that what you mean?"

Jerry leaned over the bed and kissed her hand. "Yes, I'm afraid that's it. And that's why I'm so glad it was a good one for both of us." He smiled at her.

The intensity of the wave of relief that pervaded her did not surprise her; she welcomed it.

Jerry continued to kiss her hand, saying, "It's been marvelous, but we both knew it had to end sometime, didn't we?" He paused and continued in the same tone. "Anyway, maybe it's just as well. Martha has been asking funny questions about where I go on Wednesday afternoons—she knows I have no classes.

After all, Milly, I wouldn't want anyone to ever find out about us. I certainly wouldn't want that to happen to you, of all people."

He released her hand and smiled at her. Milly did not smile back. The bastard, she thought, the unmitigated bastard, always scared, always a frightened rabbit.

"Of course. I understand, Jerry." She tried to put some emotion into her voice, but knew she didn't need to. He wouldn't notice anyway.

"I knew you would, Milly. I just knew it!" Jerry said explosively. He looked at his watch; Milly knew the next words by rote, the variations were so minute. "Lord! It's time to go already. I've got to hurry," and he disappeared into the bathroom.

Milly could not resist shouting, "Don't worry, Jerry. You'll make it. Martha doesn't expect you for another twenty minutes unless you've changed the schedule."

Jerry's voice came through the half-opened bathroom door. "Can't hear you. The water's running."

"Doesn't matter," said Milly to herself.

Within minutes Jerry reappeared, knotting his tie as he came towards her. "You're a brick, Milly. I'm so glad you took it so well; but it's what I expected of you." He bent down to kiss her unresponsive lips.

"Goodbye, Jerry. I'll see you in class before you take off."

"Of course you will." He smiled his most charming smile. "But it's not quite the same, is it?" he said playfully, and laughed. Then he went to the door, opened it, looked outside, and disappeared, closing the door softly and carefully behind him. That he had omitted his routine farewell embrace did not occur to her until much later.

Milly put her head back on the pillow and lay still for a long time, reflecting on what had just happened. In every romantic novel she had read, the break-up of the lovers involved a scene of high passion, swirling emotions, recriminations, accusations, even tears. She felt none of these things. Jerry had behaved with appropriate smallness of spirit and she knew that he was glad to be removed from a situation that persistently aggravated his fears. Jerry was a little man, she mused, and she had been an utter fool to have become involved with him in the first place. Nor would she ever have done it, she consoled herself, were it not for Judd's growing withdrawal and indifference to her. Maybe the presidency would change that; it would satisfy his greatest ambition. Perhaps then they would come to each other again as they had in the past.

She arose slowly from the bed. Looking at the stained and rumpled sheets she shuddered in sudden revulsion. She could hardly wait to get home and take a shower in her own bathroom. She felt befouled, somehow polluted. Then she thought of Suzanne. She'd phone Suzanne at The Las Palmas Spa. That's what she needed to feel clean and whole again, the kind of punishing, cleansing massage that Suzanne had always given her. Besides, Suzanne was a friend by now; she would understand.

She looked around the shabby room and said to the walls, "Thank God, I'll never see you again."

Fully dressed a few minutes later, she took a last look at her image in the cracked bathroom mirror, opened her purse, reached for her perfume atomizer and sprayed herself copiously. She strode to her car, determination in her step.

When Milly entered her driveway she noticed Suz's Porsche was already in the open garage.

As she fumbled for her house key, the door was opened for her. It was Suz.

"Hi, Mom. I've been waiting for you," said Suz. "You look lovely." She mimed sniffing as she leaned forward to kiss Milly. "And you smell so good, too. What is it?"

"It's Joy, darling. I still have some left from that trip your father and I took to Paris," said Milly.

The mother and daughter walked into the hall together. Milly noticed that Suz seemed distracted, a little tense, so that she was not surprised when Suz turned to her and said, "Mom. Got a few minutes? I've got something important to tell you."

"Of course, darling. Let's go into the study. What's so important?"

Once in the study, where the afternoon sun laid slashes of sunlight on the polished mahogany desk and the ornate, comfortable Victorian chair, Milly sat down, lit a cigarette, and looked up at Suz expectantly.

Suz did not sit down. Instead she began to pace, trying to remember exactly what she had planned to say.

Milly said nothing; she waited calmly, puffing on her cigarette.

Finally Milly broke the silence. "Well, darling. Here I am. What is it? Anything wrong?"

Suz stopped in the midst of her walk, smiled broadly, and answered in a rush. "Wrong? Just the opposite. Everything's wonderful and I want to tell you all about it." She sat down opposite Milly and took her hand. She seemed nervous and uncertain of herself.

"I don't know quite how to say this, Mom, and I don't know how you're going to take it. You may not like it."

Milly patted her daughter's hand, her eyes beaming. "Try me, Suz. How can you tell till you try?" she said cheerfully.

Suz breathed hard. Then, without any pauses, she said, "Okay, here I go. You remember I've told you a little about a new man I met at school? His name's Jake Isaacs. He's wonderful, Mom, just wonderful! He's a straight-A student, he's captain of the basketball team, he's gorgeous and wise and—" She stopped and waited for her mother's response.

Milly continued to pat Suz's hand. "And what, darling? He sounds sensational, Suz; but that's not what you wanted to tell me, is it?"

"Not really, Mom." She drew in her breath, looking very solemn. She looked directly into her mother's eyes. "I'm in love with him, Mom. Not only that. He's asked me to marry him and I've said yes." Suz's gaze was still focused unmovingly on Milly's face; her chin was rigid as she waited for her mother's reaction.

Milly's response to Suz's statement dispelled all her fears. Smiling, she held out her arms and embraced Suz ardently. "Why, Suz, I think that's marvelous! If you love him he must be everything you say he is, and that's good enough for me. But I'm glad you told me." She disengaged herself from Suz long enough to add, "You're not planning to marry right away, are you, Suz? We'd hate to lose you so soon."

Suz's answer was instantaneous. "Oh, no. Don't worry about that. We haven't even discussed that part yet. But he's already got a job," she interposed hastily. "He's assistant basketball coach at Oxy; at least he will be as soon as he graduates this June. You'll love Jake. He's terrific. There's only one thing."

"What's that, darling? Is he a kleptomaniac?" asked Milly, laughing.

Suz joined in her laughter. "No. It's nothing to do with him. He's perfect!" said Suz with conviction. "It's his parents. You and Dad may not approve," she continued, and then with defiance she added, "I like them very much even though you may not."

Milly smiled. "Maybe *they're* the kleptomaniacs, then. What do you mean, not approve? In the first place you're not marrying his parents, in the second place, they may not approve of us, and in the third place, it shouldn't matter one bit either way. At least that's the way I see it, and I can promise you your father will feel the same way if Jake is even one-half as remarkable as you say he is."

Suz flung herself onto her mother and showered her with kisses. "Oh, Mom," she said. "I hoped you'd say something like that! You're terrific. You see, his parents are immigrants; they come from Russia. In fact, Jake was born there, in Odessa, I think it was. And they're not like us." She hesitated and then went on. "They speak with an accent and they live in the Fairfax district. His father's a tailor and his mother works, too. They're not educated or sophisticated the way you and Dad are." She hesitated again. Then, rapidly, "But they're great people. They're warm and kind and loving and they've had a hard time in America. And I want so much to have you like them!"

Milly's response was slow and serious. "Listen to me, Suz. I said before that if you love Jake as much as you say you do, that's all that counts. As far as his parents are concerned, why shouldn't we like them? I know a number of what you call educated and sophisticated people who aren't worth saying hello to." For a moment the image of Jerry Horton flashed before her, but she banished it immediately. "Let's not worry about Jake's parents. Let's talk about Jake. When are we going to meet him?"

"Oh, Mom! I love you! I've been telling Jake that his background didn't make any difference, and now he'll know how right I was!" Her eyes were shining and she got up and whirled around the room.

Milly's smile was loving and tender. "When are we going to meet him? When is he coming to the house? Name the day."

Suz stopped whirling long enough to reply. "I thought we'd wait till Dad takes over Global. I know he must be concerned with that a lot right now. But I wanted you to know right away. Should I tell Dad or will you?"

"You're right, Suz, to wait until the Global thing is settled. But I don't think it's fair to your father not to let him know about you and Jake in the meantime so he'll be aware. Would you like me to tell him? Or would you rather do it yourself?"

"Anything you say, Mom. But if you do it, don't forget to explain how fantastic Jake is, and how much I adore him. That's important."

Milly smiled. "I have a feeling you can describe his virtues a lot better than I can. And I really think you'd prefer to tell him yourself, anyway." She got up and put her arms around her daughter.

Suz returned Milly's hug and kissed her. "Okay. I'll do it. There's a lot to tell about Jake, and all of it is marvelous. I'll wait and pick a time when Dad seems relaxed." She released herself from Milly's arms and danced happily around the room while Milly smiled at her joy. "Oh, Mom! It's simply wonderful being in love. It's the best feeling in the whole world!"

"I know it is," said Milly quietly, remembering that night when she had slept with Judd for the first time. What had happened to that night? What had happened to Judd? What had happened to her?

By now Suz had stopped dancing and Milly embraced her again, hugging her tightly to her body before she released her. "I've got a couple of things to say to you, Suz, before you rush upstairs to phone Jake, which is what I'm sure you want to do. I think they're things you'd like to know about before you tell your father the good news." She smiled in anticipation of what she was going to say.

"What's that, Mom?"

"One is this. Do you happen to know where your father's parents came from in Russia?"

"No. Where?" asked Suz.

Milly grinned. "Odessa. And one other thing. Your father's real name isn't Judd. It's Jake."

Suz looked up at her mother's smiling face and burst out with a peal of laughter. "Oh, Mom! I can't wait to tell Jake. That's sensational!"

XV

Josie had just completed her filing and was tidying her desk before saying good night to Mr. H and going home to Martin. She closed and locked the last file, put the newly sharpened pencils into the Toby jug Mr. H had given her and reached into her desk for her purse. It had been a very long day, she thought to herself, long and puzzling. In fact, the last two days had been very strange indeed.

It had all started right after Prompton Warwick's visit on Tuesday. Josie knew, of course, how much Mr. H detested Warwick after he found out that Warwick represented Kerry for work in those porn films. In fact, she couldn't understand why Mr. H had even seen him at all, because he'd given her strict instructions never to allow him in his office. It was obviously something to do with that piece of paper she'd brought in to him from Warwick. She'd got that detective, Charles Darnton, on the phone right after Warwick had left. That had been late in the afternoon, around 5:30; Mr. Darnton had returned the call about ten minutes later. It must have been a very short conversation because Mr. H came out only a few minutes later and had left without even saying good night, totally ignoring their usual end-of-the-day meeting.

Josie knew his unusual behavior had something to do with Mira Dalloway because following the second call from Mr. Darnton on Thursday, Mr. H had called her on the intercom, his voice tight and rasping, and instructed her to cancel any checks sent for bills incurred by Mira Dalloway and to immediately advise any stores where she had charge accounts that all future bills were to be sent directly to her home address at 747 Spalding Drive. That was all he'd said; he didn't ask about any calls or messages and said to tell all callers he was unavailable. When she'd reminded him that he hadn't had any lunch, he had told her to send out for coffee and a sandwich. When she'd asked him what kind of sandwich he wanted, he'd become very irritable and said any kind at all.

She looked at the bulky folder labeled Mr. Haber— To Do; this was the second day he'd ignored it when she brought it in for him. In fact, he hardly seemed to notice her presence in the office. When she told him that he must have forgotten to look at the folder, he looked at her with unseeing eyes and said, "It doesn't matter, Josie; it really doesn't matter one bit." Not knowing how to answer, she retrieved the folder and returned to her own desk. She also took back his lunch tray; only the coffee had been drunk. The sandwich was untouched.

Josie sighed and opened and closed her purse absently. Her heart ached for Mr. H. She wondered whether it was only something to do with Mira Dalloway; it might also be his growing restiveness over the decision on Global. She had noticed that he'd gotten more nervous as the days went by, and each morning during the past week when he entered the office he'd asked whether there was any call from Gabe Donner or Jackie. She was certain he would talk about what was troubling him eventually, and she sensed there was nothing to do in the meantime except wait. Poor Mr. H.

He looked so haggard and worn that Josie couldn't help wondering whether he was ill. Once—it was that same Thursday right after Mr. Darnton's call—she'd even said to him, "You don't look well, Mr. H. Is there anything I can do for you?" He'd only lowered his head and mumbled, "Nothing, Josie. Nothing. Not a thing. I've just got something on my mind, that's all. Good night." As she went out she noticed his private phone was turned off.

Judd sat slumped in his desk chair. What a stupid, utter fool I've been, he said to himself. He could still hear Darnton's report on the phone. Yes, he had tailed Kerry on Thursday, and yes, he had seen him going into 747 Spalding Drive, and yes, he had not come out for several hours, and yes, it was Kerry, all right; he had watched him go to his car and verified the license plate number. Judd took his desk pad and doodled *Kerry* several times. His first impulse had been to call Kerry in, confront him. But by now reason had intervened. It wasn't Kerry who had betrayed him; it was Mira. It might been anyone, why not Kerry? It was Mira who had double-crossed him, the bitch!

He pounded the desk and exclaimed aloud, "The bitch! The bitch!" and suddenly the ludicrousness of what he was doing made him realize how ridiculous his attitude was. He laughed ironically. What could he have expected? It was he, Judd Haber, who had been the trusting fool; it was his insane—yes, that was the word, insane—infatuation with a whore. Yes, Mira was a whore. What could he have thought would happen? It was a salutary lesson for him. He opened his desk drawer and took out the crumpled piece of paper with the scrawled *Mira Dalloway* that Prompton Warwick had given him. He placed it next to the paper on which he had doodled *Kerry*. Then very slowly he tore both pieces of paper in half, and in half again, and dropped them into his wastebasket.

Somehow that gesture triggered a wave of relief. Throwing those two pieces of paper away arrested the agonies he had endured ever since Prompton Warwick had told him about Kerry and Mira. He straightened his shoulders and pressed his digital watch for the time. Milly again. By now he was convinced that Prompton had been speaking the truth when he'd said he didn't want money for his silence. But (Prompton was right) he didn't trust him not to inform Milly. He knew Prompton hated him; if Prompton did anything, it would be to tell Milly and destroy the only thing left in his life that meant anything to him. And now that he was losing it he knew how much it really mattered. His eyes caught his calendar pad. Milly again.

Judd picked up the heavy metal ruler and ner-

vously cradled it back and forth in his hands. He
shuddered as he imagined Prompton talking to Milly
and telling her all about Mira. He knew how much
Prompton enjoyed destroying and humiliating him in
every possible way. Would he tell her about Kerry too?
No, probably not. Prompton's main interest was in
Judd. Prompton had made that hideously clear when
they talked. Besides, Prompton was aware that he,
Judd, completely disapproved of Kerry for a dozen different reasons and he would assume that Milly felt
the same way; Judd knew that this was not so, that
Milly was protective and caring to Kerry. Granted
that Prompton was the scum of the earth, he seemed
to have some affection or friendship for Kerry and it
was more than likely he would not try to bring him
into it. Judd could recall what he'd said about Kerry
that afternoon in his office. He'd called him "a nice
kid" and said he "liked him a lot." Prompton was a
shit; but for some reason he thought of Kerry as a
friend. It didn't sound as if he wanted to embroil
Kerry in any way.

Judd relinquished his grasp on the ruler and
walked slowly back and forth in his office, his eyes
narrowed, his brow furrowed. He knew Milly would
never forgive his infidelity. It would be the end of all
they had built together, the dreams they had once
shared. He had been a stupid middle-aged man trying
to escape reality. He could already envision the loath-
ing and contempt she would feel for him, the detestation, yes, the hatred.

He arrested his pacing, sat down again at his desk

and put his head in his quivering hands. What could he do to spare Milly the ignominy of knowing?

There was a gentle knock on his door and Josie entered. "Just wanted to say good night, Mr. H. Anything I can do before I leave?" she said.

Judd looked up from his desk and then, as if making a sudden decision, said, "Yes, Josie. There is. I want to talk to you. I've got to talk to you. You know me better than anyone on earth except . . . " He hesitated. "Except Milly."

Josie saw that his eyes were red, but he seemed to be in control of himself as he went to the bar, drew his glass of scotch and Coca-Cola for her. It was as if the last few days had never existed, but Josie knew that it was these last days that he wanted to talk to her about.

She sat down as he handed her her drink. "If there's anything in this whole world that I can do to help you, Mr. H, you know I want to do it."

He was in his chair, holding his untasted drink in his hand. His voice was calm. "I want you to listen to me, Josie. Just listen. That's all I ask. I've trusted you with my whole life and what I'm going to tell you is a part of it that you may not know."

Josie did not answer; she felt there was no need for a reply.

Judd swiveled his chair around so that he was not looking directly at Josie. He fixed his eyes on a Rouault lithograph in black and white as though he had never seen it before.

"We've known each other a long time, haven't we,

Josie? How long has it been?" asked Judd.

"It'll be nineteen years in November, Mr. H, November 16, to be exact. That'll be our nineteenth anniversary together. I'm sentimental about that, Mr. H. That's why I know the date," she said smiling.

Judd gave her an answering smile as he turned his chair to look at her. "I'm ashamed that I didn't remember myself, Josie."

"A good secretary always remembers dates, Mr. H, and that's a particularly important one for me."

"I suppose you've been wondering what's been going on with me the last few days, haven't you, Josie? I know I haven't paid much attention to you or to the office in general. Come to think of it, what have you been telling Jim and the others when they asked for me?"

"Oh, that was easy, Mr. H. I just said you were working on a complicated deal and didn't want to be disturbed. Anyway, Mr. D has been out of town in Vegas working on the Three Grandees opening; he doesn't get back till tomorrow afternoon, and Miss M never asked for you. And you know Mr. B; he's always knee deep in his ledgers and wouldn't even notice you were unavailable unless somebody told him." Her tone was competent and reassuring.

Despite the turmoil that had been besetting him following Prompton's revelations, Judd's grin was unforced as he gazed admiringly at his secretary. "Josie, you're a miracle. I should have known you'd handle it somehow. And what about the phone calls and the correspondence? What about those?"

"That was easy, too. On the business calls I told everybody that you were unavailable and would call back. They're all in your folder, but I guess you haven't been looking. On the letters, I answered some myself; the others can wait. They're in your folder too."

"You're right, Josie. I haven't been looking." He fixed his eyes on the Rouault again. "Any personal calls?"

"Well, Sid Schwartzman called yesterday and said it was a personal matter. I told him what you said about not yet and he seemed satisfied."

Judd finally asked, "Any others? Personal, I mean." He turned his chair to look at her again.

Josie answered promptly. "Yes, Mr. H. There were several calls from Miss D. She seemed quite upset that she couldn't reach you. Quite upset."

For an instant, Judd's cheeks reddened in anger. Then he relaxed and said wryly, "I imagine she would be after her charge accounts were cancelled."

Josie's voice was impersonal. "She didn't mention that, Mr. H." She wondered when Mr. H. would tell her what she knew he had brought her in there for, when he would talk about Mira Dalloway. She wanted to put her arms around him, to comfort him somehow. She didn't have long to wait.

Now Judd fixed his gaze again on the Rouault and began to talk, slowly at first, then faster. "Josie, I suspect some of what I'm going to tell you you already know or have guessed." He stopped for a second, breathed deeply and went on. "I've been having an affair with Mira Dalloway. It's been going on for some time now. But you knew that, didn't you?"

Josie's eyes began to mist. She knew how hard this was for Mr. H to say. "Yes, I did," was all she said.

"Good. Then you'll understand the rest easily enough. Prompton Warwick found out about this—how doesn't matter—and also found out at the same time that Mira Dalloway had been double-crossing me with someone else, making an utter goddamn fool out of me!" Judd's voice rose as he spoke, but when Josie started to speak, he continued as if not wanting to hear her. "I've been a fool, Josie, a stupid, credible, fumbling fool!"

Josie's voice seemed to come from a great distance. "Were you in love with her, Mr. H?"

Judd swiveled his chair around to face Josie. "No. I can say that honestly, Josie. No. I've only been in love with one woman in my life."

"Mrs. Milly," said Josie quietly.

"That's right, Josie, Milly; but I needed Mira Dalloway. I wanted her, Josie, the way a man wants a woman. She was in my blood. You must know what I mean."

Now Josie's eyes began to water. Mr. H would never know how well she understood this need, this wanting, this overwhelming craving for sexual satisfaction, this blind desire, this shameful lust for another human being. She could see herself in Martin's arms, pleading for his hands on her naked body, hating herself as she succumbed to his fierce caresses. She knew what Mr. H had been going through. She knew it all too well. She also knew what courage he must be drawing on now to tell her this, to tell her what she could never have told a living soul about herself and Martin.

"Yes, Mr. H, I know what you mean. I really do, and I'm sorry all this has happened to you." She reached over and squeezed his hand in her own, something she had never done in all her years with him.

"Thank you, Josie. Thank you for understanding. I had to tell someone who would understand, I just had to!" Judd exclaimed, holding her hand in his. Then he continued, now looking directly at her, "Tell me, Josie. You know me. You know all my family, everything about them. What shall I do? What would you do?"

"Is Mr. Warwick going to tell Mrs. Milly?" Josie asked.

"He says he won't, but how do I know whether he's lying or not?" answered Judd.

"Then there's only one thing to do, Mr. H. Tell Mrs. Milly. Tell her the whole story. Tell her yourself. You said before there was only one woman you loved and that was Mrs. Milly. Be sure to tell her that, too."

Judd leaned across the desk so that his face was very close to Josie's. His eyes were pleading. "Do you think she'll ever forgive me? I've been such a fool! Thank God I know that much now. But it may be too late."

"I don't know whether she'll forgive you. I do know she loves you and I do know she'll understand. You must tell her, Mr. H. You must!"

"I can't Josie. I can't do it! You don't know her the

way I do. She'll be horrified!" exclaimed Judd.

"All I know is that she loves you. You've got to count on that, Mr. H. Tell her the truth. She deserves that much." Josie paused and then continued. "We all make mistakes in life, Mr. H. Sometimes we pay for them, sometimes we don't. But we're all fallible and I'd bet my bottom dollar that Mrs. Milly knows that, too." Josie knew she was talking as much about her own marriage to Martin as about Mr. H's present dilemma; in her case there was no one to understand.

Judd took her hand in his and pressed it with affection. "Thank you, Josie. Thank you for listening, and thank you for your friendship. I believe what you say, Josie. I only hope you're right. I'll tell her; I'll tell Milly the whole story from beginning to end."

"Do it, Mr. H. You must," said Josie.

"I will, and I'm grateful to you from the bottom of my heart. We've talked over a lot of problems in the years we've been together, and I've always appreciated your advice. I shouldn't have burdened you with this, Josie; but I couldn't help myself. I had to. I needed you this time more than I ever have in my whole life."

Josie smiled, dabbed at her eyes with a handkerchief she pulled from her purse and rose from her chair. "I'm very fond of you, Mr. H; you must know that by now. And I know what courage it took for you to tell me all this. It was no burden; I'm honored that you wanted me to help." She started to walk toward the door.

Judd jumped up to open the door for her. As he did

so, he bent down and kissed her gently on the cheek. "Thanks, Josie. Thanks."

Halfway through the open door she stopped for an instant and then said, "Good luck, Mr. H."

"Thanks, Josie. You've been wonderful to listen to me."

After Josie had left, Judd returned to his desk. What a magnificent friend Josie was! How kind and understanding. He had told her everything— everything but Kerry's involvement. She had said he had courage to tell her, but he couldn't tell her about Kerry. His own son! That he couldn't and wouldn't do. That kind of courage he didn't have.

XVI

Judd drove very slowly, ignoring the insistent horn-honking of several cars behind him that passed him in a burst of speed. He would tell Milly tonight, right after dinner. But how would he begin? How could he ever make someone like Milly understand what had drawn him into an affair with someone as unlike Milly as Mira Dalloway? What could he say to her that would make sense, when there was no sense to be made? He couldn't tell her he'd fallen in love with Mira; that would be a lie. He had never loved Mira; when he had told that to Josie he knew he was telling the truth. He had never loved any woman but Milly; but how could he tell her that and in the next breath describe his relations with Mira, his lust for her body, her hands, her mouth?

He turned his car in at the Bel Air gate. A black Jaguar exiting onto Sunset Boulevard slowed down as he approached and Judd could see it was Al Jackson at the wheel. Al waved and stopped his car as if to talk; but Judd lifted his hand in greeting and stepped on the accelerator. He didn't want to talk to anybody, anybody but Milly.

As Judd fumbled with his keys at the front door, it was opened by Albert. "I just saw you drive in, Mr. Haber. Have a pleasant day at the office, sir?"

Judd felt like barking a curt "No," but caught himself just in time. "Just another day, Albert, just another day. Is Mrs. Haber in her room?"

"No, sir. She's out. I think Miss Susan knows where she went. She's in your study waiting for you. Would you like me to bring the drinks there, sir?"

"That would be fine, Albert. Please do."

"Of course, Mr. Haber."

When Judd walked into his study he found Suz on the couch. She was just lighting a cigarette and as she put the match into the ashtray, Judd noticed the butts of three other cigarettes, one still smoldering. She jumped up nervously when she saw him, put her cigarette down, and ran to kiss him.

"I've been waiting for you, Dad. You're late. I thought you'd never come."

Judd found himself smiling. "Never is a long time, Suz, and it's only 6:30. You know I rarely get home before that. Must be something very important on your mind. I'll bet you want your allowance increased. Is that it?" He ran his fingers tenderly over her cheek and kissed her again.

There was a discreet knock at the door and Albert entered with two glasses and the pitcher of martinis.

"You can leave them on the desk, Albert," said Judd. "And thank you very much."

"Not at all, sir. Happy to oblige," answered Albert, pouring out the drinks before withdrawing from the room.

Judd sat down at his desk chair and raised his glass to his lips while Suz sat down opposite him and did the same. Neither spoke for a moment as they savored the stinging taste of the martini.

"Before we get to the question of your allowance, where's your mother? Albert tells me she's out and you know where she is."

"Oh, Mom's at Las Palmas. She's been trying to get an appointment there for a couple of days; no luck. But she just got a call from Suzanne about two hours ago—she's her favorite masseuse—there was a cancellation or something, and she decided to take advantage of it. She'll be back in couple of days, maybe sooner, she said; she told me to tell you when you came in."

Judd was taken aback. He had nerved himself to be ready to tell Milly all about Mira. It had never occurred to him that she might not be available. Maybe it was just as well; he was still tense and unsettled over the shocking events of the last few days and he wanted very much to be calm and rational when he told her. Of course, he could phone her at Las Palmas, but it was hardly something to discuss over the phone. He'd have to wait till she came back. It would be time enough to face her with what he had to say.

Suz had finished her drink and reached for another cigarette from the chased silver box he and Milly had bought together in Tokyo. "She said to be sure to tell you that she'd planned your favorite dinner for tonight. Let's see; I wrote it out so I wouldn't forget."

She fumbled in her purse and pulled out a piece of scratch paper. "Here it is: endive salad, filet mignon with julienne potatoes, asparagus, and lemon mousse for dessert. How does that sound, Dad?"

"Sounds great, Suz. If I eat like that every night I'll need to be going to Las Palmas myself," Judd said, chuckling. "I must say your mother takes good care of me, doesn't she?"

"Why not," said Suz, "she loves you. That's what love is all about, isn't it? Making the person you love happy." Suz was delighted that the conversation had taken this accidental turn. She thought this could lead naturally and easily into her telling Judd about Jake. She smiled at Judd and patted his hand.

"That's right, Suz. That's as good a definition of love as any, I guess. Let's drink to your mother."

They clicked glasses together.

"To Mom," said Suz.

"To Milly," said Judd, his voice strangely grave. His next sentence was almost forced out of him. "Where's Kerry? Is he home tonight for dinner or out as usual?"

"Kerry? Oh, he's out as usual. We'll have the whole dining room to ourselves. Just the two of us."

Judd reached forward to take Suz's hand. He brought it to his lips and kissed it with exaggerated gallantry. "That's fine with me. We'll have a father-daughter dinner. Nothing wrong with that when the daughter is as pretty as you, Suz." He looked at her hair as a streak of sunlight from the half-drawn shutters caught it. He added, "and has such beautiful red hair in addition."

Suz smiled at his praise, leaning forward to press his hand. "It's not red, Dad; it's auburn. And you can thank Mom for that. I had nothing to do with it."

"I guess I should thank Milly for many things. I'm afraid I don't do it often enough." His tone was suddenly low and freighted with emotion.

"You sound sad when you say that, Dad. Something troubling you?" said Suz.

"Nothing really. Nothing to bother your pretty red—I mean auburn—head about," said Judd, shaking off his moodiness, thinking to himself how many, many things Milly had done for him through the years, and how he had accepted them unthinkingly. What a fool he had been!

Suz puffed at her cigarette. There was an uncomfortable silence that Judd finally broke, tearing himself away from kaleidoscopic memories of Milly when she had looked just like Suz.

He drained his drink. "And now, young lady. What is it? Must be something; you haven't been home to dinner much these past few weeks. Is it the allowance? Or am I way off base?"

Suz looked at her empty glass. "Way off this time. It has nothing to do with money; but in a way it does have to do with why I've been out to dinner so much. I've been wanting to tell you about that."

Judd leaned back in his chair and swiveled it around so that he faced Suz directly. "Okay. I'm listening."

Suz drew a deep breath. "I've been seeing a lot of

Jake Isaacs; you know, that Oxy senior I told you and
Mom about and—" Her voice faltered and she hesitated.

Judd patted her hand reassuring. "And what,
Suz?"

Now the words came quickly. "Dad, the only way I
know how to tell you is to come right out with it. I'm in
love with Jake and he's in love with me. And he's the
most wonderful man in the whole world, and I know
he's just right for me, and I don't care what anybody
thinks or says, we belong together. There! I've said it.
Surprised?" She folded her hands and shot a look at
Judd, defying him to gainsay what she'd said.

Suz's tone and delivery were so earnest and her
pleading eyes so eager for his response that Judd
smiled despite himself. "Surprised? Yes, to tell the
truth. I must say you've kept this Jake Isaacs pretty
much of a secret. I know you've mentioned that you
were interested in him, and I guess it's my fault that I
didn't pay enough attention. Have you told your
mother?"

Suz nodded her head vehemently. "Yes, Mom
knows. I told her."

"And what did she say, Suz?" asked Judd.

"All Mom wants is for me to be happy, and she
trusts me enough to believe I'm doing the right
thing."

Judd stroked her hands. "So do I, Suz. I trust you,
too. When did all this happen and why didn't you tell
us sooner so that we could have met the young man?
Sounds to me as if you didn't trust us."

"Oh, Dad! Of course, I trust you and Mom. But Jake is odd about some things—mainly his family. All he knows is that you're a big shot in Hollywood and that we live in Bel Air, and he's worried about that. I've kept telling him he's crazy and that you and Mom wouldn't care where he lived or anything like that, especially when you come to know him. He's really wonderful, Dad. I mean it. You'll see. He's captain of the basketball team, he's got a scholarship to help pay his way, and he's handsome—six feet tall, curly black hair, and the most beautiful smile in the world. He's just terrific!" Her eyes sparkled as she finished describing Jake.

Judd smiled at her enthusiasm. "I'm sure he is, Suz, if you say so. Do you want to tell me about his family, since you say that bothers him?"

This time the words came easily to Suz. "They're poor, Dad. His father's a tailor and his mother is some kind of seamstress. And they live in the back of his father's tailor shop right off Fairfax Avenue. I've been there, and they're wonderful people, Dad. They're kind and loving." She stopped for a breath and went on, determined to tell Judd all she could. "They're immigrants from Russia, Jake was born there. In Odessa." She waited for an answer.

Suz did not have long to wait. "Odessa," said Judd. "That's where my father and mother came from. We already have something in common."

Suz smiled happily. "There's more, Dad. Jake and I are engaged." She added hastily, "I don't mean we're going to get married right away. Jake's graduating this spring and he's going on to get his master's in anthropology. And he's got a job, too. Assistant to the coach of the basketball team. And I know you'll love him. I just know you will, Dad."

Judd rose to his feet, came around the desk, and put his arms around Suz as she rose to meet him. "I'm sure I will, Suz, as long as you do. When we started this conversation you said that your mother wants you to be happy and she trusts you. That goes for me, too, Suz, and as long as we can still have you with us for a while before you go off and become Mrs. Isaacs, all I can say is that I'm delighted. When can we meet your Jake?"

Suz hugged Judd tightly in her arms, rocking him back and forth and kissing him again and again. "I knew you'd understand, Dad. Mom said you would and she was right. Thank you, thank you, thank you. I thought I'd invite him for dinner right after you become president of Global. That way we could have a sort of double celebration. Is that okay with you?" She held him out at arm's length, and he leaned forward and kissed her gently.

"Of course, Suz. Anytime you say. Could be any day now."

Suz released herself from his embrace and reached for the telephone. "That's marvelous, Dad, and so are you. Mind if I phone him and tell him everything's okay? He's waiting; he knows I was going to talk to you."

Judd reached for the phone and pressed the intercom button. "Not before I do this." Judd cradled the phone in his hand. "Hello, Albert. Albert, is there a bottle of the Moet and Chandon on ice? Good. Let's serve it for dinner. Miss Suz and I have something to toast. Thank you."

Suz held him in her arms again, her eyes glistening with joy. "Oh, Dad! What a great idea. Being in love is simply wonderful!"

Judd extricated himself from her grasp. "I know, Suz, I know. Even middle-aged people know what being in love is. I'll be waiting in the dining room for you." He went toward the door and turned around just before he reached it. "Oh, there's one thing, Suz."

"What's that?" she queried.

Judd grinned. "Don't forget to tell him that my name's Jake, too." As he started to walk towards the door she was already dialing and as he closed the door behind him he could hear her excited voice: "Darling! Guess what?"

When Milly entered the massage room in her terry-velour robe—courtesy of the Las Palmas management—Suzanne was already there awaiting her. The two embraced like the old friends they had become; Milly had been coming to Las Palmas off and on for six years and a warm and trusting intimacy had developed between these two women, an intimacy that knew nothing of class barriers.

As Suzanne's skillful hands had kneaded and stroked and pounded Milly's body in the sterile whiteness of the massage room, the initial, formal client-masseuse relationship had been slowly erased through the years. In fact, by now Milly's visits to this elegant spa were uniquely to Suzanne's domain. In the beginning, she had been tempted by the glowing brochure descriptions of the mud packs and herbal wraps and had once even tried Las Palmas' highly touted ice facial; but that was a long time ago, before she had realized that growing old was inevitable. Now she accepted the marring marks of middle age with grace and without defiance. Now she only came to Las Palmas when the world was too much with her, when her nerves were frayed and she felt she could not cope with some especially disturbing reality. It was then that she sought Suzanne, not only because of the physical relief and solace Suzanne brought her through her expert ministrations, but as much, if not more, for the sage counsel she offered. That was why, after Jerry had announced the end of their affair, she had phoned Suzanne for an appointment. She knew she needed her. Suzanne was not only a superb masseuse; she also had wisdom that stemmed from her peasant background in Brittany, and Milly felt an urgent need to confide in her.

After the two women had exchanged greetings, happy to see each other again, Milly doffed her robe and lay down on the mat while Suzanne covered her with a scented sheet. She dipped her hands into an oil-flecked lotion and began the stroking of Milly's body, first gently and then with increasing speed, talking as her hands moved up and down.

"And so, *ma petite*, where have you been? I haven't seen you in months. Have you forgotten your Suzanne completely?"

Milly always smiled at the *ma petite*. Milly had never considered herself "petite"; she was almost five feet five. She knew, though, that to anyone of Suzanne's Amazonian proportions almost all women were "petite." Suzanne was a woman who towered above most members of her sex. She was six feet tall, as she had once told Milly, with a shock of coal-black hair that she kept in place with an equally black velvet band. Devoid of make-up, her skin a luminous white, she moved with the grace of the athlete she was. Her hands—her stock-in-trade—were large and supple and capable of developing tremendous pressure when needed. As she had once told Milly, "I'm just like a man, only a little different," pointing laughingly to her large breasts.

Suzanne had once been married, many years ago back in her native France, to a farmer whose land adjoined that of Suzanne's family. The marriage did not last long, for as Suzanne had explained to Milly, "All Pierre wanted from life was to get up, work in the fields all day, eat dinner, make love, go to sleep, get up and work in the fields, eat dinner, make love and go to sleep. I wanted more; I wanted to come to America; I wanted to live and all he wanted was work, eat, and love. For me that was not enough."

That was over ten years ago. Through the aid of a cousin who worked in the exercise classes at Las Palmas, Suzanne got a job as a maid. Restless and ambitious, it wasn't long after that that she attended a massage school and reached her present status at the resort. When Milly had once asked her what happened to Pierre, her black eyes twinkled and she chuckled. "Who knows? But I'm sure he's found someone to feed him and make love with. In my village of Delon there were lots of girls for men like Pierre."

"Turn over, *ma petite*. I want to do your back."

Milly turned over obediently and subjected herself to Suzanne's miraculous hands. Slowly all the tensions of the past few days began to dissipate, and as the tempo of the massage decreased to a soothing series of gentle caresses, Milly closed her eyes and almost fell asleep. For a moment she tried to remember the feeling of Jerry's hands on her body, but they were so unlike Suzanne's movements that she banished them quickly from her thoughts. Jerry had very little notion of tenderness; his foreplay had always been rapid and feverish, punctuated now and again with an "are you ready?" She soon realized that the only interest he had in her body was as a means for his own satisfaction.

"You feel good now, eh, *ma petite*?" Suzanne's voice seemed to come from far away.

"I feel wonderful, Suzanne, just wonderful," Milly answered drowsily.

"Good. I'm glad." Suzanne's strokes became more and more rhythmic, her hands gliding softly over Milly's thighs.

Milly opened her eyes and closed them again, giving herself over completely to the pervading sensation of comforting warmth. Then she thought of Judd—was it that Suzanne's hands were now caressing? How thoughtful and tender and understanding he had been in their love-making, how his fingertips had traced a lingering line from her face to her breasts, how undemanding he had always been so that when the moment came for their bodies to interlock, the rush of pent-up passion had been like a rainbow of colors exploding in the heavens. That had all been long ago, she reflected. Suddenly she surprised herself by beginning to cry.

Suzanne leaned over. "What's the matter, *ma petite*? Did I hurt you?"

Milly raised herself on one elbow and wiped her eyes with the sheet. "Oh, no. I'm sorry, Suzanne. It had nothing to do with you."

Milly sat up straight, now wiping her eyes with the tissue Suzanne had handed to her. "Oh, Suzanne. I've been such a fool. You'd never believe it."

"If you say you were a fool, why should I not believe it? We can all be fools now and then."

The tears came again unbidden to Milly's eyes, and Suzanne cradled her in her strong arms. "What is it? Do you want to talk about it?"

Milly stopped crying and wrapped the sheet tightly about herself. "Yes, I do. I'd like to tell somebody and you've known me a long time."

Suzanne drew up a small white stool, sat down with her hands folded across her mountainous breasts and said, "Tell me, *ma petite*. Tell me if it will help you."

"Okay. I will. I'll tell you all about it. You don't know the man, anyway, but maybe telling someone will help me understand it all a little better."

"Oh, so it's a man, eh? It usually is," said Suzanne.

"As I said, Suzanne, I've been a fool, a complete fool. I've been having an affair with someone, a teacher I met at school, and—" She stopped and did not continue.

"And what?" said Suzanne.

"And it's over. It just happened a few days ago."

Suzanne leaned forward and patted Milly's arm. Then she spoke. "Did you love him?"

"No. I didn't love him. Ever. I did it because it seemed the only thing to do at the time. You see, I was in love with my husband."

Milly could not forebear smiling when she saw the puzzled look on Suzanne's face. "That doesn't make sense, does it, Suzanne? Okay, let me explain what I meant."

And then Milly found herself pouring out the whole story, Judd's growing neglect, Jerry's ushering her into a world of books and knowledge which she worshipped, how their student-teacher relationship had suddenly become one of friends and then lovers, how it had all climaxed that first afternoon in the Romancero Motel, and how ashamed and humiliated and *unclean* she felt—it was the best word she could think of—now that it was all over.

Suzanne had listened impassively during Milly's recital. She waved a hand in the air, a gesture of dismissal. Then spoke. "This man, this teacher. He sounds like Pierre. All he wanted was to make love. Only you didn't have to feed him."

Milly found herself laughing, and Suzanne joined

in. "That's true, Suzanne. That's all we did," said Milly.

Suzanne leaned forward and kissed Milly on the cheek. *"Ma pauvre petite,"* she said. "And now that it's over, you feel . . . *sale*, dirty. Is that right?"

Milly looked straight into Suzanne's eyes. "I feel dirty. That's it exactly."

"You haven't asked me what you should do about this now that this man, this teacher, is no longer in your life," said Suzanne. "But I'll tell you anyway because I think I know what's bothering you right now and why you don't know what to do about feeling dirty. But first I have a couple of questions, *ma petite*. You told me you didn't love this man. Is that right?"

"Right," said Milly. "Never."

"Do you still love your husband?" asked Suzanne, her eyes fixed on Milly's face.

The answer come from Milly's lips with a certainty that astonished her. "Yes. I do."

"Then tell him all about it," said Suzanne.

"I can't do that, I just can't," said Milly.

"Why not?"

"Because I'm so deeply ashamed. I told you, I feel unclean. I just can't. He'll never forgive me," said Milly vehemently.

Suzanne's face was graven. "He will, and you can. It will be with you forever otherwise. And don't wait. Tell him as soon as you go home tomorrow. You can do it. You told me."

"But you're a friend! He's my husband!" exclaimed Milly.

"A husband is better than a friend; he knows you better," said Suzanne. "I'm sure I'm right."

"But what I've done is disgusting! How can I tell him? It's so shabby, so cheap, so rotten." Milly rocked sobbing back and forth on the mat.

Suzanne took Milly in her arms once again. "Tell him. It's the only thing to do. You say you love him; you owe him that much. Tell him."

Milly extricated herself from Suzanne's arms, but held onto one of her hands. "Are you really sure? Do you think he'll ever understand what I've done?"

"Tell him. You have to," said Suzanne quietly, caressing Milly's hair with her free hand.

Milly hugged Suzanne, her voice muffled against her shoulder. "I guess you're right. I will. I'll tell him."

"Good," said Suzanne, disengaging herself from Milly's embrace. "And now get some sleep. I'll wake you in a half hour." She got up and moved toward the door. She turned back to Milly just before she reached it. "And when you do, don't forget to tell him you love him. That's always a good idea."

Milly looked at the closed door. Then, talking to herself, she said, "I will. I do," and she closed her eyes and settled herself back on the mat.

XVII

It was late afternoon on Saturday that the call came. Judd was at home in his study going over his checkbook when Albert buzzed to tell him Jim Banton was on the phone. Jim advised Judd that there was to be a special meeting at the office on Sunday at 10:30 in the morning and that Gabe Donner had asked him to phone all the executives. Judd's efforts to extract any further information from Jim were fruitless; all Jim could tell him was Gabe's instructions, and that he was going to try to reach the other staff members as soon as he could.

When Judd hung up the phone he slumped back in his chair and drummed his fingers softly on the desk top. So the moment had finally arrived, the moment he had been waiting for ever since Rudy's funeral. Judd Haber, President of Global Talent Associates. Judd uttered the words aloud: Judd Haber, President of Global Talent Associates. For some reason it had no resonance; it sounded hollow. Something was wrong about it, and Judd knew what that was. It was that Milly would not even be home to share the expected news. She had phoned from Las Palmas a few hours ago to tell Judd that she would be leaving sometime in the late morning around 11:00 or 12:00 tomorrow and would probably reach home about 2:00 or 3:00 in the afternoon, depending on the traffic. She seemed nervous over the phone, but when Judd mentioned her tone she assured him that she felt fine.

Judd picked up the phone and dialed Albert, explaining to him that there was a special meeting at the office tomorrow morning and that he'd like breakfast to be served promptly at 9:30.

What an odd day tomorrow would be, thought Judd to himself, as he finished talking with Albert. On the one hand the appointment to the presidency; on the other his determination to tell Milly all about Mira as soon as possible. Judd rested his head in his hands and pressed his fingers tightly against his forehead, his eyes closed. He knew he would have a restless night and decided to take a Seconal. Maybe it would help. He hoped so. Tomorrow would be a big day. What would Milly say? What would she think of him?

Lettie didn't get Jim Banton's message until she got back to her apartment about 6:30 that night. All her answering machine said was: "Jim Banton calling. Special executive staff meeting tomorrow morning at the office at 10:30. Gabe Donner expects all executives to be present. See you there." Lettie was irritated; she was taking Jenny out for brunch at the Citadel, and hated having her plans interfered with. She swore aloud in disgust and then picked up the receiver to dial Jenny at home to cancel the date. As far as she was concerned all that mattered was that her

Sunday meeting with Jenny was delayed; she didn't give one damn about Jackie announcing that Judd or Alex would be president, or even Jim for that matter. Right now she was interested in Jenny, and any idea that a new president might affect her life never even entered her head.

When the phone rang in Alex's apartment he took the call on his bedroom extension, extricating himself brusquely from the arms of Babette Morgan, a violet-eyed nightclub singer who was Alex's latest protegée-client. He listened to Jim's succinct message with an impassive face, thanked him and said he'd be there. Babette put her curly head back on his shoulder and asked, "Who's that?" Alex answered curtly, "Nobody," while his lips sought the nipple of the breast she proffered. Babette moaned in satisfaction. Then Alex suddenly pushed her to one side and reached for the phone again. He dialed Jackie's number and then hung up before the call could be completed. No, he said to himself, it's Jackie's show tomorrow morning and he could do all the thanking then. He reached for Babette and put his hand between her legs. "Honey," he said, "do you know you're screwing the next president of Global Talent Associates?" And he smiled as she took his stiff prick in her hands and slid the foreskin gently back and forth.

When Josie received Jim Banton's call she was in the kitchen, and he added a sentence by saying, "Mr. Donner wants you there to take notes. Okay?" When she hung up the phone, she heard Martin's slurred tones from the living room where he was sprawled on the couch, half asleep. "Who's that?"

"It's Jim Banton from the office; we're having a special meeting tomorrow morning. I have to be there."

Martin's voice now became querulous and whining. "And who's going to make my breakfast, for Christ's sake? Why the hell do you have to go in on a Sunday, anyway?"

"It's not till 10:30; I'll make your breakfast first. Don't worry. It's an important meeting," answered Josie, raising her voice so she could be heard.

It would be a strange morning, Josie thought. Judd would be announced as president, but she wondered whether he'd told Milly yet about Mira. He hadn't mentioned it again since that day in his office, and she felt he would have told her if he had.

As Jim Banton hung up the phone after checking Josie's name off the list in front of him on the dining room table, he turned to Margie across the table, a cup of coffee in one of her hands and a smoking cigarette in the other.

"Did you get everyone?" she asked.

"Every one except Lettie Mallon, but I left a message on her machine. She'll be there, I'm sure," he answered.

"I'll bet you get it, Jim. I said it before, and I'll say it again. You're the only one who knows what's going on there and Jackie Ruttenberg wouldn't have given you the chance to run it for a while unless she wanted you to have it. We're going to have something to celebrate. Be sure to phone me from the office as soon as it's over. I'll be waiting right here," said Margie.

Jim could not conceal his annoyance. "I've told you a dozen times that I don't want the job, that I'm happy doing what I do, and I wish you'd drop the subject," he said sharply.

"Jesus Christ, all I'm saying is that you're the best man for it."

"Just stop saying it, that's all. I'm tired of hearing it," said Jim.

"All right, if that's the way you want it, but I can't stop thinking it." Margie got up to take her cup to the kitchen, and bent down and kissed Jim lightly on the top of his head as she passed him.

Jim flinched at her caress. "Okay, okay, I'll phone you; but for God's sake leave me alone about the job."

Despite the Seconal, Judd woke up in time to come down for breakfast promptly at 9:30. In the dining room he found Suz already waiting for him at the table. She got up as he came into the room, made an elaborate curtsey, drew his chair back for him, and said smilingly, "Good morning, Mr. President-to-be. I've been waiting for you."

"Good morning, Suz. And thank you for the good wishes. But how did you know about the meeting?" said Judd, kissing her cheek.

"Oh, that was easy. Albert told me about it this morning and once he told me you said it was a special meeting, I figured out that this was the big day."

"I'm pretty sure it is, Suz," said Judd.

Judd noticed that no place had been set for Kerry, and almost with relief, he asked as casually as he could, "Where's your brother?"

"Oh, Kerry's got a brunch date somewhere. He left just before you came down. When I told him about the special meeting he said he was sorry he couldn't be here for breakfast and off he went."

"Is that all he said?" said Judd.

"That's all," said Suz, reaching for her napkin as Albert entered the room. "You know Kerry. He can be very odd sometimes."

Albert set down a champagne glass in front of Judd and one for Suz.

"What's this, Albert? You know I like orange juice in the morning," said Judd.

"It is orange juice, Mr. Haber. It's orange juice and champagne." Albert nodded at the smiling Suz. "Miss Susan told me, sir, about what a special day it was for all of us and suggested it would be fitting for the occasion."

As Albert left the room, Suz's grin was so infectious that Judd could not resist her joyous mood. "Well, if that's what it is, Suz, we'd better drink it. And thank you, darling."

Suz raised her glass. "To you, Dad, with love. And if Mom were here, she'd be saying the same thing." She paused. "And Kerry, too, I'm sure."

The thought of Milly passed through his mind like a shadow on his conscience. He wondered whether Milly would indeed say the same thing after he told her about Mira. It was a difficult thought to erase.

Judd clicked glasses with his daughter. "Thank you again, Suz, and to you and your Jake while we're at it."

Suz smiled again, a smile of pure joy. "I'll buy that. This is for you and for my Jake."

Judd arrived at the conference room promptly at 10:30, but when he opened the door he found Jackie already installed in Rudy's chair with Gabe Donner at her right. She blew Judd a kiss and he waved at her in return.

"Right on time, Judd," said Gabe amiably. "Sorry about screwing up your Sunday but this was the only time convenient for Jackie here."

"I'm leaving for Europe early next week and I wanted to get this out of the way," explained Jackie as she lit a cigarette. "But I don't think this meeting will take too long. Right, Gabe?"

"Right you are," answered Gabe as the door opened and Lettie entered followed by Alex and Jim Banton.

Everyone seemed inordinately cheerful, Judd observed, and mutual "hellos" were exchanged on all sides. Only Jim Banton, loaded down as usual with ledgers, was his usual businesslike self.

The door flew open again and Josie hurried in. She was extremely pale and her eyes were red as if she had been weeping.

"Sorry to be late, everyone," she said, sitting down immediately at her accustomed place, her pencil poised over the yellow legal pad she pulled from her worn briefcase. She kept her eyes on the page.

"Are you all right, Josie?" asked Judd.

Without looking up at him, Josie answered mechanically, "I'm fine, Mr. H. Thank you."

At this point Gabe began to speak. "I was telling

Judd how sorry we are to have fouled up your Sunday; but it couldn't be helped."

A chorus of hearty demurs was heard on all sides.

"Nothing to worry about," said Lettie, wondering how long the meeting would take and whether she could still get Jenny back on the phone and reinstate her brunch date.

"Glad to be here," said Jim, pushing his ledgers closer to him on the table.

"It was no trouble, Mr. Donner," said Josie.

Alex smiled at Jackie, ignoring Gabe, and said, "No problem at all. And may I say, Jackie, you look more glamorous than ever—if that's possible."

Jackie returned his smile. "Thanks, Alex, for the compliment."

Jackie glanced at Gabe as if awaiting a prearranged signal, and he nodded his head. She put out her cigarette very deliberately, lit another, and began to speak.

"You all probably know what this meeting is about, and it's going to be short and sweet. I'm not much on speeches, and Gabe here will fill in all the details," waving her hand toward the silent Gabe.

Judd clenched his hands under the table.

Lettie took out her compact and powdered her nose, meanwhile stealing a surreptitious look at her watch.

Alex leaned back casually in his chair, took a cigarette from a gold case and lit it, his eyes fixed on Jackie, his smile unchanging.

Jim kept his hands on his ledgers, ready to answer any questions that might be asked.

Josie dropped her eyes to her pad, her pencil at the ready.

Jackie took several puffs at her cigarette, put it out, and rested her elbows on the table. "As I said, all of you know what this meeting is about. It's about Global and what's going to happen now that Rudy's gone. Some of you may have thought that I'd want to take charge, but as I told you when we last met, that's not for me. I've got other fish to fry in my life. So let's get down to business. This may come as a surprise to all of you. The fact is that I've sold Global Talent Associates. Some of you may remember my saying that I like money, lots of it—and that's exactly what I got for Global. Lots." Jackie paused.

Only Jim Banton's voice finally broke the pervasive silence. "Are you going to tell us who the new owners are, Mrs. Ruttenberg—I mean, Jackie?" he said.

"Of course. That's what this meeting is for." She looked at Gabe and he glanced at his watch. "Okay, Gabe?" she continued. He nodded his head, rose from the table and walked toward the door. He opened it and reentered the room followed by Ed Garrell.

"Why don't you sit here, Ed," said Gabe, pointing to an empty chair to his left. Then indicating the others in the room with an inclusive gesture he said, "This is Ed Garrell, the new owner of Global Talent Associates." Then going around the room he introduced those at the table. "Alex Deming, Lettie Mallon, Jim Banton, Judd Haber and Josie Baylon. You know Jackie."

Jackie's announcement of the sale was followed so swiftly by the entrance of Ed Garrell that few of the uninformed people in the room were able to take in the astonishing news. Alex's smile remained unchanged, but his mind raced with questions and recriminations. That bitch, he thought to himself, that goddamned, double-crossing bitch! She never told me a thing about it. Who the hell is Ed Garrell? Where did she dig him up? Jim Banton shuffled his ledgers several times and thought to himself, Mr. Garrell will need me; whoever he is he doesn't know how Global runs and I do. I'm sure I'll be all right. Lettie regarded Garrell across the table and thought to herself, I wonder how much Jackie got for her percentage? Must have been a hell of a lot of dough. Anyway, it's done. Got to roll with the punches in this business. Judd buttoned and unbuttoned his coat, thinking to himself, what was Ed Garrell going to do with Global? He knew Garrell was an investor in the entertainment field, but what did he know about the agency business? What was going to happen to Global and to him? Josie's head was bent low over her pad; the sudden breaking of her pencil point was the only sound in the room and she hastily reached for a replacement.

As Garrell eased himself into the offered chair he waved at Jackie, who smiled at him. Then turning to the others he said, "Glad to meet you. Heard a lot about all of you." He nodded at Judd, the only person he knew in the room besides Jackie and Gabe. "Good to see you again, Judd."

"Thanks, Ed. Good to see you, too," answered Judd,

by now having recovered most of his poise.

Alex rose from his chair, walked around the table, and extended his hand in greeting to Garrell. "Delighted to meet you, Mr. Garrell. And I'm sure I speak for all of us around the table."

Garrell thanked him and shook his outstretched hand.

As Alex returned to his seat, his eyes remained fixed on Garrell while various voices around the room could be heard in confirmation:

"Same here."

"Best of luck."

"Welcome aboard."

"Congratulations."

Only Josie said nothing; she continued to bend low over her pad, her pencil busily moving.

Now Jackie spoke again. "I know this is something of a surprise to all of you, maybe even a shock; but I wanted you to know it before it broke in the trades tomorrow morning. Right, Ed?"

"Right," said Garrell.

Gabe Donner now addressed the group. "The rest of this meeting is in Ed's hands, and I think he wants to tell you what his plans are for Global. You're on, Ed."

Garrell's gaze swept around the room, finally coming to rest on Josie's head still bent over her pad. "One thing I want to make clear right off the bat. I bought Global as an investment." He paused and cleared his throat. "I'm not creative like all of you here and I don't intend to try to learn, either. That's just not my racket. You won't see much of me around the office;

that's a promise." He chuckled. "Probably just as well, too, since I wouldn't even know where to begin. You can think of me as a silent partner if you want to. I may own Global, but I'm not going to try to-run it. That's for someone who knows the agency business, the new president of this company. It's my ball, but he's the one who's going to run with it."

Garrell went to the door and opened it and said to someone waiting for him, "You can come in now."

Prompton Warwick followed Garrell into the room and sat down in the chair next to Garrell's.

Garrell put his arm around Warwick's shoulder, turned to the rest of the room, and said, "Gentlemen and ladies, this is Prompton Warwick, the next president of Global Talent Associates. I've known Prompton for a long time; we've made money together before and I'm sure we'll do it again with Global. Right, Prompton?"

"I'll do my part, Ed. You can count on me for that," said Prompton amiably.

"Now it's your turn, Prompton. You're the boss. I just told everyone here that I'm only a silent partner and that's what I'm going to be from now on. Silent." He laughed and Prompton joined him.

Josie avoided looking at Judd, keeping her gaze on the yellow pad. Jackie leaned toward Gabe Donner and whispered in his ear. Gabe nodded in agreement and smiled.

For what seemed like an eternity to Judd there was no sound in the room; the silence was finally broken by the scraping of Alex's chair as he rose half-out of his seat and leaned across the table, his hand outstretched, his face wreathed in smiles. "I'm Alex Deming, Mr. Warwick. All my congratulations, sir; I'm sure we can work together and I'm looking forward to it."

Prompton Warwick shook Alex's hand and said pleasantly, "I know who you are, Alex." Turning to the others, he added, "I know a lot about all of you, as a matter of fact, and everything I've learned tells me what a hell of an executive team Global has."

It was Lettie who spoke. "Delighted to meet you, Mr. Warwick. I'm sure we'll get along well together. I'm Lettie Mallon."

"Jim Banton here. I'm in charge of the books," said Jim. Judd said nothing; his face was devoid of all expression when Prompton spoke again.

"Glad to meet all of you. I know you've got better things to do on a Sunday than listen to me, so I'm going to make this brief. First, none of this Mr. Warwick stuff; my name's Prompton and that's what I want you to call me. Second, I said before that this is a hell of a team and I'd like to show you I mean what I said. All of you are getting four-year contracts starting July first with a built-in twenty-percent raise at the beginning of the third year. That means you, Alex, and Lettie here, and Jim Banton, and of course you too, Judd." He waved his hand in the air. "Don't thank me. Think about it and let me know. That's the offer. But don't get the idea I'm Santa Claus. I'm not." His eyes roved around the room, finally coming to rest on Judd's face. He kept his gaze on Judd, and his next words were delivered slowly and with considerable emphasis. "I expect every one of you to work your tails off for me and for Global and for Ed here. And I'm going to do the same. Let's get one thing straight right away. There's only going to be one boss at Global and that's me, Prompton Warwick, and anybody who doesn't toe the line—and I mean anybody!—will regret it. I know how to make a contract and I also know how to break one if I have to. Global is big now; it's going to be bigger because that's the way I want it." He paused, still looking directly at Judd, and then he glanced around the silent room, his voice once again pleasant and amiable. "Anybody got any questions?"

Again it was Alex who spoke first. "Only one. When do I sign?" He grinned boyishly.

It was Lettie's voice this time. "Sounds good to me. Count me in."

Prompton turned to Jim Banton. "And you, Jim? What do you say?"

"Me, too."

"No questions." This was Judd's voice.

Prompton slammed his hand down on the table. "Good. That's it then for now. See you all tomorrow morning. And good luck to all of us and to Global. Meeting's over." He got up and simultaneously Garrell and Gabe and Jackie also rose from their chairs.

As Jackie strolled to the door with Gabe and Prompton, she turned for an instant to say, "Bye-bye everybody. I'm off to Paris to spend some of Ed Garrell's money. Right, Ed?"

"Why not?" said Garrell, taking her arm. "Let's

go, Prompton. Shall we?"

"Good luck to all of you," said Gabe as he opened the door and ushered Jackie and Garrell and Prompton into the hall.

As the door closed behind them, Alex got up. "I'll be goddamned! That was quite a meeting. Lots of surprises, eh? Oh well, that's the way it goes. See you all tomorrow." And he was gone.

Lettie reached for her purse. "Me, too. I've got things to do." She turned to Jim Banton. "G'bye, cocksucker, see you in the morn."

"Wait a second, Lettie. I'll walk out with you. I just have to drop these things in my office," said Jim, clutching his ledgers under his arm. "Be seeing you, Judd."

Now that they were alone in the conference room, Josie raised her eyes to Judd for the first time.

"I'm sorry, Mr. H. I'm very sorry. I know how much you wanted it, the presidency, I mean," she said earnestly.

"Thanks, Josie," said Judd, his voice somewhat strained. "Maybe too much. I know it's Sunday, but would you mind coming into the office for a few minutes? There are a couple of things I need to do."

"Of course, Mr. H. I'd be pleased to help with anything." She placed her yellow pad back in the briefcase together with the pencil and they walked out together.

Once back in his office, Judd motioned to Josie to take the chair opposite him. His face was grim and Josie wanted desperately to console him, but she knew there was nothing she could say that would help.

Judd knew now what he was going to do. He realized what Prompton had meant in his office that day when he had told him about Mira and Kerry. Prompton's parting words came back to him: "There's more to come," he'd said. This is what Prompton meant by "more to come"; he wanted Judd to be subservient to him, to endure the ignominy of knowing that he was Judd's boss, the same Judd Haber who would have been the president of Global, the new Mr. Hollywood.

"This won't take long, Josie. Will you take an inter-office memo to Mr. Warwick, copy to Ed Garrell, as follows: I am herewith tendering my resignation from Global Talent Associates effective immediately." He waited for some reaction from Josie, but none was forthcoming.

Josie stood up, her face expressionless. "Will that be all, Mr. H?" she said. Then suddenly, unable to control herself, she burst into sobs and big tears rolled down her cheeks. "Oh, Mr. H! I'm so sorry, so terribly sorry!" she exclaimed.

Judd rose, went to her, put his arms around her shaking body. "Josie, Josie, Josie. Don't take it so hard. I'm fine, I really am." He reached awkwardly into his pocket for his handkerchief and handed it to Josie. She dried her eyes with it. "Thank you, Mr. H. It shouldn't have happened. It's all wrong. It should have been you. You deserved the job."

Judd patted her shoulder and returned to his desk. She sat in her chair, her expression still sombre.

"Let's forget about Global. I want you to get Sid

Schwartzman on the phone as soon as you finish typing that memo. Use his home number. You can get him here on my private phone and I want you to listen to what I say. Okay?"

"Certainly, Mr. H. And I'm sorry I cried; I've been upset about other things having nothing to do with you, and maybe that's what did it," said Josie as she went to her office before Judd could question her.

He started emptying his desk drawer into the wastebasket, but before he finished Josie was back with his resignation memo. He signed it with a firm hand and gave it back to her.

"Now get me Sid Schwartzman, please."

She dialed the number and handed the receiver to Judd. "Hello, Sid? This is Judd speaking. . . . The answer is yes. . . . that's right, I've made up my mind. . . . Yes, I'm sure. I'll call you in a few days and we can iron out the details. . . . Thanks, Sid. I'm looking forward to it."

Judd smiled at Josie's puzzled eyes. "Josie, you're looking at the new creative head of Paramount Pictures. Now you know why not being the president of Global isn't the worst thing that could have happened to me." He grinned while Josie shook his hand.

"It sounds wonderful, Mr. H. I wish you all the luck in the world," she said, beaming.

"Don't discuss this with anyone yet, Josie. I imagine Sid wants to make a big announcement." He paused. "I'm assuming you'll be coming along with me. I couldn't handle it without you, not after all these years. Unless, of course, you want to stay at

Global."

"Oh thank you, Mr. H. You know I wouldn't stay at Global now under any conditions. But I can't accept your offer." Her gaze was level. "I'm going to retire, Mr. H. I'm going home to Kansas. My folks have always kept my room for me, and that's where I'm going."

Judd couldn't contain his astonishment. "I'm surprised, Josie. If it's a question of money, I can guarantee you'll be making more than you get here."

"Oh, no, money has nothing to do with it." She hesitated and went on. "You remember I said I was upset about other things, having nothing to do with Global or you."

Judd nodded. "Yes. I remember. I noticed you didn't look well."

Then, for the first time, Josie told Judd all about Martin, how they met, about his lies, his chronic alcoholism, the humiliation of her tie to him, the agonies of shame she endured.

When she finished, dry-eyed, Judd exclaimed, "My God, Josie! He sounds horrible. I never knew. But what made you decide to leave him now and go back to Kansas?"

Josie did not answer for a long time. Then she said, tonelessly, "I'm not leaving him. He's dead. He took the car out last night and he was dead drunk. I'd hidden all the liquor and he wanted more. I begged him not to go. He had an accident; he hit a truck; they called me from the emergency room at the hospital about midnight. He never regained consciousness. He died about two in the morning. That's why I'm going home; I couldn't stay here without him. I just couldn't. Now you know."

Judd leaned forward and patted her hand wordlessly. Finally he said, "I'm so sorry, Josie, so very, very sorry."

"Thank you, Mr. H. I'll be going now. I have a lot to do before I leave." She smiled wanly, "Including my own resignation memo." She hesitated for a moment. "May I ask you a question before I go, Mr. H?"

"Of course, Josie. Anything."

"Have you told Mrs. Milly about Mira Dalloway yet?"

"No, Josie, not yet. She was at Las Palmas for a couple of days. She's coming in this afternoon."

"Tell her, Mr. H. Tell her. She loves you. I'm sure she loves you and I know you love her. Tell her." She was silent for a moment. "One thing more, Mr. H. You remember once telling me you brought yellow roses to Mrs. Milly when you were courting her and how much she liked them?"

Judd nodded.

"Well," said Josie, "don't forget them this time. Women are funny; they remember things like that."

"I will," said Judd earnestly.

"Good. And now I'll say goodbye unless there's anything else I can do for you," said Josie.

"Yes, Josie, one thing." He smiled sheepishly. "Where can I buy yellow roses on a Sunday?"

Josie returned his smile with one of her own. "I think I can arrange that, Mr. H. There's a florist on

Santa Monica Boulevard who's open on Sundays. I'll have them delivered to your car. Look for them before you leave."

"Many thanks, Josie," said Judd. He got up and hugged her. "Good luck. And be sure to write me."

"I will, Mr. H. And you be sure to tell Mrs. Milly. She's more important than Global and Paramount combined. Goodbye."

Judd stared at the closed door for a long time before he returned automatically to the unfinished task of emptying his desk drawer and discarding the contents.

Kerry rang twice, but there was no answer. He could hear bumps and thuds in the apartment, as if furniture was being moved. He was certain somebody was in. Finally he banged on the door, shouting, "Mira. It's Kerry. Open up."

When she finally opened the door he was astonished. The living room was littered with hangers, dresses, shoes, coats, underwear and clothes of every description. Two half-filled suitcases were thrown on the couch. Every light in the room was blazing.

Kerry turned from the mess to embrace Mira, but she slipped out of his arms and returned to packing one of the suitcases on the couch.

"What's going on here? And why in hell didn't you answer your phone? I've been trying to get you for the last hour," said Kerry, tossing two fur coats off a chair and sitting down.

Mira, her hair disheveled, face bare of make-up,

dressed in blue jeans and a tight white sweater, hardly looked up. "What the hell do you think's going on? I'm moving out, that's what's going on. The phone: I've had it off the hook for the last couple of hours. Just put it back on. Didn't want to talk to anyone. What are you doing here, anyway?"

"What do you mean what am I doing here? It's me, Kerry. You remember me," he said, feebly attempting humor, seizing her again as she stood up, her arms filled with dresses.

"For Christ's sake, Kerry, can't you figure it out? It's all over. It's finished. Somebody must've told your old man about us." Without waiting for a response, she disappeared into the bedroom.

Kerry knew who that somebody must have been: it had to be Prompton. Kerry knew Prompton hated Judd, but somehow he'd never assumed that he would confront Judd with information about Mira and himself. He knew about the meeting this morning at Global; Prompton had confided in him about the change in management and he had assured Kerry that his own career would be guided by Prompton himself in his new role as president of Global. Kerry had chuckled when Prompton had told him the news and wished he could have been present when Judd got his comeuppance. It would serve him right for not helping his own son. But Prompton hadn't even mentioned Mira when he had described how the meeting would go. Kerry had been convinced that Prompton thought the whole idea of Kerry double-crossing Judd with Mira was as funny as Kerry had found it. He thought their laughter would be the end of it. Obviously Prompton had other notions. For a second Kerry's eyes narrowed. If Prompton had told Milly-Mom about it that would be a rotten, lousy trick. But maybe he'd been content with making Judd squirm. He'd have to ask Prompton about that. Kerry knew his old man well enough to be sure that the subject of Mira would never be brought up. Kerry himself certainly had nothing to gain by discussing her, especially now when she was leaving. Besides, he didn't need his old man for anything now; he had Prompton in his corner, the president of Global. No, there wouldn't be any problem there.

By this time Mira had reappeared, both arms filled with dresses. She continued her packing, ignoring Kerry completely.

"I'll bet I know who told the old man," said Kerry.

"What the hell's the difference? All I know is that he's canceled all my charge accounts and that I'm flooded with bills I can't pay," she snapped, as she shoved at a jacket whose sleeves dangled outside the suitcase.

"Did you know the old man didn't get the presidency at Global?"

Mira continued to tug at the recalcitrant jacket. "So what? I don't give a damn. I've got my own problems; I'm not worried about him."

"You're right. The hell with him. But what about us?"

Mira turned to him, her face impassive. "What about us? That's simple. Do you want to pay for all this?" She waved her arms. "Just say so and I'll stop packing right now."

Kerry laughed. "Frankly, no."

Mira gave him a brief smile. "I didn't think so."

"Too bad. We could have had a lot of fun together."

Mira didn't answer, busying herself with the packing.

"Mind telling me where you're going? I'd hate to lose track of you," said Kerry pleasantly.

Just then the phone rang. Mira picked up the receiver and said, "Hello. Yes, this is Mira." She glanced at her watch. "Yes, I know. I didn't expect your call until a little later. I've had the phone off the hook. . . . Yes. Everything's set. I'll be on TWA flight fourteen, arriving at 7:30 New York time. Is Herman still with you? . . . Good. Ask him to meet me at the gate. I've got a hell of a lot of luggage. . . . Thanks, Grace. I'm looking forward to it, too. Can I have the Rose Room? I've always liked that one. . . . That's fine. It'll be like old times again. . . . Me too. . . . Bye, Grace. See you soon."

Mira hung up the phone and turned to Kerry. "That answers your question, Kerry. I'm going to New York." She picked up an empty garment bag and stalked into the bedroom. Brushing by Kerry, she patted his cheek with her unoccupied hand. "If you're ever in New York and want to get laid you can reach me at 347-8026, 252 East 55th. Ask for Grace if I'm not in. Just leave a message."

"Who's Grace? A friend?" asked Kerry.

"No, darling. She's the madam of a whorehouse.

That's where I'll be," and she disappeared into the bedroom.

Kerry started to laugh and shouted into the next room, "That's a deal. You'll hear from me. You're not easy to forget, Mira."

He could barely hear her laconic reply. "Thanks for the compliment. You're pretty damn good yourself."

Kerry leaned back in his chair, wondering what his next move should be. Too bad about Mira; she was really one hell of a lay; it was a shame it hadn't worked out but that was that. He'd see her in New York whenever he got there. Right now he had other things on his mind. He certainly didn't want to go home and face Judd and Milly-Mom. Not for a while anyway. He fumbled in his pocket for his address book. Of course, Colette. She was always glad to have him and he could stay with her until the whole thing blew over.

"Can I use your phone, Mira?" he shouted.

Her voice came out of the bathroom. "Sure. They're not turning it off until tomorrow. Enjoy."

Kerry picked up the phone and dialed Colette's number.

XVIII

Judd drove home from the office very slowly. He knew that Milly would not have arrived yet from Las Palmas and he dreaded the thought of facing her with what he had say. How do you tell your wife (whom you love dearly) that the long-anticipated job of Global's presidency was given to someone you despise, and then cap that with a confession of adultery with a whore? He thought fleetingly of his new post at Paramount, but it seemed unimportant at this point.

As he drove through the Bel Air gate and entered his circular driveway, his face was lined and grim. He had not thought of any way to tell Milly that would not hurt her irremediably. As he got out of the car, he glanced at the back seat where the yellow roses nestled in a red and gold box and wondered whether he would ever be able to give them to her.

As he slammed the car door, the front door opened and Albert appeared.

"Good morning again, sir. I saw you coming up the driveway. I'll take the car, sir."

"Thank you, Albert. I appreciate that. One more thing. You'll find a box of flowers on the back seat.

Would you please put them in the guest closet in the hall?"

"Certainly, sir," said Albert, starting the motor. As the car began to move he opened the window and said, "Incidentally, sir, Mrs. Haber is back. She arrived about ten minutes ago."

Judd was taken aback. She must have changed her plans and left Las Palmas early. He wondered why.

Albert had left the door open for him and Judd entered the house with reluctant steps. He went directly to his study. As he opened the door Milly's voice greeted him from within.

"Hello, Judd, is that you? I'm so glad you're home. I wanted so much to talk to you."

Milly was seated on the couch, a cigarette in her hand. She seemed unaccountably nervous; her hand trembled slightly as she lifted the cigarette to her lips.

She looked particularly beautiful to Judd in her tangerine silk blouse tucked into creamy raw-silk slacks. He noticed she was wearing the big ivory bracelet he'd given her as a birthday present.

"Hi, Milly," he said. "Welcome back. I didn't expect you so soon. You told me you'd be in sometime during the afternoon."

"I left about 8:30 this morning. Couldn't sleep. I had something on my mind and I wanted to talk to you about it as soon as possible."

Judd sat down at his desk. He pulled his scratch pad close and began to scribble idly. He was afraid to face her eyes. He'd hardly listened to what Milly said;

his mind was racing with words that he was afraid to utter. Milly crushed her cigarette in the ashtray. She swallowed once or twice and was about to speak when Judd dropped his pencil, looked at her, stood up and began to pace slowly around his desk.

"Milly, I have something to tell you, something that I know will hurt you, something I've been keeping from you, something—"

Milly's eyes were wide with anxiety. She interrupted him. "What do you mean, Judd? Are you all right? What is it?"

Judd stopped pacing and sat down again in his desk chair. This time his gaze was unwavering. "I want you to listen to me, Milly. Don't ask me any questions until I finish; I want you to hear it all first." He swallowed with a dry throat as Milly sat up straight on the couch, her eyes locked with his. "I've done something no decent man has a right to do, something stupid and disgusting and cheap. I've betrayed you." He blinked his eyes nervously and went on. "I've been having an affair—for a long time now—with a whore, Milly. A whore." Judd did not take his eyes off Milly's as he said the word "whore."

Milly flushed, half-rose, and subsided again on the couch. Her voice was even. "Is it all over, Judd? Is that why you're telling me now?" He didn't answer, and she continued, "Do you love her, Judd? Did you ever?"

"I never loved her, Milly. I can swear it. Never. I've never loved any woman but you. It was lust, nothing else. It's all over now, but that's all it ever was, from the beginning. All I feel now is shame, a deep humiliating shame. It revolts me that I could ever have done such a thing to you and—" he licked his dry lips—"to our love." He put his head between his hands, covered his face.

Milly's voice was low. It seemed to come from a great distance. "Judd," she said softly, "look at me, Judd. You're sure it's over?"

From behind his hands Judd's voice was muffled. "God, yes, a thousand times yes."

Then Judd uncovered his face and looked at Milly. She was smiling and suddenly she began to laugh, at first lightly and then louder.

"My God. Milly! What are you laughing about? Didn't you hear what I said, what I've done to you and to our marriage? Don't you understand what I've been saying to you?"

Milly stopped laughing, her eyes brimming with merriment or perhaps relief.

"Judd, my darling. I understood you. You'll soon know why I was laughing." Her voice became serious. "Do you remember that I told you I came home early today because I had something on my mind and I wanted to talk to you about it as soon as possible? Remember now?"

"Yes, I do. But what's that got to do with what I just told you? And what are you laughing about, for God's sake?" His voice was strained and high.

"That was cruel of me, Judd, and I apologize. But you'll see why in a minute. Judd, darling, what I wanted to tell you is this: I've also just ended an affair, a shoddy, cheap, vulgar relationship that I would never have begun had I not felt that you were indifferent to me, to our love for each other. Now do you understand my laughter?" Her eyes and voice were entreating.

Judd jerked half out of his chair and leaned across the desk. "You mean you were having an affair at the same time I was? Is that what you mean?"

Milly smiled. "That's right, Judd. Exactly. And before you ask—it's all over. Completely."

Milly continued to smile while Judd sank back in his chair. "My God, Milly! I can't believe it. It's ridiculous. It can't be!"

Milly nodded her head in agreement. "It is, and it was; but I've come to my senses. Please try to understand, Judd. I was a complete fool, and I couldn't regret it more than I do this minute."

The silence in the room was electrifying. Milly waited. Then Judd started to laugh, hearty, boisterous, relieving laughter, and Milly joined him. The ludicrous situation hit Judd with full force as he leapt from his chair and strode around the desk to clasp Milly in his arms as she rose, still laughing, to meet him. They both sank down on the couch, laughing together.

"Oh, Milly, darling Milly, I love you and I've been such a fool!"

"We've both been idiots, Judd." She leaned back and put her arms around his neck. "Let's not ever talk about it again, either of us. Let's bury it all in the past where it belongs. I think it's better if we never know any more than we do right now. I'd like to go on from here."

Judd crushed her in his arms; he kissed her neck, her face, and finally her lips. Their embrace was long. When he finally let her go, they were both smiling like happy children.

Judd looked deep into Milly's eyes and traced the outlines of her face with gentle fingers. "Oh, Milly, Milly, you're so wise and so wonderful. How could I ever have done this to you? How can you ever forgive me?"

Milly kissed his hands softly; she put her finger on his lips, enjoining silence. "We've both learned something, Judd." Then she smiled. "Do you remember when we read some of Shakespeare's sonnets together—a long time ago?"

Judd nodded.

"Remember the one that said, 'Love is not love/ Which alters when it alteration finds'?"

"Yes, Milly," Judd answered.

"That's exactly how I feel, Judd. It's over, finished—for both of us. I never want to mention it again. Agreed?" Her eyes were pleading.

Judd held her tightly in his arms and kissed her again and again, murmuring into her open mouth, "Oh Milly, my darling Milly! I love you, I love you!"

Tears of joy streamed unheeded down her face.

Judd held her out at arm's length. "What idiots we've both been. How could we have done it?"

Again she placed her finger across his lips. "It's over. Remember?"

For answer he held her tightly in his arms and

kissed her hair.

Suddenly he rose, strode to his desk, pressed the intercom button.

"Albert? Do we still have Moet and Chandon left on ice? Good. Please bring a bottle and two glasses for Mrs. Haber and for me. We're in my study." He hung up the phone and smiled at Milly. "This is one occasion that deserves champagne if ever there was one." Then he chuckled. "Albert must think I've gone out of my mind. It's the second time in two days that I've ordered champagne. This time it's for us."

Milly stood beside him, her arm linked in his. "Second time?"

"The first time was to toast Suz and her Jake Isaacs. She told me she talked to you about him."

"Yes, she did," said Milly. "And what did you tell her?"

"When she told me I said 'If you love him, that's all I have to know.'"

"I said the same thing, Judd, exactly. I've invited him to dinner next Friday night. Okay with you?"

"Perfect," said Judd. "I've got something else to tell you. I've been so involved with what I did to you that I forgot to tell you what happened to me today."

"Of course, today was the Global meeting. Suz told me. It's my fault; I didn't even ask you, darling. Please forgive me."

Then Judd told her about the meeting, about Jackie selling the company to Ed Garrell, a man Milly had never heard of, about Prompton Warwick being made president, a porn film agent he despised, about Warwick offering him, along with the other executives, four-year contracts.

He stopped there, waiting for Milly's reaction. It was not long in coming. "Isn't Warwick the man who represents Kerry for those filthy pictures he plays in?" she asked.

"The same," said Judd.

"How could you work for a man like him, Judd? You couldn't!"

Judd grinned and kissed Milly on the forehead. "I'm not. I resigned immediately," he said.

Milly kissed him on the cheek. "Good. I'm glad. But I'm sorry, Judd, very sorry. I know how much you wanted to be president of Global; I'm sure that's what Rudy would have wanted."

"You don't get everything you want in life. I've got you back. That's worth a lot more to me than any presidency, even though now I'll never get called Mr. Hollywood the way Rudy was," said Judd, with a mischievous grin. "Will you mind that very much?"

Milly grinned back at him. "You're my husband, Judd Haber. I'm Mrs. Judd Haber. That's title enough for me," she said.

They heard Albert's discreet knock on the door as he entered with the champagne.

"Where would you like it, sir?" he queried.

Judd pointed to the low coffee table in front of the couch. "Right there will be fine. Thank you, Albert."

The champagne bottle opened with a satisfying pop under Albert's expert ministrations; he filled their glasses and left the room.

Judd and Milly raised their glasses as Judd said simply, "To us and the future."

"To us," said Milly.

Judd put down his glass and said with boyish enthusiasm, "How would you like to go back to Hong Kong together for a week or so—let's have dinner again at Gaddis. Would you like that?"

"If you'll fill my glass again, I'll drink to that with pleasure," said Milly, holding out her empty glass.

Judd refilled her glass as well as his own. "I hoped you'd say that because—and I've kept this to the last— we have something to celebrate despite what happened at Global today." He pressed her hand in his. "Not that it holds a candle to what we're celebrating right this minute, darling." He smiled down at her, keeping her hand. "But in case you thought we might have to go on welfare, you are now looking at the creative head of Paramount Pictures, Mr. Judd Haber, to take effect whenever we get back from Hong Kong."

Milly was not surprised. She said quietly, "I knew there was something going on about you and Paramount. At least I thought so."

Judd was puzzled. "What do you mean?"

Milly smiled at him. "Well, if you look in the living room you'll find the biggest horseshoe of flowers I ever saw in my life labeled *To Judd from Sid Schwartzman*."

Judd laughed. "Leave it to Sid for a gesture like that. Well, now you know the reason."

"When Suz showed it to me I was flabbergasted. But now I understand."

"It must be something!" said Judd. "A horseshoe of flowers! I've got to see that. And talking of flowers. . . ." He rang the intercom again, smiling happily at Milly as he did so.

"Albert, that box you put in the guest closet. Will you bring it in, please? Thank you."

"What's that all about, Judd?"

"Be patient, my darling. Be patient."

Albert reappeared with the red and gold box.

"Thank you, Albert," said Judd, ceremoniously handing the box to Milly as Albert left the room.

Milly opened the box and exclaimed, "Yellow roses! Oh, Judd, what a perfect thing to do. Thank you, thank you, thank you. I love them and I love you."

"I had them in the hall, but I was afraid to bring them in until . . . until. . . . "

"Until nothing," said Milly, taking his head in her hands and kissing him.

"And now on to see the horseshoe!" Judd offered her his arm and they walked out together, Milly's arm around his waist. In the hall, Milly suddenly stopped and looked up at Judd. "It occurs to me that although you may never be Mr. Hollywood, you'll still have a title."

"What's that?"

She smiled mischievously, her eyes twinkling. "Mr. Paramount."